W9-ASX-388

Christa Wolf

Divided Heaven

Translated by Joan Becker

Introduction and Bibliography by Jack Zipes

Adler's Foreign Books

Printed in the United States of America

Second Printing

1979

Third Printing

1981

Fourth Printing

1983

ISBN 0-8417-0002-8
LC 83-153130

CONTENTS

- She returns to her friends - agape comes out of filia - Eros first, then filia, then agape. - The state or her country - her return to it & her friends. Symbolic re-birth of the new.

- Order can be found in the people, socially, in the state. From bottom up - (Au Quiet disorder from the top, mere just victims)

- Story of awakened eros - they finally choose their vocation (humble, faceless, nameless, religious) instead of each other. Rita has ordered her soul. The new is really possible - we don't have to wait for state to present us with order. Rita makes her choice b/c she doesn't want to be like Manfred (?) pessimist & selfish & accepting disorder as natural.

- Human Nature is basically good but past experience makes it evil

- intelligent heroine - better half, more egoless than men, ordinary, young, neutral selfhood

CHRISTA WOLF: MORALIST AS MARXIST

I

In her first published work of fiction, *Moskauer Novelle* (1961), Christa Wolf has her two main characters, Vera Brauer, an East German doctor, and Pavel Koschkin, a Russian interpreter, discuss the future of humanity. Pavel asserts that civilization's greatest achievement will be seen in a qualitatively new kind of humanist self-realization: the individual will not become a robot or a technologically perfected monster but will become a *Mensch*. "He'll walk upon earth upright, live long and intensively, be happy and will know that this is his destiny." Vera then asks Pavel what the most important trait of this future individual will be, and he responds without hesitation: "Brotherhood. To be able to live fearlessly in face of the world. Not forced to distrust people. Not jealous of other people's success, to help people bear failure. Not to have to hide weaknesses. To be able to say the truth. Guilelessness, naiveté, softness will no longer be negative attributes. Fitness for life will no longer mean the ability to be hypocritical." When Pavel finishes, he immediately asks Vera what her projection of this future individual is, and she remarks: "Strength of character, the power to overcome oneself."

This conversation is not only key to understanding the meaning of *Moskauer Novelle,* but it is the basis for comprehending the contents and experiments of all Christa Wolf's later works, for their underlying purpose is to indicate ways in which humankind can actually become human, ways through which human beings can become the makers of their own history and not merely objects of history. Here Wolf follows in the tradition of Marxist humanism based on the historical materialism first conceived by Marx and Engels in *The German Ideology* (1845) and most fully developed in the present day by Ernst Bloch in

Das Prinzip Hoffnung (1959). All three philosophers, Marx, Engels, and Bloch, have had a profound influence on Wolf's notion of humanity and have shaped the moral and aesthetic principles most dominant in her work. More precisely, it is her use of their concept of humanity's potential for self-mastery and emancipation which serves as both an operative aesthetic and moral model in her works and which must be seen as the impulse behind her creative writing if her efforts are to be grasped in any meaningful way.

In *The German Ideology* Marx and Engels were intent on demonstrating how notions of humankind were based on false notions of consciousness and idealism. They scorned the spiritual approach to locate the essence of humankind in the social relations of production: "By producing their means of subsistence human beings are indirectly producing their actual material life . . . . The way in which human beings produce their means of subsistence depends first of all on the nature of the actual means they find in existence and have to reproduce. This mode of production must not be considered simply as being the reproduction of the physical existence of the individuals. Rather it is a definite form of activity of these individuals, a definite *mode of life* on their part. As individuals express their life, so they are. What they are, therefore, coincides with their production, both with *what* they produce and *how* they produce. The nature of individuals thus depends on the material conditions determining their production." According to Marx and Engels, human beings can only accomplish self-realization, that is, the full development of their powers, by appropriating those material objects which both restrict and aid in their task of self-fulfillment. By analyzing the struggles of human beings themselves through labor as a historical process involving social class struggle and contradictions, Marx and Engels exposed the irrational and unnecessary agents which hindered humankind's progress toward self-mastery and mastery of nature.

Their concept of humanism was derived from a careful analysis of the individual's pursuit of freedom in relation to other human beings as they produced and reproduced the means for their subsistence. Those traits developed by the individual in overcoming oppression were seen as humanistic features which should be conserved as building blocks in the movement toward an epoch where human beings joined together to make their own history. Value judgements, both moral and ethical, were not based on prescribed rules of behavior but resulted from Marx and Engels' thorough studies of the social relations of production and the contradictions. For instance, they demonstrated that the forces which prevented and worked against humankind's emancipation were negative elements and were to be negated. There was no such thing as a universal standard of good and evil. Moral and ethical principles were elaborated by humankind in historical stages within a socio-economic context where human beings have consistently sought to enjoy the fruits of their labor. Only by relating normative behavior to the productive activity of human beings can one objectively evaluate what is good and bad for the progress of humanity. Marx and Engels demonstrated that, under capitalism, human beings had become more estranged than in any other socio-economic system from their actual human potential to master their environment and themselves. In particular, Marx depicted in *Capital* how human beings were at the mercy of alien forces which could only be explained by studying various factors in the socio-economic process: the division of labor, the development of exchange value based on a free market commodity system, the accumulation of wealth by an emerging bourgeoisie, the production of surplus value by the working class, etc. Marx and Engels posited that the progress of humankind could therefore only be measured in terms of how human beings gained full control of their material powers and social relationships and altered the division of labor in a democratic manner which would allow them to live on an equal basis each according to their needs. In essence, though Marx and Engels never wrote treatises on morality, it can be seen that their moral value system rested on a *materialist* and empirical analysis of the social relations of production.

Ernst Bloch's enormous efforts to interpret the philosophical and moral ramifications of Marx and Engels' materialist approach to the question of humanism have focused on the manifold ways by which the individual can come to realize the self, that is, overcome the self while overcoming the negative features of capitalism. "Man finally wants to be more than himself in the here and now, wants to have his full life without postponement and distant future. The genuine utopian drive is not at all an infinite striving; rather, it is much more: he (man) wants to have what is the merely unmediated and so much unpossessed of the finding-oneself and the being-there as finally mediated, clarified and fulfilled, as happily-adequately fulfilled. The objective images of hope of the construction press forward unhesitatingly to those of fulfilled men themselves and to their fully mediated surroundings with them, in other words, home." Bloch's concepts of home *(Heimat)* and concrete utopia are intricately linked to his notion of the upright posture *(der aufrechte Gang)*, the highest possible state humanity can achieve. To walk upright for Bloch means not simply to put into practice the rational socialist and democratic principles elaborated by human beings in pre-history but also to give full expression to the dreams and wishes of the imagination. Such an accomplishment will allow for the full development and emancipation of all individuals. To walk upright is not possible yet, but the striving to walk upright will lead to a more humane world: "An upright posture distinguishes us from the beasts; but we are still without it. As yet it is present only as a wish, as the desire for a life without exploitation and masters. The daydream, as enduring as it is necessary, has hovered over what has hitherto taken place, and previous failures, and has looked ahead." Inklings of how human beings can walk upright are to be found in concrete utopias which indicate innovative, socialized humane ways of behavior. Concrete utopias are such experiments like the French Revolution, the Commune of 1871, the Russian Revolution, the Chinese Revolution, those moments in history where people take power into their own hands to build a more just world commensurate with their needs, wishes, and ideas, those moments in which people glimpse their own potential to free themselves and govern their own destinies. "Marx indicates that man's ultimate intention is 'the development of the wealth of human nature.' This *human* wealth, like that of *nature* as a whole, lies exclusively in the trend latency in which the world finds itself *vis-à-vis de tout* . . . . But the root of history is the working, creating man, who rebuilds and transforms the given circumstances of the world. Once man has comprehended himself and has established his own domain in real democracy, without depersonalization and alienation, something arises in the world which all men have glimpsed in childhood: a place and a state in which no one has yet been. And the name of this something is home *(Heimat)*." All of Bloch's writings have been undertaken to map out the paths which human beings have taken to reorganize and change the social relations of production to reach home so that they can walk upright, and in this sense he has located the moral element in Marxism as emanating from the efforts of human beings to produce and enjoy the products of their work without being exploited. The wealth of humankind's powers which distinguish it from other living species can only be realized in a non-exploitative social context, and Bloch taps both the intellectual and physical sources of humankind to demonstrate how human beings can *really* appropriate the material world "by and for themselves," to reach a level of productive development where the human species brings its full powers out of itself to reach its true potential.

Christa Wolf's writings are part of a cultural praxis consciously dedicated to the fulfillment of Bloch's Marxist notion of humanism. This is not to say that she began her writing career under the direct influence of Marx, Engels, and Bloch. On the contrary, her notions of Marxist humanism took shape gradually in her writing, and they are still being elaborated. The essence of humanity for Marx, Engels, and Bloch has little to do, as I have endeavored to explain, with morality *per se* but with the structure and organization of the social relations of production. Insofar as work becomes more and more non-exploitative and non-alienating, human beings develop normative behavior which set the framework for morals and ethics. Wolf's writings reveal a growing tendency to embrace this Marxist notion of humanism.

While they are decidely different in their analysis of the concrete historical situation in which her characters are lodged, each one of Wolf's works measures the extent to which society allows for the total development of humanity and her humanist vision of the future: "Prose writing can only attach itself to the currents of thought and the social movements which give humanity a future, which are free from those century-old and brand-new magic formulas of manipulation, and which do not themselves shy away from experimentation. This means, I see a profound correspondence between this way of writing with the socialist society." In addition, "prose writing should attempt to keep human beings in contact with their roots, to reinforce self-consciousness which has become so labile that many people in the advanced technological countries have sought flight in suicide or in the dead-end street of neurosis" *(Lesen und Schreiben)*.

But it is not only society which is analyzed and judged in Wolf's works. She is also most concerned about humankind's own struggle to walk upright, and here she is consciously following in Ernst Bloch's footsteps. When Pavel and Vera express their ideas about the future individual, they themselves are in a quandry and are endeavoring to achieve clarity so that they can live more humanely and prepare the way for a better future. Pavel's ideas are for the most part expressed in the *negative*. He is older, somewhat cynical, and from the Soviet Union. He has obviously suffered under Stalinism and has encountered those bureaucrats who mechanically speak about Marxism without practicing it. He wants a world *without hypocrisy*. Vera is more positive. She is ten years younger, from East Germany, more hopeful since she has been allowed to pursue her professional interests and reach a high level of development. Her great desire is *for strength* to continue building for a socialist world. The time is 1959. The novella was written in 1960 at the beginning of the Bitterfeld Movement which promised more cultural freedom in the German Democratic Republic. Vera and Pavel. Two different models of socialist individuals. Hope tempered by grim criticism. It is this combination of traits which has marked Christa Wolf as a writer of remarkable integrity, one who has demanded the realization of concrete utopias and the upright posture. Her continual insistence on the fulfillment of these socialist goals have made her more and more demanding on her readers and government. She has been openly critical of the state and party leadership of the German Democratic Republic, and she has been accused in both the East and the West of becoming too abtuse and archane in her more recent writings. Some critics have asserted that she has turned inward and abandoned Marxism, but the truth of the matter is that she has become more certain of what she wants, more insistent that the socialist cause not be betrayed.

II

Christa Wolf was born on March 19, <u>1929</u> in Landsberg, a small city city near Dresden, and until her most recent novel *Kindheitsmuster,* she has revealed very little about her childhood and her experiences under fascism. Her father Otto Ihlenfeld was a small-town businessman, and she apparently admired both her father and mother who shared a general antipathy toward fascism. *Kindheitsmuster* makes it quite clear how Christa Wolf must have been bewildered by and suffered from the initiation into the fascist system which is associated with bestial and irrational behavior in this novel. In addition, there is evidence from her essays and stories that she felt herself to be a victim of Nazi propaganda. She especially keeps returning to the traumatic break in her life, 1945-46, when she was forced to flee her home and to rethink her situation in light of the allied occupation. This is not to say that she immediately became a conscious supporter of socialism, or that she discarded all her past ideas and habits. Her experience can be best described as a "trauma of liberation." Like many of her generation, Wolf was not aware of why she was being liberated, and what liberation would mean. She was frightened of both Americans and Russians. Signs of death and destruction haunted her in the immediate postwar years. At the same time, she was compelled to adapt to the new policies of the occupied forces in Schwerin, the city to which she had moved. She worked as an assistant to the mayor, studied at the local high school, and at one point had to spend some time in a sanitorium because of a lung sickness. In 1947 she attended a gymnasium in Bad Frankenhausen for two years, and it was only after she received her diploma that she read her first Marxist writings. This may sound strange, especially in a country that was proclaiming itself to be socialist. Yet, it must be remembered that East Germany was a society in a transitional stage and that there were numerous schools at that time which were still filled with teachers opposed to socialism. Educational policy was not strictly regulated and was just in the process of being developed by leading Marxist emigrés who returned to East Germany between 1946 and 1949 and also by inexperienced young men and women who were just beginning the study of Marxism.

It is characteristic and significant in Wolf's case that she did not immediately embrace socialism, but that she turned to it gradually out of a strong moral concern. In an interview with Hans Kaufmann, a professor of German literature, she made a revealing statement about her position as moralist, a statement which sheds light on her attraction to Marxism while at the same time clarifies her moralist position as Marxist: "To be sure, I do not take the same deprecating attitude of some Marxists toward the word 'morality' — and this is based on reasons which I gave earlier in another context: I cannot and do not want to let myself have anything to do with mere historical determinism which regards individuals, groups, *(Schichten),* classes, and peoples only as the objects of an irreversible, consequent historical law and which corresponds to a completely fatalistic philosophy of history. Nor do I want to have anything to do with a sterile pragmatism which sees nothing else in the morality of classes and individuals but a means to an end, capable of being manipulated or ignored depending on one's pleasure, sometimes a useful vehicle and other times useless. (Who cannot but feel at least the pain and tragedy which Brecht recorded in the lines: 'Those for whom we wanted to prepare the ground for friendliness could not even be friendly themselves.')

" 'How must the world be formed for a moral being?' Bobrowski's question is and remains stimulating because it helps the world adjust to morals worthy of humans and not morals of humans adjust to a world which is still far from worthy of humans — that would mean the physical death of humanity.

"This has, however, nothing to do with the Christian antimony of good and evil nor with the rigid juxtaposition of thinking and doing; it has nothing to do with abstract, fruitless and in the long run paralyzing demands for integrity. Yes, even our mistakes can be 'moralistic' if they continually bring us to the productive side of our contradictions and in a new way. On the other hand, one could call everything immoral which prevents us, the masses, from becoming subjects of history and not just objects. And, from this point of view, why shouldn't I regard the socialist author, too, as 'moralist?' "

Wolf's moral concerns about the fascist past and the future of German society were sharpened by her political education. In order to make her humanist efforts socially more effective, she joined the Socialist Unity Party (SED) in 1949 at which time she also enrolled at the University of Leipzig where she studied until 1953. This was the period when she met and married the essayist and critic Gerhard Wolf (1951) and came into contact with the leading Marxist professors in the humanities. Two in particular, Hans Mayer and Ernst Bloch, had a profound effect upon her intellectual development. Representatives of a Hegelian dialectical approach to Marxism, both Mayer and Bloch underscored their teaching with a moral and socialist humanism opposed to the rigid, schematic thinking of Communist bureaucratic officials who superficially applied Marxist principles to their work without regard for the actual needs and imagination of the people with whom they had daily contact. While Wolf was at Leipzig, which at that time was one of the most renowned Marxist universities in the world, she had the opportunity to come into contact with other dialectical thinkers such as Werner Kraus. Moreover, she was exposed to the writings of Bertolt Brecht and Anna Seghers, who have served her as models, not so much in the manner in which they wrote, but how they endeavored to seek new ways for incorporating the essence of Marxist humanist and political teachings culled from experience into their writings.

Upon completing her education at Leipzig, Wolf embarked upon a career as critic and editor first at the publishing house Neues Leben and then with the magazine *Neue Deutsche Literatur*. From 1955 to

1961, she wrote mainly book reviews and cultural essays while experimenting with different prose forms. These critical works are marked and marred by an idealistic notion of socialism which is almost other worldly. Wolf tended to prescribe socialist principles to the world and the arts so that her writing often rang with rhetoric. There is a hint in many of Wolf's reviews of moral righteousness and a naive acceptance of the state and party leadership's cultural policies so that her remarks seem stilted and automatic, especially if they are compared to her later more studied and critical observations of the late 1960's and early 1970's. It is almost as if the moralist dedication to socialism negated any awareness of the fact that the change in social relations had not kept pace with the economic changes which had been occurring in the German Democratic Republic, changes which involved the nationalization of the major industries, transportation, education, health, and agriculture. The mistakes and conflicts of early socialist planning are justified by the superficial posing of a *good* new society, i.e., the socialist German Democratic Republic against the *bad* old societies, namely the capitalist West.

Yet, despite this mechanistic moralist stance which hampered her critical approach to literature, Wolf was definitely becoming more conscious of the crucial contradiction underlying the development of the GDR state which emphasized the quantity of production over the quality of change in the social relations of production. How to make humankind the subject of history and not simply the object was one of the key questions she raised in her first fictional work, whereby she took a position that the world must first be humanized to allow all individuals to reach their full potential. *Moskauer Novelle* concerns a chance re-encounter between Vera Brauer, a young East German doctor, and Pavel Koschkin, a Russian interpreter, in Moscow during 1959. They had first met in 1945 when Pavel had served with the Russian forces occupying Vera's town, and it was there that

Vera had committed a grave mistake which resulted in an injury to Pavel's eyes, eventually forcing him to abandon his plans to become a medical doctor. Ironically, it was Pavel, who had inspired Vera to become a doctor, and, when they meet in Moscow, it becomes apparent to Vera that her achievement had been made possible through Pavel's loss. Indeed, he has led a frustrating life and reaches out for Vera at a time when he is faced with a decision to leave Moscow with his wife and embark on a new career. Vera, happily married though she is, falls in love with Pavel and must fight her urge to begin a relationship with him. She needs the help of an older friend, who is an experienced, noble party worker, and she perceives that to love Pavel is to encourage him to fulfill his responsibility, that is, to stay with his wife and seek a new life with her on Russia's frontier. In other words, she must learn *to carry herself upright,* to avoid making another mistake like the one she had made as an adolescent, to act with compassion in the name of socialism.

Though this novella is obviously contrived and sentimental, it is significant in that it focuses on Christa Wolf's prime concern as writer. From the very beginning, Wolf focuses on human relations and subjective needs within a socio-moral context. Implicit in this story is a critique of barbaric conditions under fascism, false consciousness, and bureaucratic behavior. Wolf relates to her characters in her function as narrator just as she wants them to relate to one another. In most of her works the female protagonist is closely associated with her, generally born the same year, generally having gone through the same experiences. The practice put forth in the narrative is an extension and model of experienced practice which sets alternative guidelines for future socialist practice. These guidelines are not rigid. They provide the framework for future experiments. In this regard, *Moskauer Novelle* merely sets the stage upon which Wolf has conducted more sensitive, subtle and far-reaching experiments.

In 1962, Wolf moved to a small town Kleinmachnow near Berlin and abandoned her post as editor for *Neue Deutsche Literatur* to concentrate on her prose fiction. This was the period in which she participated fully in the Bitterfeld Movement, a cultural program organized by the state, which began in 1959 and called upon writers to become more familiar with work conditions in factories, firms, and elsewhere and make them the subjects of their art. It also encouraged workers to write about their own experiences and to develop their creative talents. Writers and workers were to share experiences, to learn from each other, to sharpen new skills and insights. Between 1959 and 1962 Wolf had lived in Halle and worked part-time in a wagon factory. It was there she gathered material for her second major work, *The Divided Heaven.* This novel was published in 1963 and immediately became the subject of attack and praise in the East and the West. East German critics argued that Wolf did not accurately portray the party and that too much emphasis was placed on the voluntaristic, if not anarchistic behavior of the leading male figures. West German critics deplored the choice made by Rita to remain in East Germany and saw the novel as propagandistic and sentimental. These positions will be considered later in a more detailed analysis of the novel. What is important to remark upon here is that *The Divided Heaven* marked the turning point in Christa Wolf's development as moralistic writer. Though some of her idealistic and naive notions of socialism still remained, she committed herself in this novel to a critical perspective which saw the necessity for working people to assert themselves actively in the social relations of production in order to bring about changes to correspond to their needs and drives. This meant steering a course in opposition to the state and party leadership in the GDR, not openly antagonistic, but definitely in opposition to those bureaucratic and exploitative tendencies of the government. The moralist was giving way now more to the conscious, critical and self-critical Marxist.

The publication of *The Divided Heaven* coincided with the announcement of the New Economic Policy of the German Democratic Republic, which, on the one hand, was aimed at diminshing bureaucratic red tape and giving more autonomy to regional planners and, on the other hand, was tailored to induce greater production through traditional monetary rewards without changing work procedures and the hierarchical relations between workers and administrators in factories and other institutions. Hence, the very same pressure conditions which led Manfred in *The Divided Heaven* to abandon the German Democratic Republic, Rita to attempt suicide, and Meternagel to work himself to the bone were not overcome: the gray banal existence which emanated from alienating work conditions persisted, and, while it appeared that Christa Wolf might perhaps enjoy her laurels as one of the most celebrated young writers in the GDR — 180,000 copies of *The Divided Heaven* were sold in ten printings, and she was awarded the coveted Heinrich Mann Prize — the very opposite happened. After being nominated to the list of candidates for the Central Committee of the SED in 1963, then being chosen to hold a speech at the second Bitterfeld Conference in 1964, and finally designated a member of the P.E.N. Center of the GDR, she engaged in open conflict with the cultural policy makers of the state at the 11th plenary session of the Central Committee. In particular, she defended the writer Werner Bräunig's partially published novel *Der eiserne Vorhang* as representing a just critique of inadequacies in social relations of production against party functionaries who considered it anti-socialist. By 1967, her name was stricken by the party leadership from the list of candidates for the Central Committee, and she was regarded with distrust and suspicion by the SED. This conflict was heightened by the publication of her short story *Juninachmittag* in 1967 and her novel *The Quest for Christa T.* in 1968.

The conflict had been inevitable from the beginning. Wolf's commitment to socialism was based on an idealistic notion of Communism and a strong serious acceptance of party dogma as though they were moral principles which were established for the common good of the people. Thus, her first book reviews and essays and later *Moskauer Novelle,* while conforming to party strictures, expressed more her devout belief in socialism as moralist. By 1963, the naiveté of her devotion yielded to a more sober critical attitude toward the actual material development of socialism in the GDR. Her reflections became more penetrating and probing as did her actions and writings.

The Quest for Christa T. has generally been regarded in both East and West Germany as an indictment of how the GDR state regiments life to such a suffocating extent that individuals cannot reach their full potential. The plot line of this novel is deceptively simple and commonplace. It concerns a young woman, born in 1927, who grows up in a small village, apparently the only child of the village school teacher. There is something odd about her, something strikingly different, which makes her seem out of step with her times. After studying at the gymnasium, she is forced to flee her village due to the invasion of the Red Army. In the immediate postwar years she teaches in an elementary school and falls in love once or twice. About 1951 she decides to return to the University of Leipzig to study German literature. As she seeks more meaning in her life, she has doubts about her profession and even contemplates suicide. However, she does manage to complete her degree in 1954 and becomes a teacher at a high school. During her first few years as teacher she has several run-ins with rigid functionaries and finds it difficult to impart humanistic lessons to her students. After she meets Justus, a young veterinarian, and becomes pregnant, they marry, and she decides to seek refuge with him from her meaningless job in a small town in the north. Here she hopes to write and dedicate herself to her family. However, she cannot escape into a country idyll. While she and her husband begin building a new house, she is overcome by the senselessnes of her "new life," has a brief affair with a forester, and then learns just before she and her husband are to move into the house that she has leukemia. She dies in 1963.

The simple story is narrated in a complex manner by one of Christa T.'s oldest friends who brings together memoirs and excerpts from Christa T.'s writings with her own reminiscences and reflections. The narrative is introspective while at the same time aimed at provoking readers to pose questions about their own relationship to society. As motto for her her book, Wolf has quoted the former cultural minister of the GDR, Johannes R. Becher: "This coming-to-oneself — what is it?" The question, however, is rhetorical, for, as Wolf already knew, Becher had provided an answer with which she undoubtedly agreed: "It is the fulfillment of all the possibilities as they are given to the human being. Displeasure and discontent create sadness, and sadness becomes depression and despair since we do not live life as it is given to us to live." Throughout the novel the questions imply a critique of the truncated possibilities in GDR society. Particularly the often repeated question "When, if not now?" is reminiscent of Bloch's insistent demand for the fulfillment of past gleamings of the potential which could make for concrete utopias. Wolf, too, insists that questions cannot be begged, that humankind must be given opportunities in order to move to the creation of a more humane society. Not only must these opportunities be given, but individuals must actively seize them as they arise to pursue the humanist quest.

Enough has been written about *The Quest for Christa T.* as an experimental novel which breaks with the tradition of socialist realism in order to criticize the problem of the alienation and banality of life in the GDR. Such interpretations, while generally correct, also miss the more positive side of Wolf's work. First of all, the narrative is one filled with hope. The express purpose of the narrator, who directs her remarks largely at a socialist reading public, specifically a GDR audience, is to instill her readers with the hope and belief that things can and must be changed. Christa T.'s death can in no way be attributed merely to the state or party *per se,* but also to the general apathy of a community which has accepted the everyday regimented routine as a given condition which cannot be affected, and hence, dreams and wishes must remain unfulfilled. Thus, the example of Christa T. and the questions throughout the "quest" are meant to unnerve, unsettle, and provoke the readers. Secondly, the narrative parts ways with orthodox socialist realism but can still be linked to the socialist tradition of realism. Its tendency is clear: Wolf does not abandon a socialist position. On the contrary, she takes a more definite, assertively critical position on material conditions in the GDR, thereby emphasizing her allegiance to a humanistic program of socialism which demands cultural change along with the economic. While most critics have focused on Christa T. as the central protagonist of the novel, they seem to forget that the actual protagonist is the *living narrator* who has not given up the struggle to change herself and others. Her commitment to Christa T. is at the same time a compassionate commitment to the *unfulfilled potential* of socialism. Her consciousness represents what is possible to achieve even under conditions which might make one want to despair. Hope is the motive and motif of the narration, the unifying force. The narrator does not follow an exact chronological order. The pattern of the novel seems patternless. Time dissolves into timelessness in the course of the narrative so that Wolf can suggest how mankind must take and can make time significant: "We aren't anything yet, but we shall be one day; we haven't got it yet, but we shall: that was our formula. The future? The future is going to be quite different. Everything in good time. The future, beauty and perfection, we're saving them up, as our reward, to be paid some day, for untiring industry. Then we shall be something, then we shall have something.

"But as the future was always thrust along in front of us, and as we saw that it was nothing but the extension of the time that moves with our own movement, and that one can't ever reach it — then we had to start asking: *How* shall we be? *What* shall we have?

"Time cannot stop, but one day there'll be no time, unless one stops now: are you really living now, in this very moment, really living!

"When, if not now?"

Wolf's critique is directed both at the conformists and the apathetic people in GDR society who allow themselves and others to waste away. Insofar as the socio-economic system furthers this process of conformity and indifference, it, too, comes under attack. The reflections of a refracted and fragmented reality by the narrator and Christa T. expose the insipid and banal conditions under which a common person seeks to define her life through production. Christa T. is not an extraordinary person, not a heroine, and yet, she is exemplary in the manner in which she did seek to overcome herself and the "sickness" which was eating away at her. What is more important is that the narrator is also typical of the GDR society, and that she continues Christa T.'s struggle *"to become oneself with all one's strength."* This harks back to Vera's comment in *Moskauer Novelle,* and, indeed, both Christa T. and the narrator as well as Rita in *The Divided* Heaven are tentative models of the future socialist human being. Their experiences lead them to conceive their lives as experiments with the *upright posture.*

The reception of *The Quest for Christa T.* in the GDR reveals to what extent Wolf tapped the moral and critical impulse of her readers and captured the reality of their situation. The first edition, limited to 15,000, was immediately sold out. The next three editions of the novel were not published until 1973 and 1974, and the response was just as positive as the first: the novel has continually been sold out. Moreover, statistics have provided evidence to show that the novel has circulated among all kinds of readers and classes in the society. Nevertheless, orthodox party-line critics characterized Wolf as a "bourgeois" writer, too concerned with subjectivity and not enough with the development of the socialist society. Her method of writing was called psychological and introspective. Labels were invented to cast her into the mold of revisionist.

In answer to her critics, Wolf published a collection of essays, *Lesen und Schreiben* (1971), written largely between 1964 and 1971, which represented a kind of stocktaking on her part and brought home the lie to her critics. The collection is divided into four parts. The first is composed of political essays which are for the most part forthright attacks on the imperialist policies of West Germany and the USA. The second part focuses on the key postwar years when she began to change her socio-moral perspective and move toward socialism. Writing about a single day in her life, April 21, 1946, she states: "What followed even after this day is a long history which I share with many people of my generation and perhaps will be able to tell one day — I have often thought about that beginning without wishing things to be different. Just as I cannot regard my old pencil marks on the margin of that writing by Friedrich Engels without being moved. 'In place of the perishing real a new liveable reality emerges.' That was to be the process which then filled out my life. Did I suspect this on that evening? Not at all." It was apparently the hope which socialism provided her in the postwar years which led her to dedicate herself to change and to oppose the very cynicism and subjectivity of which she has been accused. In an essay about the diary as a means of work and memory, she remarks: "Objective cynicism (if there is such a thing like that) lies in this situation, that is, in a contradiction which has never before been so dangerous as now, a contradiction between the level of development of science and certain retarded social conditions. Their common origin is: lack of belief in the changeability of the world. The new and urgent question which confronts us now is the question about change, its forms, its possibilities; about the obstacles which oppose change. About the necessity to keep the revolutionary principle alive, effective."

The third part of Wolf's book is dedicated to one of the authors who has committed herself to change and revolutionary principles: Anna Seghers. The last part announces what has been one of Wolf's primary concerns in recent years: the role of technology in a society still in need of humanizing, and the role of the writer and writing in a technological society. Wolf stresses that humankind must remain collectively in control of scientific inventions which allow for the realization of full human potential without exploitation. Prose writing is like technology and science. Its function is to suggest innovative and alternative ways for creating worlds more liveable and stimulating than the world in which we presently inhabit. This world, this earth, must be considered precious and taken seriously so that the experiments of appropriation are not conducted for the sake of the experiment itself or mere accumulation. There is in this regard a moral purpose behind writing, a didacticism without dogmatism. "Prose is indeed a product of the maturation process of humanity, developed late, especially for this purpose. Prose creates human beings in a double sense. It demolishes deadly simplifications in that it introduces possibilities to exist in a humane way It serves as a storage room of experience and judges the structures of human social life from the perspective of productivity. It can snatch up and save time in that it plays out experiments on paper, those with which humanity is confronted: there it meets up with the standards of socialist society. The future will know how important it is to enlarge the playing space for human beings. Prose can push forward the boundaries of our knowledge much further beyond ourselves. It keeps the memory of a future in us awake which we should not renounce under the pain of our downfall.

"It supports human beings becoming subject.

"It is revolutionary and realistic: it induces and encourages one to do the impossible."

Indications of how to bring about the impossible were given in Wolf's next two publications: *Till Eulenspiegel* (1972), a screenplay, which she wrote with her husband Gerhard, and *Unter den Linden* (1974), a collection of three "improbable" stories, as she calls them. The Eulenspiegel story was written for a film production, and, although it does not bear Christa Wolf's stylistic imprint, the narrative does depict her concern with shaping images and presenting experiments based on past historical experiences which will point a way "home," in other words, toward fulfillment of the humanistic undertaking. The historical personage of Till Eulenspiegel is transformed into a rebel of and for the people, and the historical period in which he plays out his life is moved from the 14th century to the end of the 15th and beginning of the 16th century, in other words, to the period of the peasant revolts, the Reformation, and the rise of early capitalism. Till, apparently a naive peasant, learns to use his wits and cunning to oppose aristocratic oppressors and also to help his fellow countrymen. While the screenplay could be read mainly as an attempt to give a socialist interpretation to a folk hero and historically link the peasant-plebeian tradition to the proletarian-socialist tradition proclaimed by the GDR, there are definite signs in the narrative which indicate that the authors were also addressing actual contemporary problems in that they suggest that social change has its roots in the people. The use of the cunning folk hero has been a favorite traditional device of writers for criticizing unjust rulers and was particularly developed by Brecht in *Schweyk in the Second World War* and other plays. Here Christa and Gerhard Wolf show how an ordinary figure like Till can use his imagination and wit not only to survive situations but also to aid his compatriots to overcome oppressive conditions. Till dies; yet, his spirit is carried on in the struggles of the oppressed and he serves as a symbol of hope that better times will come if the common people actually use their talents actively to emancipate themselves.

In *Unter den Linden,* the revolutionary spirit is displayed in a more subtle fashion, often in such abstract and convoluted images that Wolf's message becomes as refracted as the world she aims to criticize. Though there is no doubt that Wolf seeks to use prose in a revolutionizing and realistic manner, the fact that she must temper her criticism, veil it behind formalist experiments, leads her dangerously close to the brink of incomprehensibility. This is also true of such other GDR writers as Günter Kunert and Heiner Müller, who at times walk a tightrope between obscuring and clarifying social and historical experience with recondite, nebulous, and introverted images. The aesthetic protest lodged in formal technique can only have effect if the imaginative elements do not become buried in an oblique language set up to defend and conceal the critique which has purposely been woven into a symbolic fabric. The broken lines of the images depend on clear referential points for their connection to reality since the meaning of the symbols are not self-containing. Two of Wolf's stories, *Unter den Linden* and *Die Neuen Lebensansichten eines Katers,* while conceived with unusual fantasy and addressing immediate social problems, become unnecessarily laborious because the content and lode of the images are unduly complex and ponderous for the very simple messages Wolf wants to convey. In *Unter den Linden* the narrator relates a dream which takes her up and down the famous boulevard in East Berlin. Her dream is a pursuit which uncovers her past and present predicaments. She wants to overcome the past, particularly the past of those friends who complied with the conformist strictures of the party. She is haunted by a discontented young woman who makes her feel that too much has been postponed, promises begged, love abandoned and betrayed. In the end she wakes up only to discover that the young woman in the dream was actually herself. The recognition brings relief since the narrator identifies with the pursuer and the pursued. The general themes of *Christa T.* are recapitulated here in an almost similar narrative fashion but the mystery of the dream-reality sequences is enshrouded in such abstract allusions that the images wane and the adventure becomes boring.

Such is also the case with *Neue Lebensansichten eines Katers,* which is a parody and also a continuation of E.T.A. Hoffmann's satric novel *Die Lebensansichten des Kater Murrs.* Here an ancestor of the genial cat Murr reports about his master's plans to design "Total Human Happiness" through scientific tests involving cybernetics. Along with two other ridiculous scholars, the master Barzel uses a system caled SYMAGE (System of the Maximum Corporeal and Spiritual Health) to eliminate all human problems, desires, and needs to achieve "Total Human Happiness." The tomcat superciliously comments on such preposterous designs while also describing the *human* weaknesses of Barzel, a married man, who desperately seeks to consummate his love for the girl next door. Obviously Barzel's plan does not work, and obviously the story is a satire on the technologists and planners who seek to eliminate human factors in the planned economy of the GDR. Wolf's attempt at satire is heavy-handed, and the story is long-winded and monotonous. On the positive side, it does contain a valid critique of the dangers of socio-technological dehumanization which belongs to her moralist program of preserving the humanist element in the socialist society of the future.

Her most successful story in this collection is *Selbstversuch (Self-Experiment),* in which a female scientist agrees to transform herself into a man for thirty days to test a special formula invented by bio-chemists. The narrative takes the form of an open letter addressed to the director of the project, an elderly gentleman, who has always been admired by the woman. In fact, she has always stood in awe of him because of his absolute dedication to science and his seemingly emotionless attitude. Like him, she has become an extremely competent, serious scientist, a woman in her early thirties, dedicated to science, however, mainly for the sake of science. The story is set in the GDR of 1992, and the transformation allows the narrator to gain distance on her predicament as unfeeling scientist in a profession dominated by men. For too long she had modelled herself after the director and other men, and now, ironically as a man, she begins to feel the restraints and emptiness of the male code of behavior. In her transitional state of man-woman she falls in love with a young woman who turns out to be the daughter of the director. The love she feels saves her from becoming completely transformed or reified as a man. In this sense the experiment, while scientifically a success, fails because the narrator refuses to accept the status of male. The result is that she sees through the director's sovereignty and rigid objectivity and discovers the secret of all males: "Your artistically constructed system of rules, your zealousness for work which cannot be cured, all your maneuvers to keep yourself at a distance were nothing but the attempt to keep your secret from being discovered: you cannot love and you know it." The story ends, however, on a positive note: "Now my experiment awaits us. The attempt to love. Which incidentally also leads to fantastic discoveries: to the discovery of that which one can love."

Self-Experiment succeeds in combining Wolf's critique of socio-technological dehumanization with a scathing analysis of male behavior in the GDR. In particular she sheds light on the manipulative nature of instrumental rationality which such philosophers as Marcuse and Habermas have demonstrated to be at the core of "one-dimensional" societies. Wolf clearly shows how *males* have rationalized society mainly for the sake of organizing and handling matter as the mere stuff of control and instrumentality.

The result is that technology is socially organized not to bring about human autonomy but to increase the domination of humankind in which even the administrators of the rationally repressive system, generally male, become caught in the web of technology for the sake of technology. Though set in the future as a type of science fiction story, the contents of *Self-Experiment* are obviously lifted from the conditions experienced by women and men today and from the programmatic priority given to science by the GDR state and party leadership. The measured and careful tone of the narrator sets the mood for the experiment. Her apparent dedication to science makes the ironic twist at the end more complete, for she appears to be the perfect specimen for the experiment and yet fails because she cannot rid herself of her feminine quality which is none other than the humanistic factor necessary for developing a socialist society in opposition to instrumental rationality.

Taken together, all three stories in *Unter den Linden* transcend the theme in *Christa T.* where the focus was mainly on the plight of a common but gifted woman. Here Wolf questions the experiments conducted by the leaders of the state and party and raises questions about alienation and communication in technologically advanced countries where rationalization of social labor leads more to the enslavement of humankind than to liberation. Since the stories are heavily symbolic and the allusions are not always clear, the critique often becomes too dense. Yet, at her best, Wolf exposes the irresponsibility of those responsible for social development in the GDR. Opportunism of academic careerists, obsession with machines and planning by technocrats, lack of human compassion of scientists — three themes, three stories which demand answers. The moral thrust of her argument for a socialist society depends on how material production and social labor affecting man's pursuit of his full powers can be shaped and changed to answer those questions in the stories. In this sense the stories continue Wolf's revolutionary experiment with prose.

More recently two chapters of her latest novel *Kindheitsmuster* were published in *Text und Kritik* (1975) and *Sinn und Form* (1976), and they supply evidence that Christa Wolf is further developing her rigorous moral exposition of past and present social conditions in Germany as Marxist. The major task she has set for herself in this novel is to come to terms with the past, especially with the fascist epoch in Germany and World War II. Similar to the style she developed in *The Quest for Christa T.* but more documentary and explicit in its historical analysis, *Kindheitsmuster* traces the contours of patterns of experiences from Wolf's childhood in view of the socio-political occurences of her present writing. The prose writing is treated as a conscious activity whch derives its meaning from making others aware of past history and the necessity to assume control of history. Behind the writing is a moral impulse which has resulted not from rigid socialist or Christian principles applied to the past but which has grown from a continuous, concentrated study of history and the material conditions which influence the actions and interactions of human beings. Thus, fascism is not perceived as being inherently evil but is revealed by the process through which people have organized their productive and social lives in a given historical period. The obstacles which prevent self-emancipation and self-realization are exposed as morally detrimental to humankind from a Marxist perspective. The act of writing in *Kindheitsmuster,* where Christa Wolf views her childhood in the figure of Nelly Jordan, functions as a *coming into herself* and prompts others to trace the patterns of their own past in hope that they can make the attempt to overcome themselves and this past in bringing about concrete utopias. The materialist basis of the writing precludes idealist moralizing and demonstrates Wolf's efforts to ground her moralism in Marxist humanism.

III

Of all her novels, *Divided Heaven* marked an important historical breakthrough, not only for Christa

Wolf as a critical writer but also for prose fiction in the GDR. Until 1963, she had largely posited socialist ideals in her reviews and fiction without scrutinizing to what extent they were actually being realized in society. That is, Wolf was not entirely familiar with work conditions and socialist practice in the GDR, and her thinking about socialist programs tended to be schematic. *Divided Heaven,* based on her experiences in a wagon factory and inspired by the Bitterfeld Movement, was her first published attempt to expose the discrepancies between the policies put forth in the GDR by the state and party leadership and the actual practice. Aside from openly criticizing some of the more regressive official policies, the novel was one of the first to experiment with flashbacks, stream-of-consciousness, and impressionistic writing in order to mirror the problematic existence of a young woman, who could be considered a true product of the new GDR state. Rita was born in 1940 which means that her formative years coincided with the shaping of the young German Democratic Republic. She *is* as the material conditions of production and social relationships *are* (or, as they should be). Wolf sees Rita defining herself as producer in a socio-historical context and relates her destiny to that of the GDR.

Most reviewers of *Divided Heaven* focus on the choice which Rita makes in the novel and discuss the sequences in regard to the Cold War, socialist realism, the propagandistic tendencies of the novel, and the idealistic criticism of doctrinaire Communism. All these points are valid for discussion and interpretation, but they often lose sight of the major area of experiment in the novel. Wolf sets up a spectrum of types, and their behavior is to be measured according to the degree to which they approach the ideal of the upright posture. On one end of the spectrum we find this ideal, and on the other, cynicism and opportunism. The backdrop for this spectrum is the German Democratic Republic of 1959-1961.

Let us briefly fill in this backdrop. This period was perhaps one of the most difficult phases which the GDR has had to endure. Not only were there grave economic crises caused by mistakes in central planning, but there was great resistance on the part of farmers to the nationally organized, agricultural program to bring about farm collectives. In addition, workers began to demand more autonomy and cultural freedom. In response, the government sought to channel and control the dissatisfaction of the workers and farmers by organizing the Bitterfeld Movement. Despite such official directives, workers and farmers began to write critical diaries and journals about work conditions and discussed them openly in committees and readers circles. In addition, professional artists and writers began producing plays, novels, and other works which revealed serious contradictions between the so-called socialist policies of the government and the needs and demands of the people. Discontent with the general mill of life ran high. Emigration (mainly through Berlin) reached a peak between 1959 and 1960. A drought in the summer of 1960 added to the difficulties in the agricultural sector. Educational reforms, though leading to greater democracy in the university, had also led to more doctrinaire teaching in keeping with official state policies. The situation of women, though vastly improved in terms of providing equal rights on a professional and economic basis, had not changed radically so that men continued to retain authority and receive the best opportunities for advancement. The overall work conditions were hard and drab since the economy was in a slump. Moreover, the work force was being depleted, and the western countries were bent on hindering and sabotaging the socioeconomic development of the GDR by stifling trade and recruiting the best skilled workers and professionals of the country. There was only one recourse left to the state and party leadership, and that was the Berlin Wall, officially built on August 13, 1961. It was to be a stop-gap measure, and most people hoped that it would lead to greater cultural freedom by making the population assume more responsibility for the socialist experiment.

The crisis of this period is alluded to right at the beginning of *The Divided Heaven* when Wolf talks about the air that weighs heavy, the water with its bitter taste, and "the silent voices of imminent danger, all fatal in that period." It is against this backdrop that we must try to understand Wolf's spectrum of types, for she uses it to put forward the questions: What was the correct posture to assume under those conditions? What postures were assumed during this period? How do they point the way to the upright posture?

In examining the types in the novel, Wolf's main character is perhaps the most credible because she is the most naive, impressionable, and flexible. She reacts to the forces which intrude upon and stimulate her, and under the pressures of those forces, she matures and shapes her own destiny. Her lifeblood is strongly tied to the people and relations of production under which she works, particularly after she is "yanked" from the alienating job she occupies in the country town, and this makes her choice at the end of the novel believable just as her attempt to commit suicide is also understandable. Rita must learn to endure while making major changes in her life. In particular, she must learn to seek the upright posture in a situation which demands the utmost from her: "There was no doubt that Rita had been through a terrible experience. She was well again but, like many people, she could not know how much inner courage she would need to look life firmly in the face again, day after day, without deceiving herself or being deceived. There may come a time when people will recognize that the fate of countless ordinary people depended on their inner courage — for a long, difficult, threatening hopeful moment in history."

The "ordinary" people with such courage are Schwarzbach, Wendland, and Meternagel. These men are all aware that "socialism isn't a magic formula," and each in his own way represents a critical model of behavior in contrast to the standard party members and official functionaries who place the party or their own selfish interests above the needs of the common people. In most GDR novels, especially up to 1963, it was considered *a propos* to present an official party member as guiding light. Generally speaking, this figure, like Walter in Wolf's own *Moskauer Novelle*, is a man of the older generation who serves as a moral model of socialist behavior and brings about a happy end after a trying period for some younger protagonist. To a certain extent, Wolf continues this schematic presentation in her novel except that her male "heroes" have all had run-ins with the party and, while committed to Communism, all refuse to comply to senseless, arbitrary orders at the expense of their fellow-workers. They stand for the humanistic quality of socialism in opposition to types like the professor Mangold, who can only memorize Marxist principles and apply them mechanically without consideration for human feelings.

Schwarzbach, Wendland, and Meternagel are all variations on the way toward the upright posture. They differ in age and jobs, but they share a strong dedication to Communism which drives them to use their ingenuity, creativity, and human feelings to perservere despite obstacles. These models are important to Rita, who needs to glimpse socialism as it might be lived out. These men become manifestations of hope for a young woman who comes out of isolation to tap a potential she never knew she possessed. Manfred, her lover, functions in the novel at the far end of the upright posture spectrum, for his cynicism leads him to despair. Unlike Schwarzbach, Wendland, and Meternagel, he refuses to struggle against the opportunist professors and careerists who flee to the West. His past and present family situation has scarred him to such an extent that he cannot believe in the possibility of trust, sharing, mutual support, and love. He perceives only hypocrisy around him and remains closed to new possibilities. Not that these possibilities are bright and cheerful. It must be remembered that Manfred comes from a generation which lost its illusions under fascism and has good reason to look upon the socialist state planning in the GDR with askance. To a certain extent, Wolf identifies with the standpoint of Manfred, but she is also careful to show that he is isolated from areas of production where great changes were being made and experienced by Rita. These changes give Rita an inkling of what may be possible in the future whereas Manfred is surrounded by intellectuals who are interested mainly in using science to advance their careers. Thus, the work conditions and the historical experiences of Manfred and Rita determine their decisons and also provide the basis for the moral judgements in the novel. There is no doubt but that Wolf aligns herself with the productive forces of the working people and depicts those elements which obstruct the emancipatory drives of the working people as negative. Nor does she mince her words. The university, factory, and other institutions are generally seen to be dominated by authoritarian functionaries. The "heroes" of the upright posture are common people and seen as being exceptional. No wonder then that Manfred leaves and that Rita tries suicide. But Manfred must also leave so that Rita and the future of the GDR can be preserved.

The gray industrial imagery of the novel against which Rita's dilemma is played out is certainly bleak. Yet, the purposeful striving of the ordinary people, particularly in the factory and at the university, to build more humane relationships under socialist work conditions, imbues Rita with hope. She gains a sense about herself as individual from the role she plays in productivity. Though there is the impression — and ironically this was probably not intended as a conscious critique by Wolf — that men tend to dominate the sphere of production and that quantity of production is the priority in the socio-economic system, Rita learns most from the manner in which men and women work together with consideration toward others in order to make their society more fit and worthy for humans. At times Wolf tends to be too unquestioning about the social relations of production. For instance, the fact that men dominate both the technological and industrial spheres and push mainly for high output in production is accepted as necessary in the development of socialism. The dangers of "instrumental rationality' in a planned economy which are later depicted in *Unter den Linden* were not yet seen by Wolf. Nevertheless, she does allude to the problematic by placing Rita and Manfred before a moral decision which has its roots in the nature of social production. In contrast to Manfred, who wants to escape miserable conditions by doing scientific work for more profit and power, Rita learns that history is "not built on the misery of the individual, but on the struggles of ordinary people to overcome miserable conditions." Left alone, that is, without the subjects of history acquiring consciousness to sense where change can occur, misery will indeed continue to pervade social conditions.

The movement of *The Divided Heaven* is toward such social consciousness — toward the upright posture. Reflections and flashbacks are used to heighten the awareness of both Rita and the reader. The stress on the subjective mode is further enhanced by the innovative actions of Meternagel, Schwarzbach and Wendland. They are men taking history into their own hands and in the name of the working people. They project themselves on the course of history, and in that they do this to eliminate exploitation and oppression, they endow their acts with a moral quality.

The Divided Heaven is filled with this moral quality which has nothing to do with Manichean or Christian antimonies but with the real possibilites for human beings to bring the nature of their existence more in line with their aspirations for a life without arbitrary constraints. Such a moral impulse in writing leads at times to idealistic representation and schematization in this novel, but it also accounts for the vigor and critique of the prose. The drab grayness of life is not camouflaged in the novel, but neither is the grim, hopeful determination of those who seek to transform the grayness into an idyllic field of red poppies that serves as a symbolic motif in the picture hanging in Rita's convalescent room. Rita recuperates. Just as Vera in *Moskauer Novelle,* the narrator in *The Quest for Christa T.* and in *Self-Experiment,* women with whom Wolf obviously identifies, Rita needs to overcome herself and possess strength of character if she is to become a human being in the socialist projection of the future. Overcoming must be understood as gaining control of productive and social life, as thinking critically and imaginatively, and concretizing one's aspirations in such a way that utopian thought will no longer be necessary. Fulfilling the message of the moralist as Marxist means the end of all utopias and the beginning of real history.

Jack Zipes   *Milwaukee*
                                               Summer, 1976

Divided Heaven

The city, on the threshold of autumn, basked in the hot sun after long weeks of rain; its breath, coming faster than usual, puffed up through hundreds of factory chimneys into the clear sky, where it hung motionless. The unaccustomed brilliance struck people as incongruous and almost unbearable in those uneasy days. The air weighed heavy, and the water, with its ugly smell of chemicals, tasted bitter. But the earth was still firm and would bear them as long as it remained beneath them.

So we returned to our daily work – abandoned for a brief spell while we listened to the impersonal voice of the radio announcer and to the silent voices of imminent dangers, all fatal in that period. We had escaped these dangers this time. A shadow had fallen over the city; now it was warm and alive again, bearing and burying life, giving and taking it away.

We took up conversations again where we had left off – about the wedding, whether it should be at Christmas or in the spring, about new winter coats for the children, about the wife's illness or about the new boss at the works.

We learned to sleep soundly again and to live our lives to the full, as if there were an abundance of this strange substance – life – as if it would never be used up.

1

In those late August days in 1961 a girl called Rita Seidel woke up in a small ward in a hospital on the outskirts of the city. She had been unconscious, not asleep. It was evening when she opened her eyes, and the clean white walls were already shadowy. She had no recollection of the room, but she remembered at once why she was there. She had come a long way back and the feeling of distance and depth remained with her, although she emerged quickly out of darkness into this sparse light. She remembered the city, then the works and the workshop and the exact spot on the tracks where she had fallen. Someone must have halted the two railway wagons which had been gliding towards her from either side, otherwise she would certainly have been crushed between them. That was the last thing she remembered.

The nurse came to her bedside, for she had seen her wake up and look round with curiously expressionless eyes.

"You're all right now," she said softly.

And Rita turned her face to the wall and began to weep. She wept all night, and she could not speak when the doctor came to see her in the morning. Neither was there any need to speak, for he knew about her case and that she was a student and had only been working in the factory during the holidays. She had not got used to many things there – the heat in the wagons, for instance, when they came out of the drying-room; it was actually forbidden to work in them while they were still so hot, but there was so much work to be done. . . . The tool chest was very heavy, too – about seventy pounds – but she had dragged it up to the tracks just where they were shunting. That was when she fainted – and no wonder, for she was hardly more than a girl. And now she was crying, which was what generally happened in such cases.

"It's the shock," said the doctor, and ordered an injection. But after a few days, when Rita could still not bear to be spoken to, he began to worry. What would he not have given to get hold of the man who, he felt certain, must have got her into this state.

Neither could Rita's mother, who came in from the village where she lived, explain what was wrong with her daughter.

"It's the studying," she said. "I knew from the very beginning that she wouldn't be up to it."

Might there not be some man behind it? Not that she knew of. Rita's old friend, the chemical engineer, had been gone six months already. Where did he go? Why, he skipped it. You know. To the West.

Rita got flowers – asters, dahlias, gladioli – bright spots of colour in the long, grey hospital day. Nobody was allowed to see her at first, until one evening a man with a bunch of roses refused to go without seeing her. Perhaps this was the man who could take her out of herself, the doctor thought. He stayed with them while they talked for a few minutes; they gave no special sign of love, forgiveness or the like, which he would surely have noticed, if only in their eyes. But although they talked about every-day things, like railway wagons, he sensed that this young man, who was manager of the factory in which Rita had worked, knew more about her than her mother or any of her other visitors. Twelve carpenters from the factory, a fair-haired little hairdresser – Rita's special friend – students from the teachers' training college where she was studying and girls from her home village came to see her while she was in hospital. So loneliness could not have been her trouble, the doctor thought.

And they were fond of her. They talked gently and studied her face, which was still pale and tired but no longer so desolate, for it was not in her nature to cling to grief. After a time she could control her tears. She wept less and less each day, and then only in the evenings.

She told no one that she was afraid to close her eyes, for fear of seeing those two wagons, huge and green and black, looming over her again. When the wagons were given a shove they ran along the tracks by themselves, only stopping when they met; and that was where she saw herself lying. Then she would weep again.

The doctor said she would have to go to a sanatorium. If she could not tell them what was troubling her she would have to weep her fill; then she would find peace again and the wounds would heal over. She was well enough to travel by train, but the factory sent a car to take her. She thanked the doctor and the nurses before she left. They liked her and wished her well, even though she had told them nothing.

The whole story was really quite ordinary, Rita thought, and of some things she was ashamed. All of it behind her now, in any case. But what she still had to get over was the horrible feeling of the wagons bearing down on her.

2

Rita had noticed Manfred Herrfurth at once when he appeared in her village two years earlier. He had stayed

4

with a talkative cousin and she had soon found out that he was a qualified chemist on holiday after studying for his doctor's degree; he had written a good thesis, too, for later on she had seen the *Distinction* on his diploma.

Rita lived with her mother and an aunt in a small cottage on the edge of the woods, and every morning, as she pushed her bicycle up the hill to the main road, she used to see Manfred at the pump behind his cousin's house, stripped to the waist, splashing the cold water over his chest and back. She would study the sky to see whether the day promised to be fine and suitable for a man resting an overworked brain.

She loved her village, with its red-roofed houses in little groups surrounded by just the right amount of woods, meadows, fields and open sky. In the evenings, when she left her stuffy town office after work, she rode home over a long, straight road which stretched right into the setting sun, villages to the left and right of it. And there in the meadow, where the lane turned off to her own village, she used to see Manfred, the gentle autumn breeze ruffling his short-cropped hair. The same instinct which drew her towards the village drew him to the main road which led to the big bypass and, if one wished, out into the wide world.

When he saw her coming, he would take off his spectacles and polish them carefully on a corner of his shirt, then wander slowly off to the woods, a tall, almost gaunt figure with overlong arms and a small, boyish head. She had longed to know what he was really like, whether he was as stuck-up as he looked, and perhaps to take him down a peg.

But one Sunday evening, in the village hall, she thought he looked much older and harder and her courage failed her. He watched the village boys and girls dancing all evening, until the very last dance and they were already opening the windows to blow away the cloud of smoke hovering over the heads of the drunk and the sober, before he came over to her and led her out on to the floor. He danced well, but without much interest, looking at the other girls and passing remarks about them.

She knew that he was leaving early the next morning. He might even go away without saying a friendly word to her, she thought bitterly.

"Isn't it hard to go on behaving like that?" she asked suddenly, looking him firmly in the eye.

Without a word, he took her arm and led her outside. They walked silently down the village street. Rita broke off a dahlia which hung over a fence. A shooting star darted across the sky, but she didn't make a wish.

They reached her garden gate. She walked slowly up to the door, disappointment mounting at each step. She had her hand on the knob (it was as ice-cold and hard as a whole lonely life, she thought).

"Could you fall in love with a chap like me?" he asked in an offhand tone behind her.

"Yes," said Rita.

She felt quite calm now. She could just see his face as a lighter blotch in the darkness and he must have seen hers like that, too. The door-knob grew warm in her hand. He cleared his throat and walked away. She stood quite still at the door until she could no longer hear his footsteps.

She lay awake all night, and in the morning she began to wait for a letter from him, astonished at the turn events had taken, but without doubting what would happen. His letter came a week after the village dance. It was the first letter really meant for her, after all those business letters at the office.

My little brown girl, Manfred called her. He wrote down everything that was brown about her, although girls had not interested him for a long time, he said.

Rita, nineteen years old, had often been vaguely dissatisfied because she could not fall in love like other girls, but she had no trouble in understanding his letter. She suddenly felt that all her nineteen years, all her wishes, actions, thoughts and dreams, had had only one purpose – to prepare her for this moment, for this letter. She felt that she suddenly knew things which she had never learnt. She was certain that nobody before her had ever felt or could ever feel what she now felt.

She looked at herself in the mirror and watched as the colour crept to the roots of her hair. She smiled, feeling curiously shy and proud.

3

Rita had known ever since she was five years old that it was always wise to be prepared for a sudden change. She dimly remembered living in blue-green, hilly country and watching her father, with his magnifying glass fixed in his eye and a fine brush in his hand, quickly and skilfully painting tiny patterns on coffee cups from which she had never seen anyone drinking.

Her first long journey came at the end of the war and scooped her up with a crowd of desperate, angry people, taking her away forever from the Bohemian forests. Her mother had set out in search of her husband's sister, who lived in a village in Central Germany, and at whose door they arrived one evening, without warning, like survivors from a shipwreck. They found refuge in the sister's house – a bed and a table, a whitewashed closet for Rita, a tiny room for her mother. And although her mother said again and again that she would not stay long, she remained there, chained by poverty and by the vain hope that she might one day get news of her husband, who had been reported missing at the front, or that he might find her here in this tiny cottage.

The years passed and hope dwindled, leaving only sad memories behind. Rita went to the village school, learnt to read, write and count with the village children, and played with them by the stream. Her aunt was a fussy, humourless woman, for her life had lacked great happiness or real grief and had dried up all her longings and, in the end, even her envy. She liked to remind Rita and her mother that this was her house, but she loved the child in her own way.

It had been hard for Rita's mother to share a hearth and her child's love. Rita was a cheerful, affectionate child, friendly to everyone, and the village people thought they knew her well; but she never confided in anyone about the things which really pleased or grieved her. A young teacher who came to the village later on realised that Rita was lonely and he lent her books and took her with him on long walks. He also knew how much she regretted having to leave school and go to work in an office. But she had insisted on doing this, for her mother had gone out to work in the fields and in a textile factory for her sake, and now that she was ailing Rita wanted to look after her.

"You'll make things harder for yourself later on," the teacher had said.

Rita had been seventeen then. Determination is

good, but it is one thing to make a sacrifice and quite another to go on working, day after day, in a gloomy office all alone, for a small branch insurance office only needs one office girl. It was hard to do nothing, day after day, but add up columns of figures and write the same letters to backsliders reminding them of their debts, to be given orders, scolded or praised by the same men who drove up and drove away again in the same cars, week after week.

The young teacher had encouraged her to expect a great deal from life. She hoped to experience extraordinary things, extraordinary joys and sorrows, extraordinary events; and the whole country was in fact in ferment, but this did not strike her as extraordinary, since she had grown up in the midst of it. She knew no one at that time who could help her to direct her insignificant – but to her important – existence into the great stream of life, no one to help her to alter a situation which had been forced upon her. And she had already begun to fear that she might get used to her monotonous existence.

Autumn came again. This was the third year that she had watched the leaves fall from the two big lime-trees outside her office window. She would never see anything new out of this window, she often thought. In ten years' time the post-bus would be stopping there at noon sharp, and her hands would be dry and grubby, so that she would feel she must go out and wash them even before they called her for lunch.

Rita worked all day and read novels all evening, feeling more desperately lonely as each day passed, until she met Manfred and began to see things she had never seen before. That year she noticed that the trees lost their leaves in a shower of colour, and the post-bus sometimes came late. She was linked up with life again by a clear sequence of thoughts and longings. And she was never unhappy or bored, even though she did not see Manfred for weeks at a time.

Then he wrote that he was coming for Christmas. Rita met him at the station, although he had told her not to.

"Look," he said, "the little brown girl in a brown fur cap, like in a Russian novel."

They walked over to the bus stop and stood waiting in front of a shop window.

"This is just what I wanted to avoid," he said. "Waiting here in the slushy snow, looking at watering cans and babies' baths and not knowing what to say to each other."

"Well, we can let the story go on," said Rita. "How about this? 'Come, we'll take the blue bus which is just coming round the corner,' the heroine said to the hero. 'I'll take you home and then you'll come with me to meet my family, who still don't know you exist, or that they have to get to know you so that they can invite you to share our Christmas goose.' Is that enough for today?"

They laughed and jumped on the bus. She went with him to his cousin's house and he went with her afterwards to see her mother and aunt, who scrutinised him in silence. Very manly, thought the aunt, but too old for that child. A "chemistry doctor", thought her mother. If he takes her she'll be set up for life and I can die in peace.

"Do come and share our Christmas dinner," they said.

Rita remembered that Christmas in the snow-decked village, for snow had fallen on Christmas Eve, as it should. They walked silently along the empty village street, arm in arm. She wondered if things would ever be like that again. The two halves of the world did not quite fit into each other, and they had walked along the seam as if it had not been there, she thought.

When they reached her door Manfred took a narrow silver bracelet from his pocket and gave it to her, awkwardly. Rita had already realised that she would have to have tact enough for them both. She drew off her thick woollen gloves, letting them fall in the snow, and laid her hands on Manfred's cold cheeks. He stood quite still, looking down at her.

"So warm and soft and brown," he murmured and blew her hair out of her face. The blood rushed up to his eyes and he looked away.

"Look at me," she whispered.

"Like this?"

His look sent a quiver through her.

She kept her trembling hands hidden all that evening, but Manfred saw them and smiled. She could not keep her eyes away from him. She was almost hysterically lively, too, but her aunt and her mother either did not notice it or had long forgotten how a girl tries to hide her feelings. They were very busy with the dinner.

Later on they raised their glasses.

"To success in your examinations," said Rita's mother to Manfred. "Let's hope all goes well."

"To your dear parents," said her aunt, although they still knew nothing about his family.

"Thank you," he said drily. Rita could still summon a smile when she remembered his sour expression. Manfred had been twenty-nine at that time, but he would certainly never, at any age, have been a loving son-in-law.

"Last night I dreamt I was spending Christmas at home," he said. "My father drank my health. And in my dream I grabbed up all the plates and glasses I could lay my hands on and smashed them."

"Do you have to shock people like that?" Rita asked him later on at the garden gate.

He shrugged. "What's so shocking about it?"

"Your father . . ."

"My father is a typical German. He lost an eye in the First World War, so he didn't have to fight in the second. And he's still doing the same sort of thing – giving up an eye and hanging on to his life."

"You're not fair to him."

"If he leaves me alone I'll leave him alone. But he'd better not try drinking my health, even in a dream. Why don't you like to admit that we've all grown up without any help from our parents?"

They spent New Year's Eve in a small hostel in the near-by mountains. In the afternoon they went skiing down the gentle slopes and in the evening they joined in with the other young people seeing in 1960. The night they had alone.

Rita found out how this cold, offhand young man longed for warmth and intimacy. She was not surprised, but still she wept a little in relief. He grumblingly wiped away her tears with his fingers and she beat his breast with her fists, first gently and then angrily.

"What's the matter now?" he murmured.

And she wept again. She, too, had been alone.

Later on, she turned her face to his and searched for his eyes in the dim glow from the snow at the window.

"Listen," she said. "What would have happened if you hadn't had that last dance with me and I hadn't asked you that funny question? Or if you hadn't said a word when I went into the house?"

"I can't imagine," he said. "But I'd planned it all beforehand, you know."

4

That was how he had always been. Proud to the last and hard to pin down.

"After all, I'm not the first girl you've been in love with, am I?" she had said, on one of the few Sundays they spent together.

"No, not the first," he said gravely.

"Have you had many?" she asked after a while.

"Several."

"Oh, well," she said, after worrying over this for a while, "I suppose I shall have to get used to all kinds of things."

He lifted her chin and looked into her eyes.

"Promise me something. Don't ever try to get used to impossible things just to please me, will you?"

She laid her head on his breast and let him stroke her hair, swallowed, sniffed and thought comfortably that he was hardly likely to ask the impossible of her.

The weeks between the Sundays became desperately long – a tear sometimes dropped on his letters. But she was surprised when her mother once asked her whether she was happy, for she felt that she was really living for the first time.

Manfred, who had some experience of women and of love, understood more clearly than Rita what was special about their love. Never before had nights spent together tied him to a woman. Each time he had begun a new affair his feeling had cooled quickly and each new relationship had meant less to him. But the very first word Rita had said to him had made a bond between them and had gone straight to his heart in a strangely humbling way. He had tried for a few weeks to break away from her, until he had realised that it was more than he could manage.

He was suspicious of this love; he tested Rita in various ways, and she passed every test, smiling and quite unconscious of what he was doing. He was charmed by her ignorance of her own virtues and he discovered them for her as well as for himself. At first he had been annoyed with her for awakening hopes which he had buried; then he surrendered hesitantly to them.

"You're still a child, my little brown girl," he said. "And I'm almost an old man. It won't work out for us, you know."

"Oh well," she said, "I'm used to people thinking they're cleverer than I. But at least I have sense enough not to let go of a man who's seduced me."

"I'm ruining you."

"I'd rather you did it than anyone else," she said.

Their lives had lain before them and anything had seemed possible except that they should lose each other.

In March a man had come in search of likely talent to take up teaching – a tall, dark man who carried all he needed in a big brief-case. There was no space available for him, so Rita cleared a desk for him in her office and helped him with his letter-writing.

She watched him at his work. He was on his feet all day long and in the evening he would turn up with a few questionnaires filled in by prospective students. He would show them to Rita and comment on them.

"One ought to get one's hair cut more often," he said as he handed her the particulars about a blonde hairdresser who worked in the hairdresser's at the corner.

"Foremen are the bane of my existence. It's like drawing blood from a stone to get them to give up a single man. But I've caught the foreman himself this time," he said triumphantly one day.

He would hang up his coat and sit down for a chat. Rita told him what the local officials thought of him, for they had a habit of coming in to tell her how hard it was to get labour – as if she could help them. But Schwarzenbach listened without comment and made no excuses for taking people away. He smoked and talked about all sorts of things, until she even began to think the newspapers were interesting. He asked her about people she knew and wrote down their names in his notebook.

Rita returned home late every evening and she got more and more excited the longer Schwarzenbach stayed. She was realising for the first time how a hand from above could influence the lives of ordinary people like the little hairdresser, the foreman or the clerk at the town hall. She wondered why she had never given these people any special thought, and why it was necessary for someone like Schwarzenbach to come and persuade the most ordinary people to get out of the old rut and try something quite different.

"That's twenty – not bad for this little area," said Schwarzenbach on his last evening but one.

"Nineteen," Rita corrected him, suppressing a faint feeling of disappointment.

"Twenty," he insisted, and calmly handed her another questionnaire. It was not filled in, but her own name had been printed on the first line.

Rita sat looking at the paper in silence for some time. She had always wanted a little sister, she thought. The training college was in Manfred's town. It was a railway centre and the streets were noisy, with bright lights at night . . . . and later on she would shepherd a group of singing children along her own village street.

"I don't believe I could manage it," she protested.

"Of course you can. Why not? You just fill in that form now, and I can get home a day earlier than I expected, and make up for the time I've spent playing up to you like a bridegroom."

Rita always took her time about things, but once she had taken an important decision she could follow it up quickly. She had got used to the idea and felt that it was absolutely right by the time she had filled in the form. She had waited long enough, she thought. Something had to happen soon. And it would bring her closer to Manfred who had given her the self-assurance she needed to make this decision.

She was ashamed that she could write down the whole story of her life on half a page. After this, she thought, she ought to add at least one worth-while sentence to it each year.

Schwarzenbach glanced over what she had written and slipped the form into his brief-case.

"We'll be seeing each other again," he said, for he was a lecturer at the teachers' training college.

The two hours which followed, before Rita got home and broke the news, stood out clearly in her memory. Everything looked different now – the shabby little country town which she knew so well, the people to whom she spoke, the road home. Someone had come and told her to drop what she was doing and start a new life. If that were possible, anything was possible, she thought. Why, this sleepy little town might even wake up and become a centre of interest. Who could tell what important decisions might not one day be taken in her little office?

As Rita cycled along the straight highway the last rays of the March sun retreated behind the woods. She wondered how many times she would ride along here again – and began to say good-bye.

Just before dusk the whole landscape, which sloped down on either side of the road, took on a curious clarity. The remaining wisps of snow showed up sharply against the brown ploughed fields. Tomorrow the first warm breeze would break up all these contours and new, harder ones would take their places. Snowdrops were waiting a few inches under the earth. Rita smiled. How well she knew all this, for it was a part of her. She thought with gratitude of every bird's call, of the cool river, the morning sun and the summer shadows under the trees.

She rode faster. She hardly felt her legs, but the wind blew harder. Her cheeks glowed. Yes, she would go and who could tell what might come of it.

When she got home her cheeks were rosy and her eyes sparkled. Her mother was worried, as was to be expected – in her experience everything new was worse than the old. She burst into tears as Rita talked, but denied that she was thinking of herself.

"Whatever will Manfred say?" she worried.

She had never felt really happy about Rita's friendship with Manfred, but hoped that something would come of it.

When her aunt was told of Rita's decision she went out without a word.

"Nobody seems to understand how I feel about it," she wrote to Manfred. "I just want to be a teacher, that's all. You understand, don't you?"

She had certainly made up her mind in a hurry, Manfred replied. He supposed he would get used to the idea in time. At any rate, she could come and live with him at his parents' home, although she probably would not be able to stand it for long.

Dear little brown girl, you don't know much about life, he wrote.

5

Manfred knew how it felt to be busy and yet have no interest in what he was doing. He wondered now, when he no longer felt indifferent, how he had got into this state of mind. When had it started? When had he begun to lose interest in things? Why had no one spoken to him about it until Rita came into his life and asked him if it was hard to behave like that?

He felt a completely new excitement now, as he dipped his bunch of synthetic fibres into different coloured liquids, the composition of which he constantly varied, putting them to the most complicated tests and selecting the best and strongest dyestuffs for the next, even more exacting test.

His experiments were nearly finished. Only a short time ago he had been quite unable to think beyond them. What was he going to do when they were finished? Now, suddenly, he found himself planning. He thought of big workshops – steaming, ugly-smelling places, but beautiful in his eyes because fibres would be dyed here according to his method. He himself, in white overalls, would pass down the row of boilers, examining the samples, correcting the composition of the solutions. People would value his opinion because he understood his job and was not overbearing. Modesty, which he had always thought silly, suddenly seemed to him a good quality.

Then her letter came. So she wanted to be a teacher. But why hadn't she asked him first? He thought of getting home at night to find the table covered with exercise books, the room full of backward children needing help, or worried parents. She would not be there just for him he thought jealously.

Oh well, she'll never keep it up, he thought. She's much too sensitive. She'll soon find out what it's like and give it up. And he wrote to her in this mood, too. He was annoyed with her for expecting him to make a compromise. But he would have to make sure that he did not lose sight of her, so he told his mother briefly about Rita and insisted that she should have his old room. He had moved into an attic some time ago.

His mother protested tearfully. Manfred listened unmoved, for he had known exactly how she would react.

"I have my reasons," he said shortly. "She may not be able to stand it here for long in any case."

"Oh, how can you say such things?" she began, but looked quickly away, for she knew how cold and obstinate he could be about things which were important to him. She was thankful that at least the ugly scenes between Manfred and his father had ceased – ceased since he had lost all affection for his parents.

One cool Sunday in April Manfred brought Rita to his parents' home.

"My coffin, divided into living coffin, dining coffin, sleeping coffin and cooking coffin," he said.

"But why do you say that?" Rita protested.

She, too, felt uncomfortable in this neat, silent road, amongst these neglected old villas, in these big, gloomy rooms.

"Because nothing really alive ever happens here," he said, "at least, not that I can remember."

"But your room is bright," Rita comforted herself. She felt she would have to take care not to get discouraged amongst all this silent old furniture.

"Come, I'll show you where we're really going to live," said Manfred.

They stood looking in at the door of his attic room and Manfred watched her to see if she understood what this untidy room meant to him.

"Oh," she said, and looked slowly round at the desk under the little window, the couch, the shelves of books, a couple of bright prints on the walls, and the chemicals in the corner.

"I see I shall have to attend to the flowers," she said at last.

He drew her to him.

"You're good," he said. "As good as a girl can be. And for that I'll make you the finest salads in the evening, and in the winter we'll make toast on top of the stove."

"Yes, that's how it shall be," said Rita solemnly.

They began to laugh and spar with each other, until they were exhausted and lay down side by side, waiting for the night. Spring came in with the shrill whistle of an engine from across the river in the valley below. The little room hung like a swing somewhere in the blue-black sky, swinging so high and so smoothly that they could only feel it move when they closed their eyes. They swung up to the stars, down over the lights of the town and up again towards the sickle moon. Back and forth they swung until they were dizzy, holding each other close and caressing each other as lovers do.

The lights below faded slowly, then the stars above and, last of all, the moon, in the reddish-grey glow of dawn. They stood side by side at the window, the breeze blowing in upon them. First a glimpse of the town below, then a few trees and a strip of river appeared out of the night. They turned to each other and smiled.

6

That smile had always been in danger, she thought, but it had remained between them as a wonderful, secret sign for a long time, even behind a veil of tears.

The sanatorium was white, like mourning itself. Rita moved in while it was still warm, but summer was drawing to a close. A breath of air and leaves fell. What was the use of all this magic at the very end?

Rita smiled wearily at the new doctor's quiet reserve. Was he really not curious? She would soon find out. She had plenty of time, she thought. It did not matter how she spent these few weeks. There were certainly some important things happening somewhere, and she would surely find out about them some time. Now she just took the little glass smelling of tranquillizer from the nurse's hand, drank it down at a gulp, lay back to wait for sleep to come – and it always came and held her till morning.

When she awoke she saw a meadow, green and dotted with red poppies. At the foot of the hill, where the red was very thick, she saw a slender woman with a sunshade in her hand and a child walking beside her dressed in exactly the same ruffles and frills as the woman. Higher up, farther away, a few people strolled along, enjoying the meadow and the poppies. There was a row of poplars at the end of the meadow, and between the trees she saw a little, square white house with a red roof, such as children paint. In the pale blue sky, clouds such as we remember from childhood but seldom see moved gently across the sky. The people in the picture did not look up. They missed those clouds, for they had been dead nearly a hundred years – and the painter, too. But he had seen all that.

But I can stand here at the window and look out over the old trees in the park and see the sky and the clouds as often as I like, Rita thought. That's the advantage of being alive – not much of an advantage, but something, after all.

Rita had never seen a meadow full of poppies – and she knew all about meadows. At first she could not bear the picture, because of its pleasant, long-forgotten sweetness; but why shouldn't meadows have looked different a hundred years ago, she thought. And that pale, slender woman, too. Then she noticed that the picture changed with every change in the light, and that pleased her. She felt this was real.

Rita had known nothing about big towns, except for a day's shopping or a short visit. She had been curious about everything and everybody. Her heart beat faster when she went to see the scene of her coming adventure. She had made up her mind to be patient, thorough and brave.

She had noticed that this was several towns in one; they had grown together like old trees. She and Manfred had walked round the boundaries of each and covered centuries in a few hours. The city centre attracted her; it had not been built for such traffic or so many people and it cracked at every joint during the busy hours of the day. She loved the crowds, let herself be pushed and shoved, and then stood back in a quiet corner, waiting for the lights to spring up all round her.

She had also been a little afraid. Nobody took any notice of anyone else here. It would be easy to get lost, she thought. Young people sat down in trams and let old women stand, cars splashed mud on to people's legs, doors were slammed in one's face in shops, and loudspeakers called to shop-girls when they were wanted elsewhere. . . .

She had wandered along the streets lined with barrack-like workers' houses, reading the signs at many street corners: "Here fell Comrade . . . during the March Uprising in 1923. . . ."

These two hundred thousand people did not live in these streets because they liked them – she could see that from their faces. But there was a different kind of alert tenseness, steadiness and tiredness about them. They had certainly not chosen to come here; what had made them come, she wondered.

Rita climbed up the ancient tower on the market square. She stood there for a long time, searching amongst the hills for her old home, but she could not place it. The wind swept unhindered across the wide, treeless valley into the city. Every child here could tell which way the wind was blowing from the smell – chemicals, malt coffee or lignite. And over everything hung a cloud of industrial waste gas which made breathing difficult. You found your way here according to the tall chimneys of the big chemical factories which stood like sentinels on the outskirts of the city. None of this was old – not even a century old. Not even the light,

we in the present think future is bad
she likes vitality & life — crowds
nostalgia — climbs tower, wind, smells,
breathing difficult — future is smothering

filtering through dust and smoke, was more than a generation or two old in this landscape.

She did not believe in premonitions, but she had felt, as she looked out from the tower, that she would sometimes be sad. There would be a hundred thousand faces around her, but she felt that she might be more lonely here than she had ever been in her own little village.

Even in these days, she thought, it can be a new experience for a girl to come and live in a big city.

A slanting ray shone direct on the tower. She watched the clouds scudding faster across the sky, for the April wind was in a hurry to clear it. The sun would soon be shining on the street below, she thought, as she climbed down the steep steps. She loitered on her way home along the old, tree-lined street with its shabby villas.

Manfred looked up from his books when she came in.

"There isn't an empty space anywhere," she sighed, "except up on the tower. . . ."

But when he went out with her he could reveal many hidden beauties and treasures to her, for he had grown up in this city. Telling her about his childhood seemed to help him to throw off the fears, the bitterness and shame which had gathered in his heart. Even the things he could not tell her weighed less heavy on him and he felt freer than he had done for a long time. Later on, he often thought of that spring, of the city washed clean by frequent showers, Rita's bright face against the grey, crumbling facades, the bare park, the hurrying people – and the river.

They had wandered through the poorer quarter beyond the street where they lived, past decaying wooden steps and dark courtyards, musty-smelling entrances with worn-down tiling, where he had played at Red Indians as a boy, and had come out, to Rita's surprise, by the river. It had become more useful and less friendly than Manfred remembered it, and it was covered with a scummy foam from the chemical factory which smelt ugly and poisoned the water for miles, so that children could no longer swim in it, although it was bordered by meadows and its banks sloped gently.

But the seasons still came in first along the river valley; the frosty breath of winter blew in from the river to cool the city and the first touches of colour appeared amongst the spring green of the shrubs along the river banks, to spread into the crowded city and bloom gaudily in its small front gardens.

The river could still reflect faces, too, if one leaned far enough out over a quiet spot. Manfred had never seen a woman's face beside his in the water, and it touched him unexpectedly to see Rita's face there beside his own. He watched her holding a little black beetle gently by its legs, then drew her up beside him and gazed so long into her eyes that she looked away shyly.

They walked along the path in the quickly approaching dusk until they came to where the river flowed past the last of the town houses. Then they turned back, suddenly longing to be amongst people again.

They ended up in a tiny cinema, in the middle of a children's film. The old projector creaked and the screen flickered, but the children did not care, and neither did they.

They were fascinated by the face of the little boy hero in the film – a clever face, made for joy or sorrow, not for evil or stupidity, it reflected disappointment, despair and happiness in turn, sometimes distorted by dirt and hunger, by cringing, cunning or hatred, then regaining its purity and goodness.

When at last the boy, trembling with the hope of

happiness, set out with his parents in a shabby old truck, in the depths of winter, the pent-up suspense of the children in the audience burst in a long drawn-out sigh. The lights went up. Manfred saw that Rita's face was wet with tears and that she was still crying.

"Whatever shall I do with you, child?" he murmured.

7

The weather changed during the night. The wind veered to the east, a storm sprang up and towards morning there was a hint of frost in the air.

It was Rita's first morning at the railway-wagon works. Manfred had thought the whole thing rather a joke, but Rita was determined to keep her promise to Schwarzenbach, who had insisted that a teacher should know what a big factory looks like from the inside. Manfred's father had found her the job at the works, where he was sales manager.

She felt shy, and there was no one to bolster up her courage, so she made up her mind to go straight ahead, keep her eyes open and, if she made a mistake, to see that it didn't happen twice. She would just try and work things out for herself and not let anyone notice how awkward she felt.

She walked briskly and was at the tram-stop when the first pale, cold, grey streaks appeared in the sky. It was cold and she was glad to push her way into the crowded tram-car. Then she counted the stops until it was time to get out.

The wind cut sharply through the poplars which lined the long avenue. It blew up clouds of dust and the workers held their brief-cases up in front of their eyes.

They waved and called out to each other, walking in groups of two or three and talking loudly. Only Rita was alone and she walked quickly, threading her way between the groups. She turned up her coat collar and held it with her hand, so that her face was half-hidden.

At the gates she looked round again. A glint of sun lit up the tips of the poplars and a few silvery leaves glistened. The sun and the wind would soon change them, she thought.

Inside the gates the seasons meant very little except as dates to mark the stages in the year's work.

It was only a narrow doorway, and not a gate through which she passed into a very ordinary factory yard. She would lose her way here every day, she thought. The best thing would be to get here ten minutes early.

She asked the way to Ermisch's workshop. The first man she asked had never heard of it, but others came up and began to argue about the best way to find it. Rita tried to remember the most important directions – to the left past the wall newspaper WAGON BUILD-ERS! FULFIL THE MARCH PLAN! – March? Why just March? – across a triangular yard, then into the jaws of a huge hall full of half-finished grey wagons, past the welders' shop on the right, through another hall and at last up some wooden steps and into the carpenters' sheds.

Here she was at once surrounded by all the twelve men in Ermisch's brigade, including Günter Ermisch himself. Ermisch was a man who liked to make up his mind quickly, but even he did not quite know what to do with her.

What's the sense of this? she thought angrily. It certainly was a silly idea of Schwarzenbach's. I don't think I'll go through with it, after all.

The men made no jokes, but she felt that they were thinking up a few for a more suitable occasion. Remembering that first day a year later, Rita could hardly believe she had once been such a naive little girl up from the country.

Ermisch, a wiry, dark-haired man in his thirties, had done some quick thinking, however, and decided to put Rita in with Rolf Meternagel and young Hans – a stroke of genius, as they all quickly realised; Meternagel was too old for Rita, had a grown-up daughter and thought of nothing but his work, and Hans was too young, not very enterprising and not too quick on the uptake. They grinned as the three went off together, looking shy and uncomfortable.

Little was said the first few days. It soon came out that Rita had not the faintest idea of what she was supposed to do. They had to stand by her in the narrow compartments and corridors of the unfinished wagons and show her every hand's turn. They would have got on much faster without her, but young Hans enjoyed the feeling of being able to show her how to do things.

"Fitting window frames looks easy," he said. "But it takes a bit of learning."

Rita listened carefully when Meternagel explained things to her – how to hold the screws, how to handle the borer so that it would not slip. She liked him and it was not long before he was calling her "my girl".

She began to look about her. The works was one huge, dirty, screeching confusion, a huddle of halls and workshops, huts and houses, with tracks criss-crossing in every direction and wagons, cars and electric carts shuttling back and forth – all squeezed into a triangle, far too small, between the main road, another factory and the railway.

"We're building more wagons here than ever before," said Meternagel. "We shall be stacking them one on top of the other before long."

"Or maybe not," muttered Herbert Kuhl – cool Herbert, they called him.

"What was that you just said?" asked Meternagel irritably.

"Oh, nothing," said Kuhl with a shrug. "We're a famous brigade, after all."

"We are," said Meternagel.

Rita looked round, but they all went on eating as if nothing had happened. Nobody took the trouble to tell her what this curious little squabble was about.

So far she had not exchanged a single word with Herbert Kuhl, for she was still shy of him. He never joked, seldom spoke and took no notice of her at all. He seemed to have no interest in anything, she thought, and was thankful that she did not have to work with him.

Günter Ermisch handed round a newspaper article which was about them. It was headed "The Busy Twelve". They all read it in turn, chewing their sandwiches and saying nothing. Ermisch pinned it up on the wall newspaper.

The coffee out of the big can tasted of aluminium and did not brace her at all. Her back and shoulders ached, for she always went at things too energetically in the mornings. But she managed to get through the afternoons as well. She walked slowly back along the poplar-lined road, with the wind and the sun behind her.

At first Manfred had expected her to show signs of boredom or disappointment. He had often noticed that she had little patience and could easily be distracted

29

if she felt she was doing something which did not seem useful. He liked to give her a blouse which suited her, or to show her how she should do her hair, and she accepted all his suggestions without hesitation.

But after a time he realised that she was just as determined to be a teacher as she had been to get to know him. Sometimes she was so tired in the evenings that he was sorry for her and got thoroughly annoyed at all this waste of energy.

"Why don't you give it up?" he asked.

"I can't just leave," she said.

"But of course you can if you want to," he urged.

"Well, then, I don't want to," she answered.

They all sat round the big family table for the evening meal.

Herr Herrfurth would unfold his napkin, lift the lid of a dish and politely wish them a good appetite.

He was still a handsome man, slim and tall, his hair thinning but hardly touched with grey, and his glass eye was barely noticeable. Rita did not think him so bad, but Manfred seemed to hate him. His mother, whose sour politeness made Rita shy, merely irritated him.

There was almost nothing to talk about with them. It was impossible to think of anything farther removed from the superficial and precarious restraint at the Herrfurths' supper table than the eruptive confusion of the works. And she understood neither the confusion in the works nor the tense silence at the Herrfurths' table. She sat there like someone at the theatre, watching the changing lights and scenes on the stage and the players acting, but lacking the clue which would link up these fragments into a complete play.

Sometimes, on one of his good days, Herr Herrfurth hit upon a subject which he could discuss at length;

well-rounded phrases rolled off his tongue and they had only to nod from time to time until they were fully informed about the harvest prospects that year or about the weather in Europe.

Unfortunately, Frau Herrfurth could not bear to listen to her husband for long. She punctuated his smooth flow of talk with short, acid comments which added a certain dramatic quality to the conversation.

She paid a good deal of attention to Rita, too; although she could not quarrel with her openly she made up for it with oblique comments.

"In the old days," she would sigh, "young girls prepared for marriage in boarding school. Nowadays they send them to factories amongst hordes of strange men."

Frau Herrfurth took great pains with her looks. Her short white hair was carefully tended and she wore rubber gloves for housework. Her hats exactly matched her suits. She despised her husband and had perhaps gathered sufficient reason for this in the thirty years of their married life, but she took good care that he did her credit when they went out together. Under the influence of bitter, spiteful thoughts, her features had sharpened and were almost masculine, so that there was something incongruous about the powder and make-up she used. She slimmed, too, on a rigid salad diet, did her slimming exercises daily to the instructions of a West German radio programme, and held herself as stiff as a ramrod. It was difficult to believe her capable of the hysterical fits to which she sometimes abandoned herself.

When Rita was there Herr Herrfurth felt that he ought to show disapproval of his wife's scathing political comments.

31

"Really, Elfriede," he would protest mildly, but his wife ignored the hint. She would wait long-sufferingly until he had finished his brief, moderately correctional remarks.

"But surely you've finished for the day, Ulrich?" she would say. "You've left your Party badge on your other suit."

He had his revenge, however, when his wife turned fond eyes to her son and tried to draw him into conversation. Rita watched anxiously as Manfred's expression changed. He would glance coldly at his mother and barely answer.

When the uncomfortable meal was over and they could at last leave the room, followed by a few pained words from Frau Herrfurth, they withdrew each evening to the magic of their own little attic room, quickly shrugging off their annoyance. Manfred never talked about his parents when they were alone. Rita would take out her English grammar, feeling that she was at least doing something towards her future studies, and Manfred sat down to his formulae.

He could quickly lose himself in his work. He would turn on the old radio which stood on a corner table, thrust his hands deep into his pockets and begin wandering round the room, with one eye on his desk. Rita sat quite still until she saw that he was ready. He would whistle softly, bend over his papers, still hesitant, then start searching wildly amongst them, piling charts and calculations in a heap on the floor. At last he would find what he wanted, sit down and begin to write.

Rita studied his profile – the narrow temple, straight nose and absorbed expression. She realised that he always had to overcome a certain inner resistance, a feeling of inadequacy, before he started work. But she took care not to tell him what she was gradually finding out about him. And for this very reason he had no secrets from her.

"What are you doing just this minute?" she would ask him.

He read out a sentence, sprinkled with formulae and Latin words.

"And what does that mean?"

"That your next pullover should be a better shade of blue if I leave it lying for a definite length of time in one particular liquid and not in another."

"That's fine. Do you think blue is my colour?"

"Of course, cobalt blue and no other."

Then she would knit a few rows of the thick brown cardigan she was making for him. It grew as slowly as the year grew towards winter. This calmed her and made her sleepy. Her thoughts wandered like clouds through her mind. Too much was happening to her during those weeks – the strangely exciting days at the works, the strained evening meals at the family table, and the anxious letters from her mother. But as she sat there in the evenings with her grammer and her knitting she felt sure that things would turn out well.

8

"A visitor to see you," the nurse announced one afternoon. "We're letting him come in even though it's not visitors' day."

Rita sat up quickly.

Rolf Meternagel came in quietly, stooping a little as if the ceiling were too low, and sat down beside her bed.

"Well," he said. "How are things going? I thought

somebody ought to come and tell you what's going on."
He was out helping with the potato harvest – just his
luck to get the job again – and there was a truck full
of potatoes waiting outside. The driver would not wait
more than ten minutes for him – not in this God-
forsaken place, anyway.

"I'm so glad you've come," said Rita.

He looked desperately tired and she could see that
he had had his cap on all day, for there was a ridge in
his hair.

"But it's cold out today, Rolf," she said, as he wiped
the sweat from his face.

"It's not only the heat that makes you sweat."

"What's new?" she asked.

He glanced at her, wondering if she really wanted to
know.

"One thing, we're putting in twelve windows a shift
now," he said.

He said it casually, but they both knew how much
hard work, quarrelling and intrigue lay behind it. The
papers carried brief reports on such things every day,
but Rita knew exactly how Meternagel felt about it.

"You really are a famous brigade," she said, and they
both laughed.

"You know, railway wagons were just the right thing
for me," she said. "I should have got used to the work
somewhere else, too, of course, but I can't think of
anything better than our locomotives whistling as they
go off in the evenings with two new wagons . . . ."

She often used to wonder where they went – to Siberia, the Taiga, the Black Sea. . . . She often drew a
single thread out of her red head scarf and tied it round
a pipe – a little thread of hope that she might one day
follow. . . .

And the tears welled up again as she remembered how Manfred had always teased her about that red scarf – little Red Riding Hood, when will the wolf come and gobble you up?

"Aren't you allowed up yet?" Meternagel asked hastily. Surely she wasn't going to start crying again?

"Oh yes, each day a little bit longer."

He had been thinking about how he had rushed around at the works eighteen months ago like a dog worrying a bone, insisting that they would soon be putting in ten windows a shift, and how they had all thought he was crazy. And now here he was calmly announcing that they were doing twelve a shift. He was glad that Rita had been pleased and surprised and he felt sure that once she was on her feet again she would find plenty of things to be pleased and surprised about.

"Do you remember how I described our brigade to you?"

"Oh yes, I remember very well."

He had watched for a while as she cautiously appraised the men in his brigade, then had taken her aside one day.

"Look here, child, you know we're a famous brigade, don't you?"

"Yes," said Rita obediently, thinking of the bonuses and newspaper articles that had been written about them, but also about the quarrelling between Meternagel and Kuhl.

"Well, of course, that's the most important thing about us. But the second most important thing is to know how to deal with famous people," he said, with a twinkle in his eye.

He had told her enough about the men to help her not to be too cautious or too free with them, and to understand that the brigade was a little kingdom in itself. He told her which of them were trying to improve things and which were simply there to earn their money, and about open and concealed friendships and enmities. He explained the undercurrents which sometimes burst through to the surface in a harsh word, a bitter look or a mere shrug. And she began to get along quite well with them all.

"But still, I should like to know," she said now, following up her own train of thought, "how you knew all that then."

"Knew what?" he asked.

"That it wouldn't stay like that."

Meternagel laughed, stood up and held out his hand. It was time for him to go.

Rita would never have guessed that there was so much dynamite in Meternagel's name. She had mentioned him one evening at supper when Herr Herrfurth politely asked about her work. She felt at once that this was not the first time his name had been mentioned here, for the atmosphere at the table changed. But the tension might have passed if Frau Herrfurth had said nothing.

"So he's still there!" she exclaimed.

"Surely you don't imagine that everyone Father trips up simply disappears?" said Manfred sarcastically.

Herr Herrfurth jumped up. He was quite suddenly in a violent fit of rage. He began to shout until his voice cracked. He seemed in danger of working himself up into an hysterical fit of uncontrollable irritation at his son's tone and constant harping and criticism; but then, just as suddenly, he broke off and sank back exhausted in his chair. Manfred went on eating stolidly.

Herr Herrfurth wiped his face with his handkerchief and murmured something about the inconsiderateness of the younger generation. Rita believed he was in the right.

Manfred stood up.

"We've had that old record too often. I know it by heart," he said. "In fact I'm not interested in anything you have to say."

His mother jumped up and stood in his way as he made for the door. She clutched at him, begging him to have some consideration for his father.

Manfred turned pale, pushed past his mother and left the room.

Rita felt the pain in her heart as the door closed behind him. She was desperately sorry for his mother who fell back into her chair, sobbing.

How would it all end, she thought, feeling utterly alone.

She had waited a long time for Manfred in their room; when she could bear it no longer, she went down and waited for him in the road. He came back shortly before midnight.

"You could have gone to bed alone for once," he told her.

She shook her head.

"The next time you do a thing like that you must take me with you."

He leaned against the rough wooden gate and Rita could not bring herself to go near him. She thought of how he had waited in the meadow for her, evening after evening – and not so long ago, either. She had thought then that she knew all about him.

I shall always be the one who has to make things right between us, she thought, and if I don't find the right words now, quickly, his face will stay the way it is and he'll go away forever.

He began to move away, but she sensed that he knew she would not let him go alone.

"I could go on bottling it all up, but I may as well tell you a few things now," he said after a while. "It's all quite ordinary, as you'll see. But I simply can't get over it . . . I had almost got used to things, but then you came and everything seemed suddenly just as unbearable as it used to be."

He found it hard to explain what troubled him, and she longed to tell him there was no need to explain or confess to her. But she thought it might really help him to talk to her. Looking back, she wondered whether she had done all she could to help him to throw off these ugly memories.

9

"Rolf Meternagel isn't really so important," Manfred began. "I don't even know him. If you say he's a decent chap, I believe you.

"Last year he was still foreman in your works. He didn't tell you that, did he? They say he had a good chance to get on, too. But he had the bad luck to have dishonest or at least slapdash people working under him, and he had my father as his boss. My father looked on for months, knowing perfectly well that the accounts sent in to him with Meternagel's signature were fixed. He didn't say a word until he thought he had enough evidence piled up. Then he had a big checkup made and it turned out that three thousand marks too much had been paid out in wages. Meternagel lost his job, of course. He kicked up a terrible fuss, and that didn't improve things for him, either. He's been in your brigade ever since. And why do you suppose my father did it like that? After all, he's generally such a coward and not a bit independent. He just likes to keep out of trouble. I guess he needed something of the kind to distract attention from whatever he was up to himself."

Rita walked along silently beside him, fitting her steps to his. She waited for him to go on.

"You say I'm not fair to him. Let other people be fair. I haven't been able to stand him as long as I can remember. . . .

"The first thing I remember – I've heard it as often as other kids hear about the Sleeping Beauty or Red Riding Hood – is the story of my birth. This is how it goes. There was once a man and wife who loved each other as people only love in fairy tales. (She wouldn't really have married him at all if she hadn't been nearly thirty and hadn't frightened all the other men away with her highfalutin' notions. She had to take him, although he was only a shoe factory salesman.) But that doesn't come into the fairy tale; I just put that bit in. According to the fairy tale they loved each other dearly but were not blessed with children. (Mother has told me all about her miscarriages, but that's not part of the fairy tale, either.) At last the longed-for wonder child – that's me – it was a premature baby and not likely to live, so the doctor said.

"So along came the good fairy, Sister Elisabeth, who nursed the little weakling, feeding it with baby-food in a spoon until it was strong enough to go back to its mother. Mother now had this precious child to cling to and was determined never to let it go. That's the end of the fairy tale, and where I really come in."

It was a relief to Manfred to talk at last. He could not explain everything, but Rita was sensitive and understood much more than what he could put into words. There were so many undercurrents, fleeting memories and pictures. He thought of a photo in the family album in which his mother was still beautiful and had a gentle expression which she must have lost later on during her married life. He had often tried to recall how this change had come about, when she had last been cheerful, active and warm-hearted, and to imagine what she might have been like in other, happier surroundings.

"I know she's to be pitied," he said. "I used to hear them quarrelling and my mother weeping in their bedroom, every time she found out that he was deceiving her. He was buyer in a shoe factory by that time, mainly due to her constant pushing. He was away from home a good deal, had the use of a car and could cut a bit of a figure. My mother was almost always offended about something, so he found plenty of other women who were willing to play up to him, although he really wasn't cut out for a double life. . . .

"Of course, he joined the SA in good time. I remember him standing in front of the mirror in the hall, admiring himself in his new uniform, and mother looking on. I must have been four then. I saw their eyes meet in the mirror and I was more frightened by that understanding look than I had been when they quarrelled. I cowered behind the coats.

"After that my father got friendly with his boss. He was made head clerk – fit for society, so to say. We used to visit with his boss on Sundays; and he sometimes visited us.

"I had had very few friends, because mother would

40

peer out from behind the curtain and call me in if she thought I was playing with the wrong kind of children. But later, on Sundays, I was sent out to play with the boss's son. Herbert, his name was; he was three years older than I, and he would push me into fights and I always had to take the blame. My father took no notice of me, aside from hitting me so as to show his boss who was master in our house. . . .

"I hated him long before I went to school. And that's the only thing I'm quite sure about now."

He tried to look into Rita's eyes, but she turned away. Manfred reached for her hand, and then let his arm drop.

"I've got along all right so far without telling all this to anyone," he said more gently. "Perhaps I shouldn't have told you, either."

Rita shook her head. She tried not to think too much about what he had told her, that could wait until she was alone. What she had to do now was simply to listen. Perhaps things would seem less dreary next morning. She could not tell whether she would be equal to the new situation, but it was too late to draw back.

"I was always good at school," Manfred went on. "They used to call me 'seven months' child'. But my mother turned up regularly to complain to the teacher, so they stopped teasing me and left me alone. I lied like a trooper at home, inventing friendships that never existed.

"When they made me join the Hitler Youth the war had already started. My father was 'indispensible' by this time, so we had no trouble. Everybody was glad to get a pair of decent shoes in those days."

Why am I telling her all this? he wondered. Has she any idea of what things were like, then? Why, she

41

wasn't even born! It's a queer thing, the new generation starts somewhere between us. She can't possibly understand that we were all injected early with this cynicism that's so hard to shake off.

"Where was I? Oh yes. I never missed Hitler Youth meetings, although I disliked them. I jumped over walls whenever I was ordered to, with my eyes shut, too. I'd have done much worse things than that. Nobody need try to tell me that you can't frighten people into crime. But they didn't drag me into anything. I guess I wasn't the type.

"In the end, though, when my father eventually had to join the home guards, I did get in with a gang of boys about my own age. They knocked the nonsense out of me and made me what people called 'normal' in those days. I smoked and was rude and rough and slouched about the streets, and at home I put my feet on the table. I shot at the teacher's desk with an old Colt one day, during a history lesson. The teacher was a real Nazi, so I'd have been chucked out if they hadn't had to turn all the schools into hospitals just at that time.

"We idled about all through the summer and saw exactly what a mess the grown-ups had managed to make of everything, with all their cleverness and knowing better. We just laughed aloud at the posters which told us everything was going to be better and different. Who was going to make it different, we wondered. The same people who had got us into this mess? Our school opened again in the autumn. Our old Nazi song-books were still in our lockers. The new people had not even had time to get rid of all the old stuff.

"My mother had burnt Hitler's picture one night in April 1945, and ever since then that autumn landscape – you know, the one over the desk? – has covered up the pale patch on the wallpaper. It's exactly the same size as the old picture of Hitler. But of course, the wallpaper has been changed since then.

"When my father came home in rags a year later, his old brown uniform was gone, too. My mother didn't just have it dyed, like lots of other people who had no little stores of shoes to sell on the sly.

"My mother branched out in a big way. She organised a whole black-market business. She's the one who kept us from starving. My father was a nobody, a doubtful character, and he had no self-respect left, either. He's often assured me that he was only a fellow-traveller, and that's true. A German fellow-traveller. He never had any convictions of his own and he didn't have anything special on his conscience. People needn't be afraid to shake hands with him. There may be a few old letters at the factory which might embarrass him now, but they would only be embarrassing – nothing worse.

"Meternagel has known him since that time, you know. That may have something to do with the way my father behaved to him.

"My mother moved heaven and earth to get him back to work. And she succeeded. She has him completely under her thumb now."

And she's lost me completely, he thought, although she won't admit it.

He had got over his hesitancy, and was even a little afraid that he would not be able to stop talking, although it was now long past midnight. The streets lay cold and empty before them like lonely valleys. They had passed the gate for the third time, and Rita was cold and exhausted.

But she stayed patiently by his side.

"One day Father turned up with a Socialist Unity Party badge on his lapel," Manfred went on. "I burst out laughing, and ever since then the very sight of me irritates him."

His father hadn't been the worst of them, either, he thought. But other young people had been luckier than he; had found genuine friends just when they needed them most. But where were the really honest people? Perhaps he had not searched long enough. And in any case, could he not be a thoroughly decent person himself without having to rely on others?

"We finished school without taking much trouble over examinations. We fifteen-year-olds were the oldest to have no list of dead and missing hung up in our classroom. . . .

"One of our teachers discovered that I could act. You may not believe it, but very soon I was reciting poems at town entertainments – all of it sentimental stuff without any real depth of feeling. *Beloved Spring, how you shine around me in the glowing morn,* or *Your hands are needed in these hard times!* And in our cellar club I sang all the latest hits."

God! he thought, those were queer times! And Rita had just begun to read.

"My mother used to sit in the front row, with tears in her eyes, at every performance. She set her heart on making an actor of me. That would have made up to her for her own dull life.

"But the happiest day of my life was when I finished high school and was admitted to the natural science faculty at college. I took up science partly to spite my mother, you know, and she wept and raged, just as I'd expected. But all of a sudden I didn't get a kick out of it any more. Nothing has been fun since then. The only thing that gives me any satisfaction is my work; there's just enough exactness and just enough scope for imagination about it for me. And then there's you, my dear, you're good, too."

10

Looking back, she realised that this was the night when she had sensed that danger threatened. She had kept silent about it, for she did not want to hurt Manfred when he needed her so much.

She began to find her way about the works, and gradually lost the feeling that everyone was watching her. She still could not understand how it was possible for two gleaming new, dark green railway wagons, smooth, solid and spick-and-span, to emerge each day from that hasty confusion, that shouting and cursing. By the end of the shift the wagons were waiting to be shunted slowly out on to the testing track outside the works. The last fitters sprang off, with their tools in their hands, just as the wagons moved off. Rita used to watch them and the foreman, until they were finally turned over to him, the foreman would shout and curse and wave. Everyday Rita and the men laughed at his antics; then they all stood around and watched the little train until it disappeared into the distance.

"When you just think . . ." young Hans used to say. That was his favourite expression. "Don't you try any of that," the others would say good-humouredly.

Things had seemed to be going smoothly. The men did their work well and there was no quarrelling. Even Meternagel kept a check on his tongue. During the noon pause, they would sit together on rough planks in a green corner of the yard, their legs stretched out in front of them, hands deep in their pockets. They blinked peacefully into the mild autumn sun, watched the clouds wandering slowly across the sky and enjoyed the unusually clear midday air.

Far outside the town jet planes broke through the sound barrier with an ear-splitting crash and were suddenly right above them, flying very high and at a tremendous speed. They followed them lazily with their eyes and felt even more peaceful by contrast.

Her biggest day was perhaps the one on which they celebrated the five thousandth wagon built in the works since the war. It was also their brigade leader's birthday. The works yard had been tidied and the wind blew sharply across it. On the shorter side stood the wagon, decorated with flags and bunting, with 5,000 and the date – April 20, 1960 – painted in big letters on it. A band played and there were speeches and applause. Rita, standing between Meternagel and young Hans, clapped cheerfully with the rest. She had been drinking nothing but malt beer. But everything amused her and she giggled about everything. The dance group, in white blouses and coloured skirts, jumped up onto the wooden platform. She laughed as she saw Ermisch pushing his way into the front row – they had forgotten to invite him onto the platform and this was his way of drawing attention to himself.

At last a heavy shower sent them scuttling for shelter. Everyone had known it would rain, because the air smelt of malt coffee, which meant a west wind. A few scraps of paper blew up against the wooden fence and then the yard was deserted.

The brigade withdrew to the nearest pub to celebrate Ermisch's birthday. They were known here and several tables had already been reserved and were set up in the window corner. . . . Let the rain pour outside! Ermisch was treating them to beer and schnapps and they all were busy drinking.

The light was dim in the narrow, smoke-filled little room.

Rita sat with her lemonade glass in front of her, wondering how much she should drink and how long she ought to stay. The bartender dashed back and forth, for they were his best customers. Smoke rose up from the tables like an evil-smelling fog, and they drank and shouted and laughed. Rita grew quieter and quieter.

She had never before had a chance to look at these twelve men carefully. The eldest of them was sixty – a grey-haired man from East Prussia.

"Hey, Karssuweit, tell us the story about your master, the Baron, and the eggs!" somebody called out. They always called him by his surname. He had been a carpenter on a Junker's estate and even now he looked a peasant amongst these town workers. Young Hans, who was never called by any other name, was drinking with them for the first time and was proud of himself. He hadn't had much luck in life so far and had not even plucked up courage to look for a girl friend yet, but he was always in good spirits.

". . . and then he went over to the harvest hands and said: 'I bet you I can eat fifteen eggs at one go.' Nobody believed him, so he just picked up the egg basket and began to eat, and he got through sixteen. . . ."

Ermisch always interrupted the old man here.

"And all you silly asses admired him for eating your eggs!"

He roared with laughter, his face as red as a turkey-cock, and the whole brigade roared with him, as if this were the best joke they had ever heard. Karssuweit always fell into the trap and turned sulky.

Most of them had quite ordinary, every-day faces. Few of them were young. They had managed to get through life so far, but perhaps it was better not to inquire too closely how they had managed – certainly not without rebelling or cringing, according to temperament, or without having been in difficulties and searching desperately for a way out. . . .

"That's nothing," Franz Melcher said to his neighbour. "Paris was all right. But have you seen Bedouin women bathing at the spring early in the morning – quite close up, through your telescope. . . ."

There was a sudden hush. Melcher glanced quickly at Rita and stopped talking.

Someone struck up a song – *The water roars down from the mountains* and they all joined in lustily. These men had left so much behind them – brothers killed in the war, friends killed in prison, women all over Europe and traces of themselves all over the world. But their experiences were less than useless to them here.

Rita thought that Herbert Kuhl looked even more detached and ironical than usual. He did not join in the singing, either.

Someone else came to their table – Ernst Wendland. This was the first time Rita had seen him. He looked much too young, quite an unlikely person to be production manager of such a big enterprise. He was stocky, fair-haired, a little pale. Ermisch motioned him to sit down. Rita felt that he was doing his best not to damp their cheery spirits. He clinked glasses with Ermisch and cracked a couple of jokes, but he was obviously not in good form.

The noise did not die down after he joined them, but

something changed. It was no longer the same party. Rita suddenly saw them all as if from a distance, sitting there at the table in the dim public-house light, as if she were looking back into the past, and she heard their voices more distinctly. Wendland had disturbed the atmosphere because he had tried to fit in. They seemed to sense a hint of disapproval and they began to sing loudly and defiantly and bang their glasses on the table.

Wendland said little. He drank his beer quickly, rapped the table with his knuckles by way of good-bye to all, and went away again.

"I knew that would happen," said Meternagel, breaking the silence which followed his departure.

Rita had no idea what Meternagel meant. Young Hans, disappointed at the change of mood, tried to turn things against Wendland.

"Pretty young for the job, huh?"

They all laughed. But nevertheless the party soon broke up after that.

"Your beer tastes lousy. Drink it yourself!" somebody shouted to the bartender.

It had stopped raining when Rita went out, and the air was warm and soft. She was tired but excited, and she felt like going for a long walk, perhaps down the road out of the town, and on to the wind-swept meadows. . . .

Manfred was waiting for her when she got out of the tram.

"Have you been waiting long?" she asked, surprised.

He shrugged his shoulders. "If I say I've been waiting a long time, who knows, you may get up pity and come home late every evening, stinking of beer and smoke."

She laughed and rubbed her face on his sleeve. So

here she was, coming home, waited for and expected to give an account of herself and grumbled at for staying out late. It was not much use dreaming about long walks in the meadows.

They met a man coming out as they got home. He had stopped by the gate to light a cigarette, and Rita recognised him by the light of the match – it was Ernst Wendland. She greeted him shyly. He looked up and realised that he had seen her amongst the twelve men in the public house. He raised his hat and went off quickly to his car, which stood under the next street-lamp.

"Who was that?" asked Manfred.

Rita told him.

"I seem to have met him somewhere . . ." he said thoughtfully.

Herr Herrfurth sat in his study, thoroughly upset. Without thinking of his quarrel with his son, he began to tell them what had happened. The old works director had not returned from a business trip to Berlin. He had probably wanted to escape the responsibility for the break-down in production next month; he must have seen the catastrophe coming. Ernst Wendland had been appointed director in his place.

11

Rita always connected bright red sunrises with dark smoke rising up against them, grey, confused days and worried dreams with the weeks that followed.

Not only she but everybody at the works seemed to feel that a great deal now depended on them. The factory was neither very big nor very important and it had never had much attention from the authorities; but it seemed as if the tension which had spread all over the country had suddenly gathered at this one point. Even people over there in the West began to take notice of it. West German newspapers wrote about the "once flourishing Mildner Wagon Factory now facing ruin" – a mixture of truth, half-truths and downright lies. Their former director spoke over a Western radio station. He had known for a long time, he said, that he stood at a lost post, but only recently had friends helped him to make the only possible decision and free himself from the difficult position in which he had found himself. But he sent greetings to his workers, who knew his liberal attitude, from the happier part of Germany, and urged them to do the same as he had done.

The next day his speech was relayed over the works loudspeaker system. After each sentence it was interrupted and the young, untrained voice of the works radio operator repeated: "Comrades! Colleagues! That is the voice of a traitor to our works, to our state, to us all!"

For two weeks, production decreased every day. The little works locomotives stood idle. Worried commissions in white or blue overalls worked through the various departments of the factory tapping and listening against its huge body, like doctors. The men watched them, at first scornful, then thoughtful and finally thoroughly worried.

Rita's heart sank as the screeching, stamping, whistling noises in the workshops gradually subsided. She compared the resigned, long-suffering expressions on the men's faces with the newspaper photographs which still hung on the walls of the locker-room. There were more and more delays and ugly quarrels broke out while the men waited about.

Rita had no idea what a tremendous undertaking it was to pull a big factory out of such a situation. As usual, people were pessimistic, bad-tempered and suspicious, and many seemed glad that the ship was sinking, even though they were on it.

"What's going on?" she asked Meternagel.

"What do you think? It was sure to happen. If nobody feels responsible for anything except his own little job and nobody ever looks beyond his own nose there's bound to be a big crash some time. The purchasing department doesn't know what to buy to keep production going, supplies aren't scheduled properly, the technical plans aren't there, and nobody has the faintest notion what to do next. And on top of all that, if a few items don't turn up on time, you get a colossal mess like this one."

"But how are we going to get out of it?"

Meternagel laughed bitterly and shrugged his shoulders.

Manfred understood Rita's confusion. He did not resent her continual talking about the works; he tried to comfort and encourage her, telling her about worse situations which had righted themselves in the end.

"Later on – perhaps quite soon – you'll be laughing over the whole thing," he said, not realising how right he would prove to be.

Just when it seemed most hopeless, when there was hardly any work and the men slouched about in silence, Rita awakened to the change in herself; her despair had become impatience, and a desire to help, to do her share, to be ready when the chance came to improve things.

She became aware of small things which she had not

previously observed – that Ermisch and Meternagel were eyeing each other speculatively, and that Ermisch had started it. For these difficult days had revealed that his leadership was dependant on the times: when there was plenty of work and good wages and radio reporters to be interviewed, statements to be issued and seats on platforms on May Day, Ermisch was the man. But when the going became rough, he was easily discouraged and no good at keeping up the men's spirits.

Finally, Ermisch accosted Meternagel with, "What are you staring at me for? What are you looking at, anyhow!"

But it was no use. Ermisch had to stand aside and see a rival gradually take his place; the men began to look to Meternagel, who kept calm and took things in his stride. Everybody felt that change was in the air, and Ermisch certainly did not want his brigade to be the last to make a move . . . if he only knew what move . . .

But Meternagel held his tongue.

There was conversation again at the Herrfurths' table. This made Rita feel much happier. Herr Herrfurth flaunted his white table-napkin less jauntily now, and he was no longer able to sweep aside all the unpleasantnesses of the day when he sat down to supper. The confusion at the works had broken disastrously into the well-organised calm of his household.

At first, while the flight of the old director was still being investigated, Herr Herrfurth had had serious misgivings about some of the papers – orders for material and so on – which he had also signed.

"After all, you can't look into everything yourself," he said. "And I'd like to see the man who refused to sign what the director put under his nose."

But later on, when he had escaped with a warning and had delivered his "self-critical" speech, he became less worried.

"It's not so easy to find a buyer who knows his job as well as I do," he used to say.

But he had other troubles. He did not dare to criticise the new director openly, but it was clear from some remarks he let drop that he felt uneasy.

"He's a young man with new ideas and healthy ambitions," he remarked. "And why not? But Rome wasn't built in a day."

"All very well and good, you know, his being a good organiser," he said on another occasion. "But just wait till he tries one of his new schemes on these people. It's a pity that a youngster like that doesn't have time to get the corners knocked off him. He'll soon have done for himself. . . ."

Frau Herrfurth had never been inside the works since it was taken over by the government; she had no idea of what was really going on. But instinct seemed to tell her what the changes would mean. She knew her husband, she had watched the girl her son meant to marry, and she had seen – if only for minutes – Wendland's ambitious, dogged expression. Wendland was now her husband's immediate superior. That was enough for her.

So far she had regarded everything that went on outside her four walls as a nuisance, because she had been forced to make certain adjustments in her way of life. She had always thought the current state of affairs silly; it couldn't last long. Now the thing had happened for which she had been hoping. The very existence of many of the changes was threatened. She observed the efforts which were being made to avert a catastrophe.

Nobody could be forced to make these efforts. Only people who felt that they were facing a real personal loss would have the energy to exert themselves. At last she realised that something really important had been going on around her in the last few years; these fanatics, she understood now, had actually succeeded in infecting other people with their madness. Now she would have to make some decision. She began corresponding again with her widowed sister in West Berlin.

12

While these events were taking place, Rita had gradually ceased to be regarded as a new-comer at the works. She knew exactly which tram she must catch in the mornings if she wanted to meet acquaintances, and in the evenings she went home with Rolf Meternagel, who lived not far away. They exchanged a few words about work, or about the coming Sunday, before they parted – always at the same corner where, in the course of their acquaintance, a lilac bush had already put out buds, blossomed deep purple and the blossoms withered again.

"How long are you going to let all this go on without saying anything, Herr Meternagel?" Rita asked, one afternoon in June.

He knew at once what she meant and was annoyed that his exaggerated caution should have struck her, as well.

"And how long are you going to call me Herr Meternagel?" he grumbled. "The name's Rolf, as everybody knows."

There was a silence. Rita said good-bye, shyly.

"Come a bit of the way with me. You've plenty of time," he suggested.

They walked on in silence. He glanced at her with a frown, as if to make quite sure that he was talking to the right person.

"I suppose you know I've had what they call a 'retrogressive development'?" he said at last, in an offhand tone.

She realised that although he had never talked openly about this to anyone he must have thought about it constantly.

Rita never forgot what Meternagel told her then. What surprised her most was that he considered his story quite ordinary. Only much later did she realise that he was right in this. He was one of those people who had been pushed suddenly from darkness into light and at first had moved uncertainly in the glare.

"After all, what was I before?" he said. "A skilled carpenter, and proud of it. But they could do what they liked with us. They seemed to have waited till we were old enough to start their war."

So he had gone along with them, been wounded several times and had more than once been the sole survivor.

Rita wondered how old he was, and when he told her he was nearly fifty she was surprised, for his clear, bright eyes made him look younger.

"After that I was put to tree-felling and building barracks, a long way East. You can take my word for it that it took time for me to cotton to the idea that that sort of work was better than shooting at live targets."

But this small glimmer of understanding had not sufficed enough for what he had let himself in for when he got home from prisoner-of-war camp. He had joined the Socialist Unity Party at once; he was thirty-six. They hadn't asked many questions, so they had not really seen how little he understood. They only wanted to know if he was honest (and even some dishonest people had slipped in and had to be thrown out later, if they hadn't learned to be honest meanwhile).

Shortly after that he had met an old friend who was on the look-out for a "reliable element" to take over an instructor's job. His friend had told him that people like the two of them would have to take things into their own hands now, and then turned his attention to other urgent matters.

The following years had flown by in a sort of wild dream. He was shoved upwards by a force stronger than any he had ever known before. They had given him jobs to do which he had never before heard of, and he had learned words and expressions which he needed if he were to handle these jobs, but there was never the time for him to find out exactly what they meant. He had slaved night and day; his wife became a stranger to him and his daughter grew up without his noticing it. And he had hardly the time to notice her as a child, either. New jobs were thrust upon him one after another. Very occasionally he had time to wonder whether he was really directing events or whether events were driving him.

He rose higher and higher, until he seemed to be watching himself from outside. He learned to use bigger and bigger words and to understand them less and less. He found his way about in many situations and learned to issue orders. He even learned to shout at people when he could think of no answer to give them.

"You don't believe that? Well, you should have seen me!" he said, with bitter irony.

Rita wondered how long it had taken him to see things properly.

And then, when he had become sure of himself, when he had given up expecting trouble, it happened: He was caught out in a bad mistake, thrown out of his job and sent as a foreman to the railway wagon works. The crash had been just as fair to society as it had been unfair to him personally, for he had tried to serve society, unselfishly and to the best of his ability. Not without bitterness, he saw younger men taking his place who had been able to study and prepare themselves while he had tried to keep things going without the necessary knowledge.

He did not say so, but Rita realised that his second demotion – the one they had talked about at the Herr-furths' table – had hit him harder than the first. Here he had failed at a job which seemed to be made for him and there was no excuse. Too much money had been paid out, signed for by him, for jobs which had not been done for weeks. A work-mate had diddled him like a greenhorn – a man he had trusted and with whom he still had to work. It was no excuse to say that the accounts had been doctored before they were given to him to sign. A foreman ought to know exactly what is going on in his department.

"So how can I start giving advice now? Those chaps still laugh at me and call me 'foreman' behind my back."

He took Rita to his home. His wife made coffee and when she had gone out he took a book with a black cover from the shelf under the radio and opened it at the first page.

Studies at Work, Rita read.

He had been looking into things carefully during the

past few weeks and nobody could put anything across him any more.

"It's all in here," he said, tapping the book. "Ermisch knows there's something brewing. He follows me about like a dog. But I shan't show the book to anyone yet. If there's anything I've learnt in these twelve years, it's not to be in a hurry. There's nothing so stupid as heroism at the wrong time. Wendland's turning the place upside down and inside out, you can be sure of that. I know him. He'll have to come to us one day. And that's the day I'm waiting for."

Rita would have given anything for a look into that book. But Meternagel had already shoved it back under the radio.

Everything had been so simple at home in the village, so easy to understand, so friendly and homely. If there is such a thing as an untroubled spirit, Rita had had it, and she was losing it now. A cold breath was clouding her mirror on the world.

So a man like Meternagel was pushed into some job and left to get on with it as best he could; his work-mates even played tricks on him and made fun of him. She could hardly believe it of those men whom she saw every day. And how was she ever going to get used to such injustice, as Meternagel seemed to have done?

Rita felt that she was on the verge of growing up, that she was entering a region where only results counted, not good will, or even the effort a man put into his job if he failed at it in the end. And she rebelled against the idea.

Very little was said beforehand about the big meeting which was finally called, but everybody attended it, which was unusual. They stood or sat around in the big hall between the half-finished wagons. The heavy smell of metal, oil, sweat and tobacco filled the air, and light filtered dimly through the dirty skylights. Far away at the end of the hall she saw the big slogan in glaring red, but she did not bother to try and read it.

"Comrades!" someone called into the loudspeaker. And the casual talk about holidays and out-door dances died away.

It turned out that the commissions had sent in a report, which was read out by the Party secretary, a stocky, white-haired man. It was short, distributed the blame evenly for what had gone wrong, and there was nothing much to be said against it. But there was nothing sensational about it and it seemed odd that such a major catastrophe could have resulted from such a minor cause.

Ernst Wendland was called to the microphone. There was some clapping. Rita thought he looked taller than she remembered him. His voice was hoarse. He had slept little during the past weeks and had hardly had time to eat.

"I shouldn't like to be in his place," said somebody behind Rita.

Wendland was no platform speaker, and that was the very last thing they wanted just then. He told them plainly what the situation was — how far behind they were with production, how much raw material and semi-finished parts were not available and how short they were of labour. He gave them exact figures of the number of mechanics, carpenters and welders needed at the works and in the whole district.

"So nobody else can help us out," he said. "We've tried to catch up by doing overtime. The only thing left now is for each of us to do just as much as he can and be honest about it."

The day for the meeting had been well chosen, the tone he used was also right. During the past weeks everybody had had time to get his discontent and grumbling off his chest; now they wanted to get back to real work. They were not interested in vague promises, but they were willing to listen to sensible suggestions. When the first few got up and promised to do this or that, Ermisch began to squirm in his seat. Could he have missed his chance? Would he be too late with his men? Meternagel looked at him challengingly.

"I shall open my book now," he said.

Rita got home late and went straight up to the attic. Manfred saw how excited she was. He handed her sandwiches and tea, scolding her for keeping him waiting even before they were married.

"Well," he said, after a while. "Who's to blame?"

Rita looked up, surprised.

"Or wasn't the meeting called to haul someone over the coals?"

"Well, yes, I suppose it was," Rita said slowly. "Wendland spoke well."

"So now everything's going to be different?"

"Well, I hope so."

"Why, do you really think things will be better after the meeting than before? Will there suddenly be enough material? Will bad managers suddenly be good managers? Will the men suddenly realise what it's all about, instead of just thinking of their own pockets?"

"Maybe things won't change," said Rita thoughtfully.

The night was clear and still, moonlit. They lay awake side by side.

"There've been dozens of these meetings in all the factories. This was your first."

Even so, she thought obstinately, this one was important to me. Why should he be afraid that something I think important might come between us?

"Listen," she said after a while, "let's try not to be jealous of meetings, shall we?"

13

September passed. One night, unexpectedly, the autumn rains began, beating down steadily, forming a grey curtain in front of the sanatorium windows which did not lift again for days. The trees, blackened by the wet summer, lost their last leaves. The sodden park was deserted.

Rita assured the doctor every day that she was quite well again. But he said little and she could not tell what he was thinking. He merely nodded and thought to himself that at her age she should have got over her trouble more quickly. Sensitive people had a hard time of it nowadays, he thought. He did not like her forced cheerfulness, either, and the dark shadows under her eyes told him that she was still very tired.

She had been trying for a long time to forget, and now she was afraid that she would. When she closed her eyes at night a wave of memories, painfully sweet, broke over her; memories of his face, again and again. She traced every line of it a hundred times, but it vanished when she tried to see it as a whole. And the feel of his hands. It shook her and she had to clench her teeth. Her heart thumped heavily.

She had lost the whole of the summer, she thought. Could it really be over?

She remembered one glorious midsummer day the

year before – a day which stood out as a peak in her life; she felt she had lost the strength ever to climb so high or be so happy again.

They had left the town early and driven up into the cool mountains in the ramshackle little car which Manfred had bought the day he took his doctor's degree. At noon they reached a gay little town on the northern slopes of the Harz Mountains, and after their lunch they joined a group of tourists climbing up to the castle huddled on the mountain peak. They toiled up the two hundred stone steps to the top of the look-out tower to stare out silently at the West German town which could always be seen from there on clear days. It shimmered in the distance like a mirage.

"You'll see," said Manfred as they climbed down the mountain again, "the guide-books will soon be advertising a 'glimpse of West Germany' as one of the sights of the town."

Later on they had watched a village fête, taken a turn on the carousel and tried their luck at the shooting-range. Towards evening they wandered back along the cobbled street, tired and happy.

Suddenly, in front of a small, lantern-lit garden café, Manfred halted.

"Of course," he said. "Of course. Now I know where I've met him before."

Rita followed the direction of his eyes, and saw Ernst Wendland sitting at a table talking to a younger man.

"Where was it?" she asked, surprised.

Manfred hesitated. He seemed to be recalling exactly what had happened, to make up his mind whether he should be pleased or annoyed at this renewed meeting.

"Never mind," he said. "Let's go in."

But he made for the other young man, not for Wend-land. The former looked up when Manfred spoke to him, hesitated for a moment, with the same look of uncertainty on his face as Rita had noticed on Manfred's. Then he jumped up and shook Manfred's hand.

"You must remember him, too, you know," he said to Wendland.

"That's right, and I remember where it was, too."

"So do I," said Manfred.

They all sat down and began to explain things to Rita. The younger man, Rudi Schwabe, had been at school with Manfred. He was older and had been secretary of the school youth organisation, so that everybody knew him there.

"He once helped me out of a bad patch," Manfred explained with exaggerated casualness. "I told you about our cellar club, didn't I? Well, all of a sudden it was supposed to be a centre of political opposition. The whole thing might have ended pretty badly for us. There was a big meeting and they all had their knives sharpened, but Rudi Schwabe and Wendland got us out of it. You were in the Free German Youth town committee, weren't you?"

"That's right," said Wendland. "It looked too much as if the school had it in for you. That's why we were able to help. Still, I'm not so sure, even now, that the whole thing wasn't political. . . ."

"Of course," said Manfred irritably, "if you accept the theory that everything anyone says, does, thinks or feels is politics. After all, we're the political generation, aren't we?"

"That's a bit sweeping, isn't it?" said Wendland. He glanced at Manfred in a considering, but not unfriendly way.

The waitress brought ice and whipped cream. They ate in silence. Suddenly all the lanterns round the café lit up and a modest little band began to play. Rudi Schwabe bowed politely to Rita, but she plucked up courage to put him off, for she wanted to dance with Manfred first.

Manfred was still disgruntled.

"Did you notice Schwabe looking at Wendland first to see whether he ought to laugh?" he asked. "He used to be different. He could take a risk. But he doesn't seem to have learnt much . . . all-round functionary — what sort of job is that, anyway?"

Rita did not bother to answer, but whirled around faster and faster. She was delighted with everything, the little dance floor, the pale apricot sky, and all the people in holiday mood. She was glad, too, that Manfred had introduced her to people he knew and that everybody must see that they were engaged. She liked Wendland, he was calm and deliberate, so different from Manfred.

"Do you realise that this is only the second time we have danced together?" she asked.

"So it is. We can still count our blessings one by one."

"You like that, don't you?"

"Yes, I like to have something to remember for always, even if it's only a small thing."

"Then remember all of today, and forget the way you feel about Wendland," she said.

"But you don't know the whole of that old story."

"But I know you. And you look now the way you always do when you're in the wrong and don't want to admit it."

"So now you're going to start improving me?"

"You never wanted a wife like that, did you?"

"No, indeed, but what's the use of regretting it now?"

Later on, when she danced with Rudi Schwabe, Rita was glad to see that Manfred and Wendland seemed to be talking quite amicably together. Manfred told her afterwards that Wendland had asked him what he thought of Schwabe. He had not felt like beating about the bush, so he had said Schwabe seemed to have changed a good deal. He remembered him as a pretty rough sort of chap, but he seemed quite tame now. Wendland had laughed, apparently not much surprised.

"Well, you'll be seeing more of him now," he said. "He'll be in the Dean of Studies' office."

But this did not affect Manfred, for he had very little to do with the university authorities.

They walked together a little way down the road. It was quieter now. Wendland walked beside Rita.

"How's Meternagel's brigade getting on?" he asked. Rita laughed. So he knew quite well who had the most say in the brigade. She glanced across to see whether Manfred could hear what they were talking about, and lowered her voice, as if what they were discussing were nobody's business but hers and Wendland's. She had not told Manfred that he had been right; nothing had changed since the big meeting.

"They're quarrelling all the time," she said.

Wendland understood at once what she meant.

"Meternagel's making too much fuss, eh?"

"Well, he's right, you know. Why don't they listen to him?"

"Are you disappointed?"

"Yes, I am," she admitted.

"I often feel like that, even now," said Wendland.

A curiously friendly feeling had sprung up between

them, encouraged by the darkness and the happy day she had had. But she did not stop to think what could have put Wendland into the same frame of mind.

"People are so suspicious of each other. One is always coming up against it," he said. "But have you noticed that it only seems to worry younger people? I suppose as you get older you get used to it. Older people probably wear their suspicions like a second skin."

He was silent, as if he felt this was a good enough explanation, and she thought over what he had said. She found it pleasant that he spoke so easily, without irritation. And she realised for the first time that it was difficult to talk calmly with most people.

They stopped in front of a tiny cottage in a row.

"This is where we're staying," said Wendland. "Once a year, on Mother's birthday, we all meet here, my brothers and sisters and I. Rudi Schwabe is with us this year, too."

He put a finger in his mouth and whistled shrilly. A slim little boy, with big dark eyes, appeared at once.

"My son," said Wendland.

Rita was surprised. She tried to imagine what his wife might be like. There was an unexpected expression on his face – tender and a little sad.

Then Wendland, Schwabe and the little boy disappeared into the house. The two men stooped under the low doorway and the little boy imitated them. A bright strip of light shone out into the road for a few seconds, a whiff of food filled the air, then the door shut and Rita and Manfred were alone again in the dark.

They strolled along to the next restaurant, a little old wine cellar, found seats in a corner, and Manfred ordered a meal which astonished Rita.

"There's still something you don't know about me," he said, "and that's how much I like food; grapefruit for breakfast, like the American President, sandwiches and tea at eleven, like the English, a French meal at midday, good German coffee and cake in the afternoon and a big, solid Russian meal in the evening."

"I hope you know I can't cook?" said Rita.

"I'll do the cooking," he said.

They drank cool white wine with water. Their hands touched as they clinked glasses. Things can begin again, over and over again, with him, she thought. They knew each other just well enough to feel safe together and just little enough to surprise each other continually. Even the brief confidential talk she had had with Wendland, which she did not tell him about, brought him closer to her.

"Do you know, I've never had a meal like this before?" she said after a while. "I've never had such a wonderful day, either, and I can't even imagine what wonderful days we can have."

It was late when they got back on to the highroad. The moon, hidden behind a thin, even layer of cloud, spread an eerie blue light which ended in a sharp line where the sky met the black earth. Rita was fascinated by this light, hard and soft at once, for which she could find no name nor anything to compare it with.

Suddenly, to their left, exactly on the line dividing heaven and earth, an island of light appeared.

They swam quickly towards it. Soon they could make out different colours and strengths of light, yellow chains on the ground and scattered red lamps above. Then the black shadows of chimneys appeared against the lighter sky. An acrid smell poured into the car and they closed the windows.

They were back in the realm of industry.

When Rita was already in bed, with her face to the wall, she heard Manfred come in softly behind her. Paper rustled.

"Just this minute somebody is twenty years old. It's midnight," he said.

Rita turned round. He stood there with a big bunch of carnations. She counted them. There were twenty.

"Thank you," she said. "Oh, thank you!"

14

No one could have foreseen that those first warm summer days would be followed by weeks under a glowing sun, an unearthly body which sent its scorching rays over the land. People got up tired and watched the sun's slow, majestic course across the pale sky with burning, dazzled eyes. The meadows dried up, corn withered on the stalk, trees cast off dead leaves and put out new shoots in the middle of summer. Strangely fat, sweet, juicy fruit ripened in the gardens in such quantities that it could not be gathered fast enough and at night ripe apples and pears fell to the ground.

Rita barely noticed nature's ominous indifference. What she remembered most clearly about that summer was Rolf Meternagel's face; his eyes, which had always had a sceptical, detached gleam, were now watchful, hard and relentless. Sometimes, when she felt most desperate, those eyes were what kept her going and she realised later on that it was this haggard, dogged man who, probably more than anyone else, had saved her from succumbing completely to useless longing for a vanished dream.

For she had seen him take-up a big responsibility, of his own free will, without thinking of any reward and, like a hero in some old legend, set out upon a seemingly hopeless struggle. He had sacrificed sleep and rest and put up with people laughing at him, quarrelling with him, ignoring him. Rita had seen him in such despair that she could not believe he would ever laugh again; but he had held on grimly until the unexpected happened – the others came over on to his side and began to do what he suggested, and at last he could relax. All this stood out vividly in her memory.

Rolf Meternagel opened his book, handed it round and showed them a figure, underlined in red, on the last page – a figure running into hundreds of marks: "Time wasted in our brigade last month."

They shrugged their shoulders. It was nothing new to them. They glanced at Ermisch, who was scribbling in his notebook. He said nothing.

"I've been looking into the reasons," said Rolf Meternagel.

"Why don't you talk to the director about it?" somebody suggested.

Meternagel turned to another page. He was being patient and tactful, which irritated them even more.

"Lay-off time due to poor organisation," he read, and pointed to the number of hours. "That's only half the real total, though. What I'm interested in is the other half."

"Well, it doesn't interest me," said Franz Melcher curtly, stood up and went away.

"Do you have to go into all that?" asked old Karssuweit reproachfully.

Meternagel looked at Ermisch, who was already packing up his bits and pieces.

"Well. I suppose we might do something about it," said Ermisch, non-committally.

"If the cock crows early on the dunghill the weather may change, or it may not," said Herbert Kuhl defiantly as he pushed past Meternagel.

"You'd better look out!" Meternagel shouted after him. Kuhl never failed to irritate him. The others had got used to Kuhl's habit of jeering at them whenever he got the chance; but Rita often wondered whether he really got any fun out of it.

The next morning Meternagel brought a sheet of paper with him and stuck it up on the notice-board, between the yellowing newspaper articles dating from the days when the brigade had been famous. The sheet was headed "PLEDGE", but nobody looked at it. They all turned their backs and went on chewing their sandwiches, talking and laughing loudly, but not speaking to Rolf. Rita saw his face harden, as he made a tremendous effort to control himself. Then he jumped up, snatched the paper from the notice-board and flung it down on the table in front of them.

The pledge he wanted them to take was to put in ten window frames each per shift instead of eight.

"And don't tell me you can't do it."

"Lots of things are possible," said Melcher. "But what normal person wants to foul his own nest?"

"What do you call normal?" Kuhl put in quickly. Rita thought she saw a glint of real interest in his eye.

"What's normal?" said Meternagel in a dangerously quiet voice. "I'll tell you what's normal. Normal is what's good for all of us, what makes men of us. Abnormal is crawling, swindling and tagging along. We've been doing that long enough. But you'll never understand that – Lieutenant."

There was absolute silence. Why didn't somebody say something? Why did nobody ever tell me Kuhl had been an officer? Rita wondered.

Kuhl's cold, sneering expression did not alter, but he turned dead white. So it was possible to get under his skin, after all.

"You made a mistake there," said Ermisch later on. "You should have had it out with him then and there."

"Well, who cares? I'd make a mistake like that again any time," said Meternagel.

Not one of them had signed Meternagel's pledge.

Rita could not understand why they held back, or what they were fighting against. She thought back over what she knew about them, after working with them for three months – the things they talked about: a girl friend, a little bit of property left them by some relative, a motor cycle, gardens, children, an old mother who was blind and needed a nurse, actresses and film stars, the speed-up in the factory – and all sorts of minor worries, ugly little complications in their lives, or the simple pleasures and distractions with which they tried to fill their lives. They were clinging to all their familiar habits now, and that was why they complained so bitterly.

Gradually, however, one or two of them began to feel that they ought to put their backs into their job. One morning a single name appeared beside Meternagel's under the pledge – Wolf Liebentrau, a silent, retiring man who always got confused and apologetic if anyone so much as spoke to him or asked his opinion.

"What's got into you?" asked Ermisch.

"Well, I only thought – either I'm in the Party or I'm not," he murmured.

"Do you think I wouldn't do everything I could for the Party," said Ermisch angrily.

"Well, it doesn't look much like it," Liebentrau replied, frightened at his own temerity.

Ermisch marched up to the notice-board, licked his pencil and added his name.

So Meternagel, Liebentrau and Ermisch sat down together at the table and young Hans took up his post at the door, delighted that someone was speaking to Rolf again.

"You can't go in there now. Party meeting," he said importantly.

Two weeks later there was a new photograph of the brigade in the paper, headed "They lead the way." Much against her will, Rita had been pushed into the front row, with young Hans beside her. She studied the photo carefully, looking again and again at Kuhl, Meternagel's most obstinate enemy, who also stood in the front row, still sneering; but women, at any rate, would certainly think him handsome. And she understood why Meternagel, the real winner this time, had kept half hidden in the background; he did not need to have people looking at him, but for Kuhl the feeling that many eyes were on him might perhaps help to bring him out of his shell.

Hans bought twenty copies of the paper and cut out all the photographs. He always kept one in his pocket, along with his favourite film stars.

Rita had forgotten her own little worries and fears in the midst of all this. She could wake up at exactly the right time, and get out of the tram at the right stop without looking out. She met the same people at the same spot in the poplar-lined road; she knew all the signs of the approaching lunch hour or change of shift.

Most of the time now she was alone with young Hans in one of the railway wagons. Meternagel turned up now and again to catch his breath after talking and arguing with the others. They would show him what they had done and he would nod and slump down on the bare wooden seat. There was always time to sit down with him; they said little and let him smoke in peace, taking no notice of the electricians cursing as they drew their cables in through the window and across the wagon, or of the varnishers working on the roof over their heads. Rolf's face grew thinner and thinner, but his eyes were as sharp and icy-blue as ever. Sometimes he would send Rita on errands and she soon got to know every corner of the works and all the workers in it.

After he had rested awhile, Meternagel would pull out his clumsy old pocket-watch with its battered tortoise-shell case, jump up and dash away again.

"Everybody knows my old watch by this time," he would say with a chuckle.

Rita and young Hans went back to their work. Hans liked to go about with two big screws in his mouth – they made him feel important.

"Why does he rush about like that?" he asked.

Rita could think of several answers, but she thought they would sound too high-brow, so she kept them to herself.

"Do you suppose he wants to be foreman again, like they say?" Hans went on. "Or maybe he just wants to be on good terms with the director. You know he used to be his son-in-law, don't you?"

"What was that you said?"

Young Hans was delighted to have a bit of gossip to tell her. Until a year ago Ernst Wendland had been married to Meternagel's elder daughter, but she had gone off with someone else while Wendland was away on a training course. It had happened right under her father's nose, too, for they had all been living together. Everybody knew that Meternagel was much too soft with his girls and could never refuse them anything. Maybe he thought he had no right to interfere. But Wendland hadn't forgiven him for letting it happen and even now, although he was divorced from his wife, he avoided Meternagel as much as he could.

This had given Rita something to think about for days. She had got used to hearing curious things about people whom she thought she knew quite well, but she was surprised at Meternagel for bringing up a daughter who deceived her husband and doing nothing to prevent her from leaving a man like Wendland. She wondered how he managed with his two motherless little boys. Maybe he disliked all women now, she thought. That was what sometimes happened.

Maybe Meternagel really did want to make a good impression on the director, she said to young Hans as they worked away at their windows, but this could not be the only reason for all the work he was doing in the factory.

Hans was proud to be taken into Rita's confidence, so he showed her his favourite film stars and expatiated on their good and bad points. There was certainly no harm in dreaming that they were smiling just for him.

Rita got home exhausted each evening. Sitting down at the bright supper-table with the Herrfurth family was like slipping into another world. Manfred often turned to look at her or pressed her hand under the stiffly-starched table cloth, not caring whether his father or mother noticed, and then the table seemed to drift away from them, getting smaller and smaller, but still quite clear and bright, like a tiny magic island inhabited by exiles.

Conversation seemed to reach her from a long way off, too. The sound of her own name would bring her back to reality.

"You must bear in mind, Fräulein Rita, that the carpets have to be vacuumed every day here, for they simply soak up the dust."

"Yes, of course," she would answer politely. But her thoughts were far away from things like carpets.

Manfred was happy, for he was enjoying the feeling of having done a really good, worthwhile job which had cost him a great deal of hard work. Many people outside his own institute were now interested in the research work he had done, and he was kept busy answering inquiries, preparing his thesis for the printers and speaking to groups of technical experts in factories. He saw that he could really help and this gave him as much satisfaction as the appreciation and respect shown for his work.

This feeling of being in tune with life, which was rare for him, made it easy for him to give his mind to Rita's problems. She was often surprised at how quickly he understood what she was trying to say, even when she was excited and did not finish her sentences. He encouraged her to talk when they were out walking in the evenings, or resting in the meadows by the river. What he enjoyed most was her way of describing her workmates. Her witty remarks delighted him and she found that she had a clearer picture of many of them after she had described them to him.

"And how's your Wendland?" he used to ask. He always called him "her Wendland", and she knew he did not care to admit how much the thought of Wendland bothered him.

"We don't see him often, but there's always a feeling that he's somewhere about," she said.

Wendland and Meternagel were working together more and more and, even when things had not been arranged between them, they seemed to be playing into each other's hands. She felt sure that things were going better now, in the management and amongst the workers.

"Well, that's nice," said Manfred. "It doesn't happen often, as you'll have noticed."

He often got her to talk just to be able to look at her. Her face never palled. It was still just as smooth and clear, but he could see a new strength emerging, which pleased, but at the same time disturbed him. He felt he must make sure of her again and again. He ran his finger lightly over her face, her forehead and temples, from ·her eyebrows to the down on her cheeks. She leant back. She knew the path his hand would take, for she had first become conscious of herself through his lips, his eyes, his hands. He always looked at her with wonder and she knew that he did things for love of her which he had never done for anyone else. And his tenderness never failed to move her.

Like all lovers, they were afraid for their love. A cool glance or a sharp word could ruin a whole day.

"What would you like this minute?" Manfred would murmur, when they opened their eyes at night and saw the familiar objects in their little room by the faint green glimmer of the radio light, still firmly in their places while they had been so exalted and so far away.

"Always the same thing," said Rita. "One skin to cover us both, one breath for both of us."

"Yes," he would say, "but isn't it like that now?"

She nodded. It remained like that as long as they wanted it to be so.

One night they were awakened by the rain beating on the roof. They went over to the window and drew in deep breaths of the fresh, moist air. They stretched out their arms and drew them in again, cool and wet, and splashed each other in the face. Their eyes grew accustomed to the dark, and they could gradually distinguish between the compact black outlines of houses and the soft blackness of the sky. An occasional light flickered on the river.

No one lived higher than they and the rain reached them first.

"I dreamt that we were sitting in a tiny boat floating through the streets. It rained and rained. The streets were empty, the water rose steadily. The churches, the trees and the houses were slowly covered with water. Only we two rocked on the waves, quite alone in our frail little boat," said Manfred.

"Whoever taught you to dream such dreams," said Rita reproachfully. They stood there leaning against each other and looking out into the night.

Suddenly a light blinked on the river, pale but quite unmistakable. Rita snatched up the table lamp, held it high in the window and switched it on and off, on and off.

"What are you up to now?" he asked.

"We're the lighthouse. There's a little boat out there on the ocean, sending out SOS signals. We're answering."

Manfred took the lamp from her, held it aloft and let it burn steadily.

"Do you think they'll make the harbour?"

"Oh yes, I'm sure they will."

"And will they still find people in the sunken town?"

"Yes," she said. "The town didn't really sink and the boat has only come adrift."

"And everybody in danger can see our lighthouse signal."

"Yes, anybody who looks can see it."

"And no one will ever sink again?"

"No," said Rita.

They switched off the lamp. The strange little light on the water had disappeared – sunk or safe in harbour. The rain beat down on the roof long after they had fallen asleep again.

In the morning clear drops ran down the telephone wires from the roof, chasing each other at regular intervals, always at the same speed, endlessly and without haste.

15

Nine months later their boat had sunk and they stood on opposite shores. Had no one noticed that they were in distress or answered their signals?

Rita went through a time of profound self-questioning during those hazy, monotonous weeks in hospital and she brooded constantly over this. Had she not seen the danger herself soon enough? Since so short a time had elapsed she tried instinctively to pile up events between herself and what had happened, so as to get a sufficiently detached view of things and see the whole story from beginning to end.

The town council gave the railway wagon workers a party on the fifteenth anniversary of the nationalisation of their factory, and this chanced to be the first day for many months when they could also congratulate themselves on having finished the month's work on time. So they were ready to relax and enjoy themselves after all their recent troubles.

The hairdressers had done their best and a wave of perfume hung in the air when the girls left their coats in the cloak-room. They felt much happier in their party frocks than the men in their stiff dark suits.

Manfred had not wanted to go with her, she remembered. He was no good at playing prince consort, he said. Besides, receptions were always boring.

"Not for me," said Rita firmly. She took a long time getting ready.

They met Meternagel and his wife at the door of the hall and after shaking many hands they finally got inside, where they caught sight of Hans, buttoned into his confirmation suit, standing under a candelabra with a very pretty girl at least two years older than himself.

"He cut her out of one of his postcards," Meternagel remarked.

But the girl was flesh and blood all right. Her name was Anita and she had a roving eye. Rita looked at her and then at young Hans, as if she were seeing him for the first time. He was sweating, but doing his best to appear casual and manly.

"There's another prince consort for you," Manfred whispered.

He was surprised that she knew so many people. They wandered round the hall, looking at everyone and being looked at by everyone.

"You're the belle of the ball," he declared, and she blushed, because that was how she felt. She wore a maize-coloured dress, a present from him – he who had always wanted to see her in that colour – and many heads were turned to look at her with approval. She took his arm and tried to hide her excitement.

"It's not a bit boring with you," he murmured.

The speeches began at the huge, horseshoe-shaped table piled high with sandwiches and salad. Dignified men drew pages of notes from their breast-pockets and solemnly read out what they had unwillingly dictated to their secretaries earlier in the day. The guests listened solemnly, too, hardly daring to laugh at the jokes which turned up at regular intervals. Some speakers of course repeated what earlier speakers had said, but they always acknowledged this and everyone was satisfied.

Young Hans's protruding ears were turkey-red. Manfred wanted to laugh, but Rita stepped on his toe and he restrained himself. When it was time for supper, he wormed his way through the crowd to the table and quickly filled two plates.

"Speech-making is hard work," he said, chewing, especially when it's not your real job. Just think – you've been busy all day long in some Ministry or other – the Ministry of Engineering, let's say – and in the evenings you're expected to perform as a speaker. You just can't think of a thing to say except 'So we have constantly . . .' or 'Thus we march victoriously forward . . .' Ghastly!"

"Well, but everybody liked the speeches," said Rita.

"Did they? That's only because it's their duty to like them. They think a speech has to be long and solemn and full of big words – not the way people talk."

"Get me some more salad," said Rita, "and just try and remember that not everyone wants to scoff the way you do."

"You're right there," said Manfred. "Take young Hans, for instance."

"And Meternagel – and me," said Rita.

And then they forgot all about it, for the band began to play in the next room. Spirits rose and people collected in groups, talking and laughing.

At first only a few young couples danced. Manfred was proud of Rita as he took her out on to the dance floor. She did not glance at a single mirror on the way, for she felt she could be herself and everyone present would feel kindly towards her.

Manfred whirled her round; she could have gone on dancing all night. She danced with one young man after another, ending up with young Hans. But Manfred danced with no one else.

Hans was not very happy, for Anita had found other admirers. He admitted he had only borrowed her for the evening from a friend. Rita thought it was a shame, but Hans knew that he was too young for Anita.

Dancing with Manfred again, she felt as if they were alone amongst the crowd. It did not worry them that the party was drawing to a close, for they were sure that there would be other parties. They twirled until they were dizzy, then sat down in a corner.

It was just the moment which comes at every party before faces begin to look pale and drawn, hair turns dull and smiles are forced, before the shadow of morning dulls the glow of the ceiling lights and left-over food loses its freshness. Glasses still tinkled and dancing was easy, but each step, each mouthful of food and each smile brought them nearer to the point where pleasure and high spirits become forced and banal.

Rita shut her eyes for a moment. When she opened them again Ernst Wendland stood before her. She glanced past him to Manfred and saw that his expression had changed. It was cool, almost suspicious. She looked up at Wendland and was shocked. She saw at once what had happened. Wendland had been shaking hands and drinking with everyone, relaxing after the tension of the past weeks. He had seen her dancing and had come over to her, passing Manfred without a word. Now he stood before her with an almost tender smile hovering on his lips and a look which had completely sobered Manfred and startled Rita.

The band was still playing the same tune, but everything had changed. Wendland bent over Rita and asked her to dance. She got up, looking across uncertainly at Manfred, but he looked away with a bored expression. She was annoyed with him and let Wendland lead her on the dance floor.

"I saw you dancing," he said. Rita was glad that no one else heard the way he said it. She stiffened in his arms and he felt at once that he had gone too far. The almost drunken look vanished from his face in an instant, and his eyes lost their hungry look. It hurt Rita to see the change. And it hurt her when he spoke in his normal voice.

"A jolly evening after so much hard work, eh?"

What had actually happened? Nothing, less than nothing. So little that even to mention it would have seemed clumsy and petty. But Rita and Manfred both understood what they had seen. They wanted to put it out of their minds, and they succeeded, too.

When they returned, Manfred stood up and greeted Wendland politely. Wendland fetched three cups of coffee from a near-by table and they drank it together.

Manfred inquired about Wendland's work and said that running a big works was a heavy responsibility.

Wendland agreed, but added that one could get used to anything. Manfred replied that getting used to things seemed to be the fate of mankind, and then went into a long monologue about history being based on indifference, ending up with a remark about people all being cut to the same pattern.

Why does he have to talk like that? Rita wondered. She felt that she must keep quiet, that anything she said might irritate him.

"Possibly," said Wendland, "if you leave the difference in people's reasoning capacity out of account. . . ."

This was just what Manfred had been waiting for. He laughed.

"Don't give me that stuff! Reason was never a factor in historical development. Since when has reason ever made people happy, either? You can't reckon on that."

Wendland smiled, and Rita blushed for Manfred.

"So we may as well give up all hope?"

"Well, perhaps not hope," said Manfred, "but illusions."

Later on, Rita remembered that this was the second time she had felt vaguely uneasy. Then it struck her that they were not simply sparring because of jealousy or hurt pride. They were really concerned with the principles they were discussing.

Wendland did not bother to have the last word, for he was not taking things so seriously. He stood up to meet Rolf Meternagel and his wife, who came up rather hesitantly.

Rita was upset by Manfred's bitterness, and she knew he had wanted to go on with the argument, but she realised at once how much this handshake between Wendland and Meternagel meant.

"Well, Rolf, how are you doing?"

"Well, Ernst, pretty hard times, eh?" Meternagel grinned and Wendland smiled back.

"Yes, pretty tough. But we seem to be over the worst now. Let's have a drink on that."

So they clinked glasses, drank up and stood talking for a while.

"You've heard about our new model, I suppose?" Wendland asked.

"Of course. A tiptop job, too, several tons lighter than the ones we're building now."

"I guess you could help us with it," said Wendland.

"I?" said Meternagel, surprised. "Well, if you think. . . ."

"Of course. With all your experience. Come over to-morrow morning early and we can get together on it."

Meternagel put his hand on Rita's shoulder.

"So we'll be joining the experts, my girl. You heard that?"

"Good for you, Rolf," she answered. "But I shan't be with you any longer, you know. My time's up. Or can I stay a little longer?"

Meternagel laughed, and Rita suddenly felt happy again.

She got Manfred to dance the very last dance with her and on the way home through the dark, silent streets put her arm through his. They did not talk but were content.

Shortly afterwards the summer holidays began. Together, on foot or in the little grey car, they combed through the countryside around Rita's village, bathed in the lake and filled their lungs with clear, pure summer air. Then Manfred took his future students to the Black Sea for a fortnight and when he returned he brought with him a tiny greyish-brown tortoise for Rita. They christened it Cleopatra and put it in a sandbox in the little room next their attic.

They loved each other and looked forward to their second winter together.

16

They had no third winter together.

Now that she knew it could never be repeated, Rita's memory of the changing colours of autumn as they saw them from their little window was tinged with bitterness. They watched the leaves lose their warm, bright colours and turn pale, cool and lustreless. The changing light over the town, the bend in the river and the flat valley, the light reflected in Manfred's eyes, these would never come again.

No one could have known then what a difficult year lay ahead – an historic, trial year, people will call it in years to come.

It is hard for the living to withstand the cold, inexorable march of events. Looking back over that year, Rita felt that she had understood the difference between the relentless but permanent light of history and the chance light of day; but on many faces she had seen light and shadow alternating according to mood or to the momentary situation. She saw a vast amount of strength, passion, sympathy and talent expended upon ordinary things which were still hard to deal with, even fifteen years after the war's end.

Had Manfred perhaps been right when he said that love, friendship and optimism were impossible nowadays? That it was stupid to fight against the forces which stood between us and our desires? If they wanted their love to last they would have to keep very quiet, he had said, for fate was jealous. Had he been right? Had she demanded too much of them both? He had said she would never hold out, that she had no idea what life was really like.

He thought people had to be like chameleons if they wanted to avoid being seen and destroyed, and that was what had condemned him to loneliness and made him so bitter. But she had never wanted to lose her identity; she had not even felt that they had been born in an unhappy age until he had said so. He wanted to be born a hundred years earlier or a hundred years later, but she had never played that game with him and he had said that she had no imagination. . . .

But Manfred had, after all, realised that she was full of the adventure of her own life and did not want to exchange it for any other. He had not misunderstood or misused the desperate moods which overcame her after the first few optimistic weeks at her teachers' college.

"Do you really love me?" she had asked, one evening in early October.

"Pretty much," he answered, peering at her closely, for he realised that she meant it seriously this time. He reproached himself for not having noticed how tired and pale she looked. He put down his book and suggested a little drive, although it was cold and raining.

He turned on the radio and the heater in the car and drove out of the town towards the south, talking casually until he felt her relaxing beside him. He laughed when she asked where they were, for she had a poor sense of direction and always lost her way quickly. Then he gently persuaded her to talk.

She felt lost and lonely at the institute; nothing

special had happened, she assured him, nobody had criticised her or hurt her feelings, but nobody had taken much notice of her, either.

"But they're all so clever. They know everything already. Nothing surprises them any more," she said.

"Oh well, that's nothing new," said Manfred easily. "You'll see, they'll be different as soon as something happens to them."

"But nothing ever will happen to them," said Rita, "that's just the trouble."

Manfred laughed.

"You just wait. Something happens to everyone some time or other, you can take my word for it."

Why, something had even happened to him to shake him out of his indifference. He had met Rita, he thought.

But he should have taken her worries more seriously. He was lulled into a false sense of security by her friendship with Marion, the slim, fair girl from the hairdressers' saloon in the little town where Rita had worked, he was glad for her to have a girl friend, for he felt this could not come between them. And it was impossible to be sad with Marion, for she was bubbling over with her own joys, sorrows and problems. From Marion Rita heard for the first time what kind of people she had been living with for years in that little town, and she amused Manfred in the evenings with stories of their curious adventures.

The only time Marion could be absent-minded was when she sat poring over fashion magazines. She introduced some drastic changes in Rita's habits, too.

"I bet you wash with soap and water at night," she said. "That would be just like you. You haven't a clue about making the most of yourself. If I hadn't stopped you, you'd probably have gone on using that impossible red lipstick for the rest of your days. It's all wrong with your colouring."

Rita loved to watch Marion chattering away to Manfred, taking no notice of his polite aloofness though she was a little in awe of him and hinted to Rita that as a boy friend he would be too strenuous for her.

She confided more and more in Rita as they got to know each other better. Her name was really Marianna, but she liked to be called Marion because it was less old-fashioned. She also kept Rita up to date on all the phases of her dramatic love affair with a young mechanic from a near-by automobile works, and it was not long before Jochen was waiting for her every evening outside the institute with his motor-bike. Manfred found he did not mind playing second waiting lover on those melancholy autumn evenings; he and Rita never tired of watching Marion sail down the steps to meet her admirer, greet him like a princess and depart in a cloud of dust when Jochen took off in a dashing curve.

But Marion's cheery friendship was not enough, after all, to dispel Rita's misgivings. Manfred tried for a time to ignore the change in her – a barely noticeable change betrayed by a curious expression which sometimes flitted across her face – and put off trying to find out what caused it. But when his mother began to put titbits on Rita's plate and urge her to eat more, insisting that she looked ill – which was not surprising considering how hard she had to work, she would add – he realised that something was seriously wrong.

"You must look after her," she said to Manfred when they were alone; and for once he did not choke her off rudely, although he found it hard to believe that his mother could really be concerned for Rita.

He cautiously questioned Marion, who was flattered by his confidence but could not help him much. She could only assure him that she admired Rita tremendously and was sure that the institute was the right place for her, for she was clever – much cleverer than herself, she sighed – for she felt a little out of place there.

So Manfred did his best to help Rita through this difficult time. He introduced her to Martin Jung, a young engineer who came from Thuringia every three or four weeks to consult him about improvements he was making on a spinning jenny to be used in the synthetic fibre factory where he worked. Manfred liked and respected him because he was completely bound up in his work.

"It's my machine, you know," Martin would say to Rita when she scolded him for having no outside interests. "She leaves me no time for other girls!"

"You're too good-looking," she would say. "Handsome men are always stuck-up."

Martin took it all in good part. He was always in high spirits when he came to see them, bringing new records and chocolates for Rita. Manfred never gave her sweets; he said they were bad for her. And their little room, which sometimes seemed very quiet now when they were alone, was full of life as soon as Martin appeared. He would dance with Rita and lecture them on jazz, which he loved.

"He makes me feel like an old, old man," Manfred would sometimes say when Martin had gone, leaving the air quivering behind him.

Rita was pleased and a little surprised to find that Manfred was so fond of Martin. It had seemed queer to her that he had no man friend; and Manfred realised that this feeling of real friendship for the younger man had developed after Rita came into his life.

She still lay with her head on his left shoulder at night. His breath stirred the tips of her fine-spun hair and she still loved his warmth and he the smoothness of her skin, which moved him to tenderness. But it could happen now that he would wake up at midnight because Rita had pressed up against him, and he would see that her eyes were open.

"What's the matter?" he would ask, and stroke her hair. But she shook her head and pretended she had been asleep. She did not want to talk, for she could not explain what she felt; besides, she was not sure whether he really wanted to know what was troubling her.

It had been a grey, dull autumn that year. The leaves fell like wet rags on the sticky roads, where they were swept up into heavy, dirty balls and carted away. The fogs began in October – the particular kind of heavy, thick, bitter-tasting fog usual in the district which hung over the town for weeks. People had to feel their way along fences, the light was dim all day and there was a pervading sense of missed opportunities, lost love, pain not understood, joys untasted and a sun never seen over foreign lands. Traffic was held up. Even the strong headlights of the big, long-distance trucks could hardly pierce this reddish-white wall of fog.

On one such evening Manfred waited a long time for Rita. He made some excuse for her at supper, which his parents did not believe, for they noticed that he was worried. His mother wondered whether there had been an accident. But then she forgot all about Rita while she spread out on the table the contents of a parcel from her sister in the West – the first for several years. So now they were once more amongst those who could invite neighbours in to a cup of "West coffee". Manfred was not much interested, for he hardly knew his aunt; but he took the cigarettes meant for him and also added a few lines to the letter of thanks which his mother had written.

He inquired casually after his cousins. Photographs were handed round. He looked at them, recalling that one cousin was short and plump and the other tall and thin and both had straw-blond hair. He sat on at the table, straining his ears to catch any sound at the gate.

"Perhaps it's the tram," said his mother. "They were creeping along this afternoon, and some of them just didn't run at all. You really can't do a thing but wait."

The lamp shone brightly, as it had done years before when he had sat down at this table to do his homework. Surely his mother had stood behind him and stroked his hair sometimes, with a light, warm hand, comfortingly? Why should he feel there was something false now when she worried about Rita? And why could he not feel sorry for his father who, after all, was just a weak man who tried to do his best? He felt somehow drawn back into the stuffy warmth of this room, felt himself weakening. But he struggled against it, rebelling against a vague sensation which he could not identify, jumped up angrily and went to his own room, where he smoked nervously and listened to the news.

There was talk of an accident on the high road. He walked up and down. The room suddenly seemed too big for him. Gradually, and then like an avalanche, the conviction poured over him that something must have happened to Rita. He had overcome the first crippling feeling of dread and was putting on his overcoat to go out and telephone to the hospital when the door opened and Rita came in.

Fine drops of fog had settled on her coat and hair, and they glistened in the light when she moved. Her face was flushed and innocent. He remembered her like that many times later on when she was far away, standing there in the doorway, glittering, fresh, a little cloud of vapour surrounding her, with an imperceptible air of defiance (or had it been merely self-confidence?). And each time he could feel himself stiffening as he had done at that moment.

"Where were you?" he asked abruptly, in a self-righteous, demanding tone, empty of the concern he had felt.

"I was at Schwarzenbachs'," she said.

She ate nothing, but drank her tea. And she could not talk to him so long as he remained cold and remote. She went to bed and he sat down at his desk. But she did not sleep and he did not work. He could feel her watching him and stiffened. She was waiting for a sign from him. My God, are we children, she thought?

That evening he managed to throw off his black mood.

"You smell of the fog, even now," he said, bending over her.

She told him a great deal that night, and they talked for hours, until the fog retreated or dissolved – who knows what happens to fog when it disappears at last? At all events, the town was visible again the next morning. Things which had been hidden for a long time were suddenly there again.

"I waited for Schwarzenbach outside the institute," she said. She had felt that he was the only person who could help her for she had got to know him a little better during the evenings they had spent together. Schwarzenbach remembered how little confidence she had had in herself and had not seemed surprised when she said she wished she had stayed at home.

"So that's the way you feel. Have you time to come and talk things over?"

She nodded, although she knew Manfred would be worried.

They walked a long way in the fog, for no tram came. Luckily, Schwarzenbach lived near-by. They met his wife and two children at the door. The children rushed up to their father. They were both black-haired. They had to be fetched every evening from different nursery schools.

"He kissed his wife in the hall, right in front of me," she added.

She liked the whole family. There was no chance to sit down then and there and talk to Schwarzenbach, for all the jobs were waiting which have to be done when a mother goes out to work – getting the supper ready, washing the children and hearing about their day's doings.

All these were fairly divided between father and mother and Rita looked on happily. She was given the job of helping the elder boy with his homework.

"I felt so happy in that noisy, crowded room. At first I was surprised that Schwarzenbach seemed to like it. I should have thought he would want peace and quiet and a gentle, thoughtful wife. But she's just the opposite – much younger than he and very energetic and cheery. She has thick, black, curly hair, sticking out all over the place after the damp fog. I've never seen anything like it before. . . ."

Frau Schwarzenbach was a teacher. She stayed with them after supper, when the children had gone to bed.

"This is the girl who helped me get through those

long evenings," Schwarzenbach said to his wife. "She's going to be cross with me for persuading her to leave her peaceful village and her easy job."

"I felt better already by that time," Rita told Manfred. She felt as if her doubts were dispelling even before they talked about them.

"I often didn't know whether I was just imagining things. But the Schwarzenbachs didn't even try to talk me out of anything. They didn't tell me to be patient or that I'd get used to things, either."

Manfred had sometimes said that.

"But what was bothering you so much?" he asked.

"That's what they asked me, too," said Rita, "and it's so difficult to explain. But Schwarzenbach understood at once when I told him about Mangold and how they're always saying we ought to learn from him. I can't and I don't want to. Do we have to be like him?"

"Who's Mangold?" Manfred asked.

"I told you about him. He was a department head in some town council or other before he decided he wanted to be a teacher. He must be well over thirty. You'd be surprised at all the things he's done already. I can't think how they put up with him where he worked before. He knows the answer to simply everything. He makes us all nervous."

"My goodness, aren't you taking him too seriously?"

"Schwarzenbach says we need people who take things seriously. What's the use of people who have no feelings?"

"He may well talk," said Manfred. "The only thing for sensitive people is to get over it. You oughtn't to make too much of it. You know young people have too much idealism and some of it has to be knocked out of them. They want to alter people's way of doing things and it gets them into trouble. So when that happens a few times they draw in their horns. There's nothing new about that."

He sounds as if he'd been through some of that himself, Rita thought.

"Well, but Schwarzenbach was just as mad as I was when I told him what happened today," she said. "Mangold just stood up and corrected our social science lecturer today. He's a young man and not very sure of himself in any case – always looking round to see if he's made a mistake. Mangold said he'd quoted some important sentence or other all wrong. Of course he knows all the quotations by heart. He must have spent years learning them. He made it sound as if the poor fellow had committed a serious crime. Anyway, he blushed to the roots of his hair and could hardly finish his lecture. Mangold simply enjoyed taking a rise out of him, and we all sat there not daring to look at each other or say a word. It was horrible!"

"Well, every step forward costs something," said Manfred, "and the price we have to pay is putting up with chaps like Mangold."

But that can't be right, Rita thought. Schwarzenbach didn't think we ought to put up with it, and his wife was really angry about it.

"There's nothing worse than these know-alls," said Schwarzenbach. "At first they scuttled back into their holes and did a transformation act; now they're coming out again, hanging on to our band-wagon, pretending to help and doing us all the more harm."

"Your Schwarzenbach is a Communist," said Manfred. "But you're not. Let him fight all he likes and come to blows with anyone he likes. But what does he expect you to do?"

"I don't know. He seemed to think I agreed with him about everything."

"Well, if you want my advice," said Manfred, "you keep out of all this!"

"I'd like to," said Rita. "I'm not looking for trouble."

She fell asleep after that, with a childishly reassured look on her face. But Manfred lay awake, as if she had passed her worries on to him.

17

One morning in her fourth week at the sanatorium Rita stood on the balcony which ran along the entire south side of the building, and saw that the scene had changed – quite suddenly, without any warning.

It was the first clear, cold autumn day after a stormy night. She had slept little, but did not feel tired. The storm had howled and screamed through the park all night, and the telephone wires had droned threateningly. About midnight her own voice calling for help had awakened her and her dream broke off when she stopped screaming. She would have liked to recall the dream; it had seemed so clear and unforgettable for a few seconds after she awoke, and she felt she would have understood it perfectly if she had only been able to think about it long enough. But it retreated from her memory too quickly.

What she did remember was a familiar, long road, and how she had felt as she walked along it – a curious mixture of fear and curiosity – and strangely enough it was Ernst Wendland, not Manfred, who walked beside her, and even in her dream she had wondered why he was there. But he behaved quite naturally and kept insisting that she should forgive him but not Manfred. Then, before she could answer or ask him what he meant, they had been sitting in Rita's little room at home in the village (she knew it must be her room because she smelt the fresh, hay-scented air wafted in through the open window). She and Wendland had never been there together, and her astonishment grew.

She woke up at that point and the dream began to fade at once, retreating like a wisp of fog when she tried to grasp it. But her astonishment lingered. She felt suddenly grown up, a real individual. And for the first time she felt a desire to throw off her illness, which she did not need any longer.

The clear, hard light dazzled her a little – who does not sometimes long for the vague outlines of childhood? But she knew she would get used to this hard light, for she was not naturally sentimental.

She stood at the corner of the balcony for a long time, looking down over the park, until the little triangle of sun on the stone floor narrowed and lost its warmth. The wind had dropped. As she stood there, Rita was really conscious of colours for the first time in her life; not the reds and greens and blues of childhood, but the twenty different shades of grey in the stone floor and the countless browns in the trees and in the leaves, too, for now after the heavy rains and so late in the year, they were more brown than autumn-tinted as they fell. All this she saw under the swiftly moving ceiling of clouds, now breaking up to show more and more blue as the day advanced, until a pale, cold sun came out again and altered everything.

The sharp light and the cold air cut through the soft blanket of recent habits. She could look round again and feel that life was not impossible, for many of her problems seemed to have solved themselves in the meantime. And now she could use this new clarity like a new pair of hands. She had seen and experienced so much and this morning she was glad that she had done so, glad that she had known both bitterness and joy.

Rita went down into the park. She wanted to touch things: the wooden benches, the ridged trunk of a copper beech, leaves, twigs, dry moss. Turning again to the things which existed without help from her, she was also able to think of herself again. She saw and felt herself as a real person, and no longer as some poor thing flung down into a dark pit. She had had to pay for this new awareness.

After her talk with Manfred about Mangold she had never again felt that they were quite alone and sufficient unto themselves in their gondola room swaying high above the world.

They had talked of many things. Manfred tried to show her the world as he saw it – recognisable, familiar, but hardly affected by this familiarity, a mass of uncontrollable, contradictory matter – and man, who strove to master it, still little more than an apprentice. He felt a grim satisfaction in the mathematicians' efforts to foresee all manner of things, including things outside their field, such as the effects of economic experiments or the results of a war; for even the calculations of electronic brains did not prevent people from gambling and arming on a huge scale, in one half of the world, at any rate, he said.

"But what about ordinary people?" Rita had put in.

"Oh well, most people's lives run alongside each other – parallel lines which only cross in infinity," he said. "But they certainly cross in infinity, so they say," he added with a smile.

All the same, Manfred felt that he belonged to the prophets. He felt some satisfaction at the big share which his branch of science had in shaping people's future lives, and if he felt any impatience it was the impatience of the inventor who cannot get hold of whole cities and provinces quickly enough to try out his experiments.

"That's what people want, after all," he had said one day to Wendland, "a house that runs like a well oiled machine, cleans itself, heats itself and keeps itself in running order, a house in which a perfectly planned course of human life can proceed without interruption or inconvenience, automatically controlled bringing up of children – yes, that's part of it. At all events, an existence in which no time is wasted because of faulty technology. That's the scientific problem of our century, and it's a problem which can only be solved by us natural scientists."

"Well, hurry up and solve it, then," said Wendland.

He was on one of his visits to Manfred's institute in connection with a chemical analysis for his works. He had often passed Manfred's door in the long corridor, but today was the first time he had gone in, after a brief hesitation. Manfred, who was checking solutions in a long row of test tubes, was surprised that Wendland should want to see him, but he even appeared a little pleased and there was no sign of the aloof expression on his face which Wendland had half expected.

The hard, clear light, the strictly useful nature of everything in the big, tidy room, and the preoccupied expressions on the chemists' faces impressed Wendland particularly that day, and the politely smiling faces they turned to him seemed a little out of place.

He glanced along the row of test tubes.

"All the same?" he asked Manfred.

"Not quite," he answered, smiling as an expert smiles at an amateur. "It's the tiny differences that matter here."

Manfred took him to each of his colleagues in turn and explained what they were doing. He was more friendly than Wendland had expected and made the most of being at an advantage for once. Wendland pretended not to notice this, but towards the end of their inspection, he caught Manfred out in a quick, ironical glance; he grinned and Manfred smiled back, shrugging his shoulders, as if silently agreeing to a kind of truce between them. Why should a girl make them enemies? Could she not be a link between them?

Manfred held out his cigarette case. They went over to the big window and looked down into the busy street, which was bathed in soft, early winter light. As they smoked Manfred began to talk about what he hoped to do in his line of work.

"Well, hurry up with it," Wendland said again. "Or did you expect me to be against science?"

"Not exactly against it. That wouldn't be progressive. But maybe you think science is arrogant?"

"Oh no, it's only the scientists who are arrogant."

"You may be right there," said Manfred with a smile, "but don't you think science is pervading every-day life more quickly elsewhere than here?"

"You mean west of the Elbe, for instance," said Wendland, casually.

"Yes, that's what I mean," said Manfred. He picked up a glossy magazine from his desk and leafed through it. "Look at that, for instance. Why aren't we as far as that?"

"Well, why aren't we?"

"You'd better ask the people who're responsible."

"Why don't you ask yourself?"

That was a mistake. Manfred shut the journal and put it back on his desk. That's what they were all like, he thought. Why had he let himself be drawn out. He tried angrily to retreat into himself again. After all, he had had plenty of practice in putting up a disinterested front.

"Speaking as a chemist, you know, I appreciate the accident which put life on our planet – including people like you and me," he said. "But aren't we demanding too much of ourselves as a result of this accident? Was it such an important accident, after all? Why should we take everything so seriously?"

"Look," said Wendland in a not unfriendly tone, "you can't turn round and talk to me like that now. If I want to see a somersault I can go to the circus."

They both laughed. Manfred felt something like respect for the other man. He agreed at once when Wendland glanced at his watch and suggested they should have lunch together.

It was chilly when they left the institute and went out into the pale December sunshine, and they turned up their coat collars. They walked side by side down the shrub lined road.

"You'd have enjoyed seeing us," said Manfred later on to Rita. He told her all about the visit, but not about his inmost thoughts that morning.

Rita had never heard so much about Wendland as she heard from Manfred that evening.

When he and Wendland reached the restaurant at the corner where Manfred often had his lunch, they found it crowded, mostly with farmers, but there was a corner table free. They sat down and ordered pigs' trotters with sauerkraut, a talkative waitress brought them their beer, banging it down on the scrubbed table top and wiping up the froth which bubbled over the rims of their glasses. They ate heartily, for the trotters were good – tender and not too fat – and said little.

Then Wendland ordered coffee and began to talk while they waited. Manfred was not sure whether he had decided to talk on the spur of the moment, or whether he had been leading up to it all the morning; at all events he realised he was there to listen and he played his part tactfully. He studied Wendland's face, too, for it interested him.

"Today is a special occasion for me," Wendland began. "It's my birthday. I'm thirty-two. But don't start congratulating me. That's all over now. ... Talking about mistakes. You know how much electrical equipment a railway wagon needs. Well, we've been getting our fittings from the same Berlin factory for years. But suddenly, a month ago, the factory simply stopped deliveries."

He spoke more slowly than usual – a sign that he was upset.

They had written to the factory at once, of course, but had had no answer. They had sent telegrams and telephoned. But you can't make people talk if they don't want to. So there were all those wagons standing about, finished except for the electrical fittings. Wendland went up to Berlin to find out what was wrong. It turned out that the factory had simply stopped producing their equipment and switched over to quite a different line of production – of course on instructions from above. The manager was on holiday – an unheard-of thing so late in the year – and the man responsible in the Ministry was abroad at some conference.

"I couldn't let them get away with it, you know," he went on. "So the manager got a telegram from me, on behalf of the man in the Ministry, ordering him back from his holiday. He was pretty mad when he got back and found out what had happened, but I finally persuaded him to start producing our equipment again. After that, of course, he sent in a complaint about me.

"I was at our district office today. They gave me a pat on the back for getting our contracts filled on time, and then hauled me over the coals for the methods I'd used – anarchism, factory egoism, usurpation of official authority and all the rest."

Why am I telling him all this? Wendland wondered.

Manfred guessed what he was thinking and was glad to know that Wendland was not lecturing at him.

"Well, to make a long story short," Wendland went on, "they gave me a thorough talking-to and I didn't say a word. What was there to say? They're right, but I was right, too. Things like that do happen."

He gulped down his coffee.

"And how about your IG Farben people? Do they never make mistakes?"

"Not any more, I should think," said Manfred. "Things seem to be working pretty smoothly now, and they can kick people out if they hold things up."

"Well, that's what I said. Throw me out if you're not satisfied with me. But that didn't impress anyone. Even if they weren't satisfied with me they would still have to find someone better to take my place, is what they said. A pretty logical answer, eh?"

"Yes, if you're looking at things from above," said Manfred slowly. "But looking at it from your point of view. . . ."

"Oh well, it's no good being too thin-skinned. Something of the sort happened to me once before, in '45. An old sergeant sent a group of us young air force helpers home. Home! That was easier said than done, in those muddled days at the end of the war. A friend and I tramped for fourteen days right from Hamburg to the little village in the mountains where my mother lives. We had to crawl part of the way, and swim, for we had to get across the Elbe, too, and there were groups of soldiers on the loose everywhere, some of them old Nazis and some of them occupation troops – all against us.

"We got home with bleeding feet, but we were as happy as children to be there at last. I slept exactly one night at home. Early the next morning the house was searched – not specially for me, of course. The Soviet patrols were hunting for much bigger fish. But they found a pistol on me that I'd picked up on the way home and had been meaning to get rid of, so they took me away with them.

"Well, I spent the next three years in the mines in Siberia. Pretty tough luck, eh? I certainly thought so. You know what I scratched on the white-washed wall beside my bunk? *Did I get through the war alive for this?* Of course, I don't know what I might have done at home. Over there they sent me to the Anti-Fascist School at the end of the three years. When I got back home I went and joined the Free German Youth at once. My friend, who had thrown away his pistol in good time, went off to the West long ago. . . .

"Perhaps it's impossible to see the logic of things from above or below, but only later on, looking back."

Aha! I know what's coming now, Manfred thought. They always end up with agitation and propaganda. He stood up. Maybe Wendland knew more about him than he should and was just trying to get him to talk? But what could he know, after all? He had nothing much to hide anyway, he thought.

"I've got to go," he said. "Your problem interests me very much."

Wendland looked at him, hurt. Manfred stretched out his hand impulsively. Why do I always have to be so suspicious, he thought.

"It really does interest me," he said in a friendlier tone. "Anyway, here's luck on your birthday."

The sun was still shining palely when they stepped out into the street again. They parted at the door and Manfred went back to the institute.

18

The days passed, but they no longer slid by in a vague monotony; Rita was again clearly aware of each long, dreamless night and each short day in which she did exactly what the doctor told her.

She and Manfred had wanted time to stand still, she remembered, one evening after a party given by his professor. The thing she remembered most vividly about the professor was the neat parting in his hair; his wife, a slim, fair woman, much younger than he, had talked about him incessantly. But many of these minor details were already fading from her memory.

They had stayed in town over Christmas so as to attend this party, although Rita had really wanted to go home, to see the winter stars – perhaps, after all, not so big and bright as she imagined them – which seemed to her to have shone down over the village and the woods every night between Christmas and New Year for as many years as she could remember. A strangely harsh wind had swept in over the town just before Christmas, gnawing at it like a dog at a bone and beating up against the houses in huge gusts. It had dropped suddenly on Christmas Eve. She remembered how lonely and bored they had felt amongst the well-dressed crowds in the streets. The Christmas season had seemed an anti-climax after the weeks of preparation.

They had not cared to drive up to the professor's house in their little old car, for it would have looked very shabby beside the others drawn up at his gate. So they walked instead. Rita wondered how these people could afford such shining new cars, but supposed they attached great importance to outward appearances.

The wife of Dr Seiffert and Dr Müller's fianceé, too, looked as if they had come out of bandboxes. She would never manage to look like that, she thought.

They talked of nothing but cars for the first half-hour. The professor was an important man and a brilliant chemist; Manfred had told her how he could gather up the threads of all their work and produce a really inspired idea from it. But that did not make him interesting. He was in fact self-opinionated and what he valued most was his own success and reputation. Rita would have liked him better if he had let his work speak for itself.

"Oh yes, I've been driving my own car for thirty years. That car I have now is pretty good, you know," he was saying, and his wife did not forget to add that he had won lots of prizes at amateur motor races before they were married, but was much too modest to mention this. And they all began to extol his modesty, while he raised a hand in protest.

There were more than a dozen people at the party and it was the first time Rita had seen Manfred amongst so many. She had certainly not been so consciously critical of them at the time, but her perceptions had sharpened since then and later events had added a tinge of bitterness to her memories – perhaps more than the occasion warranted.

So long as the professor was not thinking of himself there was a trace of disappointment on his face when he observed his students around him; he might even have been thinking that a professor deserves the students he gets. He seemed to like Manfred. Rita thought Dr Müller and Dr Seiffert noticed this and she mentioned it in a whisper to Manfred. He pretended not to hear. This was no place for confidential asides and she was glad to find Martin Jung in this somewhat constrained company. He had chanced to be in town and had been invited as Manfred's friend, although he did not belong to the professor's "narrower circle".

Martin had made fun of them all and called them "idol worshippers" – including Manfred – but Rita was not quite sure whether he had meant that they were all worshipping at the professor's shrine, or at the shrine of science.

Dr Seiffert certainly talked a great deal about science, although he was continually being reminded not to talk shop. Seiffert was a tall, thin man with smoothly brushed, nondescript-coloured hair and a carefully selected wife who gave the impression of being in a permanent state of irritation. Rita thought she might have tried to make the best of her husband, since she must have married him of her own free will.

Seiffert belonged to the generation which had been dragged into the war from the very beginning; the few who came out of it alive had had a tremendous struggle to gain a firm foothold again. Not all of them had managed to do this, but it was well known that Seiffert was tremendously hard working and ambitious and that, although the professor did not particularly like him, he could hardly find fault with a man who was always so correct in his behaviour and so good at his work. Seiffert was next in seniority at the institute and next in line for a professorship; but everyone hoped that this particular professor would not give up his chair for many years to come.

Rita had vaguely realised that evening that this was the environment which surrounded, or rather restricted, Manfred at work. She looked at Dr Müller's fiancée, a small, overslim young woman with her hair done in a huge blue-black pompadour who hardly spoke the whole evening – which was just as well, for fat, rosy little Dr Müller had certainly not fallen in love with her on account of her intelligence. Dr Seiffert scarcely concealed his contempt for his colleague's taste in women; Rita could imagine him wondering what had possessed the man to get engaged to that girl and bring her here with that primitively possessive look on his face – he should have had more sense.

The dinner was good, but not very interesting, for it had been sent in from a restaurant. The young people who had not been working with the professor for long sat at the lower end of the table, doing their best to behave in a suitably dignified manner, and she would have felt much more comfortable with them than with Manfred.

Rudi Schwabe now belonged to the professor's narrower circle, for the professor was Dean of the Faculty and Rudi his contact man in the Dean of Studies' office.

Left to himself Rudi would never have come to this party, and he did his best to escape notice. But the others were not prepared to let him off lightly, since they were in the majority. Rita could not remember exactly when they began to bate him, for she had been watching Manfred and Martin Jung as they stood by the buffet in the next room.

"Keep smiling, boss. We've been passed over," Martin was saying.

"Passed over? You mean to say they're not going to use your improved spinning-jenny?" Manfred thought of all the months of hard work Martin had put into designing the new gadget for drawing off waste gases. He knew just how much this meant to Martin, but he said nothing more. Martin had been hinting that there were difficulties, but had never really discussed them in detail with him. It appeared that another design, not nearly as well thought out, had been accepted and was going into production.

"We shall have to go and look into things, Manfred. There'll be a fight, too. Some very queer things have been happening lately."

Manfred had shrugged his shoulders and gone back to the others. Martin told Rita later on that he could have taken hold of Manfred and shaken him. "You just wait! I'll show you a thing or two!" he had said to himself.

But it had been too late. Manfred had already begun to feel out of place and unwanted. All the talk about justice and equality meant exactly nothing, for there were people sitting in offices who could simply brush aside a man's hopes without giving the matter a thought.

He watched Seiffert teasing Rudi Schwabe in a sly

way. Five minutes before this would have made him angry. Now he simply felt that it was none of his business, and he felt curiously relieved, too. He could see these people and himself clearly now through Rita's eyes, but it did not seem to matter any longer, since it was not his business. For weeks he had been deeply involved in Martin's project, not only for Martin's sake, but also because of his own part in it, which would have given him some status in Müller's and Seiffert's eyes. And the shock of hearing that it had been rejected plunged him back into his old indifference; he mentally washed his hands of all responsibility for what was going on, and made up his mind not to let himself be drawn into anything again. A new feeling of cold detachment pervaded his thoughts. Real pain or happiness could only come from Rita now. . . .

Pale but smiling, he wandered back to the others and listened to them bating Rudi Schwabe. Somebody began questioning him – harmless questions at first, which Rudi answered a little too eagerly. They saw that they could go further, although the professor remained disapprovingly in the background. They asked about old-age pensions. Thirty-year-olds began to argue about pensions as if it were an urgent problem, and Rita had felt like laughing at first, until she realised that there was a hint of a threat in the air; Schwabe, as a representative of the government, was being subjected to a veiled kind of blackmail.

The names of colleagues, top men, were mentioned, who had gone off to the West because there had been delays in granting them some special privileges. Someone remarked that it was a great loss, especially for the government, since it was dependent on its scientists . . . all countries needed their scientists. . . .

And it was a pity, too, that things were being done twice in Germany, once in the East and once in the West. The word "risk" came up. You couldn't afford to take risks. The government knew now that they ought to avoid taking risks with scientists, for there were enough risks involved in the whole experiment. . . .

Rudi began to sweat. He had not been prepared for this kind of thing, but he stuck to his instructions and agreed with everything.

"Germany has always led in the chemical industry," said Seiffert. They all stopped talking to listen to him. "You can't gamble with anything so important. But the question is, which Germany is to carry on the old traditions? The West or the East? That depends on real facts, by the way, not on politics. And our brains are real facts – not the least important facts, either. The workers' state has to make the best of unpleasant bourgeois chemistry for the sake of the pleasant results it can provide. That's about it, isn't it, Herr Schwabe?"

Rudi's mild protest made little impression. Seiffert glanced at Manfred. Manfred should be the one to back him up, he thought. Seiffert was a man who knew more about other people than he permitted them to know about himself.

"Of course," said Manfred shortly, and Seiffert smiled, although it was not quite clear what Manfred meant.

The younger people looked extremely embarrassed, but said nothing. Rita wondered what they would say about all this when they were alone, and how long it would be before they took Seiffert's line, as Manfred had done.

The teasing went on. Manfred did not join in. He glanced at Rita; he saw exactly the puzzled, hurt expression in her eyes that he had expected. He was sorry for her. He had seen this sort of thing before, but he knew she would take it hard.

Had she seen him clearly then for the first time? No, she thought, it must have been earlier, but it is difficult to see a person one loves. In those few seconds Manfred seemed to shift from unclear proximity to a distance which gave her a chance to measure him and see his value. This is the moment which is supposed to coincide with the end of love, but it is really only the end of enchantment, one of the things which real, enduring love must take in its stride.

They both realised this; there was a moment of silent understanding between them when she saw in his eyes the decision not to build up hopes any more, and in her eyes he saw that she would never agree to this. She also realised that she could not comfort or encourage him and he, in a flash, understood that life could be a failure – that he had perhaps failed already. Many things which had seemed possible yesterday were quite unthinkable today; he was no longer very young and he could not believe in miracles.

Rita shivered. She fought against the desire to go over and lay her head on Manfred's shoulder, to free him with a touch from this evil enchantment. Manfred did not try to hide what he felt.

Their eyes drew apart and they could hear what was going on around them again.

Rudi Schwabe had taken up the challenge.

"No, you're wrong there," he was saying. "But some people are only too willing to take advantage of the mistakes made in the revolution."

"And why do they need to do that?" Seiffert asked politely.

"Why, as an excuse, of course, an excuse for their own laziness or cowardice. . . ."

Not much of an answer, Rita had thought, but at least he was not going to give in meekly. He was hitting back, upsetting their little game of hide-and-seek with words, breaking through the conventions.

But he had no sense of humour. It would have been much better to fence with them than to throw stones. He was not always right, either, for he defended things which could not be defended and let himself be drawn into ridiculous forecasts. The day would come when they would not care to be reminded of what they thought now, he said.

One thing had been quite clear, however; Rudi believed every word he said. He was a romantic. Rita caught herself planning what she would have said in Rudi's place. What would she have said to Dr Müller, for example?

"Revolution in Germany?" Müller was saying reflectively. "Why, it's a contradiction in itself, isn't it? The Russians, yes. They're to be admired. You mustn't think we're so blind we don't see that. But revolutions always end up in dilettantism in Germany, don't they?"

Rita had listened impatiently to Rudi's long-winded answer.

"But you needn't label us incorrigible reactionaries, Herr Schwabe," Seiffert answered. "Why shouldn't there be revolutions? But for heaven's sake spare us your illusions. . . . In any case, you ought to know as well as anybody that the revolution eats its own children, or if it doesn't eat them it puts them aside somewhere – in the Dean of Studies' office, for instance."

That ought to keep you quiet, my boy. You needn't think we don't know you were thrown out of Free

German Youth headquarters with a black mark on your Party card, and now you're trying to get back on the band-wagon by catching us out. . . .

Rudi turned bright red. So they knew all about that business. He wondered how he was supposed to do his job under these circumstances.

This was all new to Rita. She had no idea what was at the back of Seiffert's remark.

"If you ask me, I'd rather have a person who makes mistakes trying to do his job than somebody who always goes at things with an eye to the main chance," she said loudly, in the silence which followed.

Seiffert took this up quickly.

"I absolutely agree with you," he said, as he clinked glasses with Rita and Rudi and agreed cheerfully with the professor's wife that the ladies ought not to be left out of things any longer.

Rita had never spoken to Manfred about this little episode. She smiled back when Martin nodded approval, but she felt neither more nor less wretched than before. She did not even like Rudi Schwabe much and did not know what had prompted her to stand up for him. Manfred should have done it, that would have made her feel better, she thought.

Seiffert was easily offended. He'll hold this against me, even though he turned it off so neatly, Manfred thought indifferently, but he did not mention it to Rita, either. There had been too many things left undiscussed between them, Rita thought. Now, nearly a year later, after she had had time to think, she realised that she had not quite grasped what was going on that evening, for she had not endured all the doubts and heart-searchings which beset these people.

There was a great deal of drinking after that, for the

evening was spoilt and it was impossible to gloss things over. The professor mixed the drinks himself. He offered a box of chocolates and a bottle of champagne for the best name for his new cocktail. Dr Müller's fiancée suggested "Love Potion", her first – and slightly ludicrous – remark of the evening, but she won the ladies' prize. The cocktail was as clear as vodka and the men made various suggestions – "Murder", "Firewater" and so on. Dr Müller's suggestion was "Scorched Earth".

There was an embarrassed silence. Thoughts went back to the days when this idea was being shouted across huge crowded squares and put into practice in half the countries of the world. . . .

"If you can't hold your liquor you shouldn't drink," Dr Seiffert cut in.

Frau Professor ordered a taxi for Dr Müller. Small things – a dropped table-napkin, or a vulgar joke – were apt to irritate her, but she did not quite see what the fuss was about this time.

The party began to break up. The professor had not exactly sought out the most difficult situations in life, but he was no longer young and unaccustomed excitement sometimes caused a slight flutter in the region of the heart.

He filled their glasses for a final drink. For some reason, there was one glass missing and his wife jumped up to fetch another.

"Please don't bother," said Manfred, glancing at Rita, "we prefer to drink out of the same glass."

The professor applauded loudly, glad to be able to end the evening on a cheerful note. Rita blushed, feeling extremely embarrassed and exposed.

They raised their glasses. What was the toast to be?

"To our lost illusions," Manfred suggested.

The professor shook his head.

"To everything we hold dear!" he said.

And they drank to very different, even opposite things.

Manfred took a sip and handed his glass to Rita. She drank the rest in one draft, and they both wished for the same thing – that time might stand still.

Later on, Rita remembered the vague feeling of anxiety about the future which had come over her.

After that the party broke up quickly, as if they were driven by bad consciences.

19

Manfred was used to disappointment, and he liked to think he was prepared for anything. So far he had achieved all he wanted without undue exertion, for the country was hungry for talent. But he had put a great deal into helping Martin with his new spinning-jenny and he felt that the designs for it were like a birth certificate. Now that there was to be no birth and he was faced with defeat, he was surprised at his own despondency. He realised for the first time how easy things had been for him.

But it was mainly for Martin's sake that he decided early in the New Year to go with him to the works which had rejected the machine.

He had often visited factories, but this was the first time he had thought about making a good impression on people.

"So much can depend on little things, you know," he said. "Should I wear a tie, for instance? Which would be better, a hat or a cap?" he asked Martin, who was watching him packing.

"Who cares? What you'll need is plenty of patience," said Martin, "and self-confidence, too. It's hard to resist self-confidence."

Rita wondered whether Manfred had noticed that Martin was cautiously preparing him for trouble. She sat watching them and did not know whether to be happy or miserable, for she was in what Manfred called her "drizzly weather" mood. As usual, she took refuge in grumbling.

"Why ever didn't you give me a budgerigar instead of Cleopatra?" she asked. "Cleopatra sleeps all winter. A bird would have sung all the time. I shall need something to cheer me up when I'm alone."

"But you're not alone," Manfred objected. "You have lots of friends. Anyway, no nice girl makes it harder for a man to go away. And in any case. . . ."

Martin knew what was coming. He always turned his back when they kissed.

"By the way, nobody at the works knows we're coming," he remarked after a while.

"I'd better unpack again, then," said Manfred, looking up in surprise.

"You don't have to come if you don't want to."

Manfred really did want to see the machine working as soon as possible and with as little trouble as possible. Nevertheless, he cursed Martin heartily for dragging him into it.

Rita began to feel better. She made coffee and put out a plate of biscuits. Martin played a tune on Manfred's plastic slide rule. She was glad to have Martin for a friend, for she could talk to him about Manfred.

"You'll keep an eye on him, won't you?" she said.

Martin bowed ironically.

"Listen, Martin. You know how rude he is sometimes. He blurts things out and annoys people."

"You're right there. He's damned rude sometimes. He just doesn't know how to talk to people. He rubs them the wrong way. He's stuck up, too. But our machine is good."

Rita sighed.

"And he's not exactly a hero, either."

"Oh well, it's the chemists and engineers who get the jobs, not the heroes."

It was nice of Martin to want to calm her fears, she thought.

"But you will look after him a bit, won't you?" she insisted.

"Look, Rita," said Martin. "Just sit down quietly and take that frown off your face. I've always admired the way you get on with Manfred. One doesn't often see anything like it. You carry on with the good work and leave me to admire him. After all, we shall only be away a week or so."

But they had seemed very long weeks to her. It was a gloomy, colourless February, without snow but with sudden cold spells and an icy wind sweeping down the road to the institute; she had longed desperately for spring – with almost unbearable urgency, like a glow under ashes.

At first she had invited Marion to come up with her to her cosy little attic room and let her friend go home alone. They sat at Rita's desk and worked away together at the formulae and figures which swam together before Marion's eyes, for a single figure could darken the whole gay, colourful world for her. Marion used to get up after a while and wander over to the window, sighing and gazing up at the real live sky darkening above her.

She simply could not understand that a real world was unfolding for Rita out of her books, but she admired Rita for it all the same. Schwarzenbach had noticed this, too.

"Didn't I tell you? Nothing much can go wrong as soon as you begin to enjoy learning," he had said reassuringly.

Manfred did not write to her. Martin sent a postcard from the station as soon as they arrived at the little town in Thuringia. And after that she had no news of them. Sometimes she lay awake all night, worrying.

"We're getting married at Christmas," said Marion. "How about you?"

"Oh, soon, I expect."

By this time Rita was going for longer and longer walks round the sanatorium. She loved the autumn scenery. She stood beside the shining railway tracks which cut through the gently sloping hills and waved cheerfully back at the stokers when they waved to her from their engines; but they made her feel a little homesick, too. The clear, cool weather suited her mood. She could take herself in hand and think clearly, and this helped her back to health more quickly. She also learned to avoid touching old scars.

She put a vase of mountain ash on her bedside table, talked cheerfully to her neighbours and to the nurses, and she began to read in the evenings. The night trains rattled past, the dry leaves rustled on the trees in the park and she began to take an interest in the efforts of poets to pierce the darkness of things unsaid.

But her real life during those last weeks at the sanatorium was compressed into fifteen tense minutes each day. Not far from the quiet white house there was a path through the fields which came out at a sharp angle to the main road leading through various small villages and country towns into the city. Rita stood at this corner, close beside the yellow signpost, each day at the same time and waited for the bus which had met the afternoon train.

Somebody must give her a sign, she thought. Somebody must disobey the order to leave her in peace. Somebody must feel that the time had come to help her to find her way back into the noisy world again. Marion would be the best person, for she did not know what her real difficulty had been.

Rita began to spend the days longing for Marion to come. Marion had left the institute long ago, in March. There had been no argument about it, for everybody liked her and wished her well. The girls let her fix their hair and told her all the news, for she was still interested in everything. Marion ought to come, she thought; she would be the best person.

And one day she really did come, and was not the least bit surprised to find Rita waiting for her at the bus-stop. She tripped along the field path on her high heels and they laughed together as if they had seen each other only the day before. They could not talk of anything without mentioning Manfred, so they did not even try to avoid his name. And Marion talked as naturally of him as if she had been talking about a house or the moon.

Although she had had no such trouble herself, Marion understood instinctively that love could cause terrible pain.

They walked along by the wood – a sparse spruce

wood behind which the sun went down in a red-gold blaze. The shadows flickered across their faces. Marion's high heels sank into the soft earth, but she had no time to bother about this in the excitement of describing her wedding preparations.

"And how's Sigrid?" Rita asked.

Sigrid sent her love. Rita smiled; Marion and Sigrid would certainly have spent hours talking about her. . . .

Rita had sat beside Sigrid, one of the quietest girls in her class. They had been friendly, but had known nothing about each other until one day Rita had seen her scribbling the same sentence over and over again on her blotting paper: "What shall I do? What shall I do?"

In the afternoon, sitting in the darkest corner of a little café, Rita had found out that Sigrid had got herself into a terrible situation. Her parents, with whom she lived, had "gone away" two weeks earlier, taking her younger brothers and sisters with them. Everybody knew what "gone away" meant. Sigrid had stayed away from home a whole night and the following day. When she went back late that evening she found the house quite empty, as she had hoped and feared.

She had hated and feared her father, and now that she was left alone the one thing she dreaded was that she would be turned out of the institute when they found out that her family had gone to the West. She had built up a complete wall around their flight. She told the neighbours that her parents had decided at short notice to go away for a winter holiday. She telephoned to her father's factory, where he worked as a welder, that he was ill; she would send in his doctor's certificate later. She wrote notes excusing her two little brothers from school.

She had worked feverishly to keep up this tissue of

lies for more than ten days, but the truth was bound to come out soon and she was sick with worry. Of course, she knew that there was only one thing to do, but she kept putting it off. Rita did not try to push her. She saw a new Sigrid beside her – terribly frightened, but trying to dig in her heels.

Then at last, at the end of a fortnight, when they were talking one day at the institute about quite different things, someone asked Sigrid where her father worked.

"He's gone to the West," she answered promptly.

Rita was the only one who was not taken completely aback. She had time to look closely at all those astonished faces staring at Sigrid as if they had never really seen her before.

"And nobody else knew about this?" Mangold's voice cut sharp and cold through the babel of questions and answers.

"Yes," said Rita calmly. "I knew about it."

So she had known about it. A fine conspiracy. A worker deserts our state, our republic. His daughter deceives this same state. And her friend, who also draws a stipend from this state, conspires with her. This will have serious consequences. His voice droned on and on.

The faces turned away from Sigrid as if they had seen enough of her. They turned towards the inept young teacher who was not as good at quotations as Mangold. But he could think of nothing better than to repeat that there would be serious consequences.

"I'm glad Marion's come," thought Rita. She walked along beside her, hardly listening to what she said. Marion was deep in a description of her new suit. She was one of those lucky people who can cheer themselves up with a new suit. She could bolster up her self-confidence in simple ways – not like me, or poor Sigrid, Rita thought.

Rita remembered every little detail of what happened that day, although she had been too much upset at the time to notice them. She thought at first that it might help to take a firm line. If they were going to make a big thing of it they had better do it at once, she told Mangold. But he flatly refused to discuss the matter and insisted that preparations would have to be made.

Nobody spoke to Rita or Sigrid – at least not where Mangold could see them – except Marion, who took no notice of their silly talk, as she called it.

"They'll throw us out," said Sigrid. "I know they will."

Rita sat silently in her room for hours that afternoon. She thought with dread of the setback it would mean if she had to go back to the village, and she knew that if Mangold got his way, much worse things might happen to her than that. She had no clear idea as to how much Mangold's opinion was worth and she was also not yet quite sure that Schwarzenbach, Meternagel and Wendland were on the right track; but she clung to the morsel of conviction which she felt she had already gained from them, for she knew very well that without them people like the Herrfurths would gain the upper hand again.

These people were only waiting for a chance to step in, and they seemed to think that they would not have to wait long. The more friendly Frau Herrfurth had lately been the more Rita retired into herself. Frau Herrfurth would retail gossip which she had heard; more and more old acquaintances were fleeing to the

West, simply abandoning their good jobs, other honest people were accused of swindling and black marketeering and exposed to all sorts of insults in court, and people were saying this couldn't go on much longer . . . and she would shake her head and pretend to be worried.

Rita wondered why she had never noticed how much alike Mangold and Frau Herrfurth were; was it possible for people to fight for quite opposite things in the same narrow-minded, selfish, nagging way?

She tried to remember what Mangold really looked like – not that she had forgotten each individual feature, for she knew quite well that he had a big nose, a soft mouth and pale, flabby cheeks. But there was no life in it, that was it, she thought; he might have been wearing a mask. She could not make up her mind whether he was really worried about the way things were going or whether he wanted to draw attention to himself. Was he merely cynical and selfish, or could he perhaps be trying to cover up a feeling of inferiority?

Rita was sick with worry. That evening she went to see Meternagel, as she had often done before. She found him with four or five other men from the works whom she knew, all talking loudly in a cloud of tobacco smoke. They were writing a complaint to the district Party committee about the constant hold-ups at work. That complaint, Rita remembered, had caused a big stir in the works and had been published in the newspapers a few days later. The men were delighted to see her, teased her about her studies and got her to write parts of the letter for them. She felt better, but she soon went away again, for she had wanted to talk to Rolf alone about her own troubles.

"Come again tomorrow," he said at the door.

She went on to see the Schwarzenbachs. Frau Schwarzenbach opened the door, and Rita hardly recognised her, for her face seemed to have turned to stone. Rita went silently past her into the sitting-room. Erwin Schwarzenbach sat slumped down in an armchair.

"Oh, it's you," he said, looking up, relieved to see she was there.

They were waiting for news from the hospital. Their little boy had had a slight pain in his right side for the past few days; then, while they were both away at work, it had suddenly become acute. He had been alone at home for hours and they had come so late. . . .

"I'll never forgive myself," said Frau Schwarzenbach. She sat by the telephone, in despair, on the verge of suicide. Her husband, too, was quite incapable of giving his mind to anything else.

Rita walked down the street again, thinking of the child as he had sat at the table, doing his sums, the neat rows of figures spreading out over the page. . . .

It was raining slightly, the first spring rain. Its soft, almost cheerful murmur mingled with faint breaths of wind to a sigh of relief at the approaching end of the long, silent winter. Rita still walked on ridges of crumbly snow, but they would soon be washed away by the warm drops.

There were few people about. And she no longer wanted to meet anyone. Fate must not have meant her to find anyone to help her, she thought, and this was not the first time she had felt so completely alone. But it had never before hurt her in this way. The town she had thought so friendly looked grim and hard.

Well, it serves me right, she thought, for believing everything like a child. How could she have been so stupid as to be taken in by all that talk about people being good if you only gave them a chance. How could she have been so silly as to think that the selfishness that stared out of most people's faces really could turn into goodness and loving kindness!

She had made a mess of things, as anybody else would probably have known from the start; and now she would have to take the consequences.

What was the use of it all, she thought, and her courage failed her.

She went home, packed her shabby trunk, left the house unnoticed and got to the station in time to catch the train home. Here she waited freezing in the draughty little station, for small country towns are not prepared to deal with unexpected night travellers. But she knew without thinking about it when the milk truck would be driving round the villages. The driver was still the same and he remembered her, too. They drove through several other villages first, but this did not matter, since she was not in any hurry to get home.

Dawn came slowly, a misty, milky-grey dawn. Then came colours; first the man-made colours, the red of newly-tiled roofs on the outskirts of the villages, the green garden fences, a poster, and later on the natural colours, the dark grey of the fields against the pale blue-grey sky, dark, silent birds, slim young red-brown beeches along the roadside, and at last a touch of blue above the dark zigzag of the woods at the edge of which, whatever else might happen, there was always the wind-swept meadow and the path turning off to the right, rising slightly and then falling steeply down into her village, which was still firmly in its place. She had only to walk through it to find the little house and all she needed just then.

20

Rita had slept through a whole day and a night. She woke to the sound of church bells on a Sunday morning. She had forgotten nothing, but felt it had been right to come home. Here there were no blocks of houses or chimneys to hide the high, veiled sky; it dominated the scene, broken only by the familiar line of woods, fields and gentle hills. Things fell into focus and she no longer felt utterly bewildered.

She went for a long walk through the land of her childhood. A small kingdom, she thought, smiling, but not unchangeable, as it turned out. The people were full of news. They seemed more alert than she remembered them. They tended to speak in low tones, surreptitiously, breaking off in the middle of a sentence with a shake of the head. She had never realised that there were so many children in her village.

She discovered new lines in the face of the landscape – fields whose headlands ran differently from the way she had always remembered them. New lines were not etched so quickly in people's faces, but Rita could feel their anxiety, their fear of losing something, and their still vague hopes that they might gain something from the changes which cooperative farming was bringing into their lives.

She met other students on holiday. They stood and talked together for a few minutes, faintly embarrassed at appearing as grown-ups where they had lately been children.

But had she gone home to find out all this? Had she expected to find some little corner waiting to receive her? Had she wanted to find a refuge?

And she suddenly felt ashamed of having run away

in despair. She realised that at some time everyone felt an urge to survey his past life, critically, resignedly or even with smug approval.

This had all happened eight months ago and she had not thought much about it since. But as she walked along with Marion, who was talking away without bothering whether she was listening or not, it all came back to her with full force. And she knew why, too. The same impatience, the same dissatisfaction with herself and with everything she knew which had compelled her to return to town the next day had seized her as she saw Marion, so composed and self-confident, step out of the bus and trip across the road to meet her.

"I think I'll be coming back soon," she said.

"Of course. Why ever not?" Marion answered.

Somewhere on her way back to town Manfred must have passed her train as he drove out to fetch her in the little grey car. Marion had told him what had happened when he returned from his trip. And Rita, when she found the note pinned on the door of their room, hurried off to the nearest post-office to telephone to him.

She met young Hans on the way. He had been ill and was at a loose end. He might just as well wait with Rita until her call came through, he said. While they waited he told her about his sister, who had looked after him since their parents died. She was married and had two children, and the flat was much too small for them all, so he would be moving out soon. Not that his sister had said anything, but Hans knew very well that his brother-in-law would like to have his family to himself.

"The kids are fond of me, too, you know," said

Hans. But Rita understood how hard it was for him to start out alone with the feeling that nobody really needed him. Perhaps they would not find Manfred, she thought distractedly; then she would have to wait until he got back.

But her call came at last. She rushed into the telephone booth and pressed the receiver to her ear. It was still warm from the last call. Manfred's voice sounded quite close.

"So I must have started off to fetch you just before you left," he said.

"Yes. And you never wrote a word – for two whole weeks."

The wires crackled and hummed between them.

I can see your face quite clearly, she thought. Don't look so aloof, it doesn't deceive me. I know you as well as I know myself. But not well enough, you'll say. You don't know everything about me, either, and there may be some good in that. At least we don't need to talk now, we can leave all that to the wires, who are used to all sorts of things . . .

Are you cross with me, little brown girl. Do you still have that frown on your face?

Of course, I've got quite ugly because no one has looked at me for two whole weeks.

Not even looked at you?

You know, when I went out in the evening I left the green light on, so that when I got back I could imagine you were there waiting for me.

Rita was not sure whether they had said all this, but these were the thoughts which she remembered quite clearly, like his face – so close to her and yet out of reach, as only a familiar face can be – and that sudden, frightening attack of weakness and longing for him.

"I'm on my way," said Manfred, and the mysterious humming of the wires broke off.

Rita had already thought out for herself anything she might have learned from that dreaded meeting for which such careful preparations were made. She acknowledged with a nod the criticism for cutting lectures and the young teacher's announcement that she was to receive a reprimand. After all, it was the least they could do in face of Mangold's righteous indignation.

Then Mangold got up and talked for a long time. Rita barely listened to him, for she knew it all by heart. She felt now, as she watched him, that she could see through him and she wondered whether no one else realised what empty, silly, mechanical phrases he was mouthing. She was ashamed for everybody who toadied to him.

Sigrid was nearly in tears. Rita smiled encouragingly, hoping that she would not go to pieces altogether. Mangold might succeed in frightening the others a little longer, she thought, but they would not be taken in by him in the end. And, as it turned out, the end was nearer than she had thought.

"On whose behalf are you speaking?" Erwin Schwarzenbach broke in at last.

Everybody turned to look at him.

"Why, on behalf of the comrades here, of course," said Mangold defiantly. "There's that resolution. . . ."

"And what's in the resolution? Does it say anything about why Sigrid acted the way she did? Does it say why she couldn't ask us for help?"

Rita had had no chance to talk to Schwarzenbach since that other evening. She felt sure his little boy must still be alive, otherwise he could not have been so normal again.

But there was no stopping Mangold. He droned on and on about the Party line – like a Catholic talking about the immaculate conception, Schwarzenbach called out furiously.

The whole meeting would have ended quite differently if no one had stood up to Mangold. Why had no one else insisted that they talk about the real human problem involved? Were they all so unsure of themselves?

Mangold insisted that things had to be brought to a head – that was how the Party got to the root of contradictions.

"What you have to do is to see that the Party is there to help people like Sigrid when they need help. What else is it there for, I'd like to know?" Schwarzenbach retorted sharply.

"But that's far too naive." Mangold went on with his tirade, dragging in world imperialism and the hard political school he had been through.

"I can well believe that," said Schwarzenbach quickly, as if this confirmed a suspicion he had had.

"I'll tell you something," he went on more gently, as if he were speaking to Mangold alone. "Even though I'm a worker's son I wanted to join the Werewolves and get myself killed when the war was nearly over. We deserved hatred then and we expected people to hate us, but the Party was patient and tolerant with us, although it expected a great deal of us, too. You know, ever since then I've had a great respect for tolerance and patience. Those are real revolutionary qualities, Comrade Mangold. Didn't you ever feel you needed them?"

Mangold shrugged his shoulders.

"When have we ever had time to think about things like that?" he asked bitterly.

"You have something there, of course. But I often wonder what would have become of me if ... How old were you at the end of the war?"

"Eighteen," said Mangold slowly, as if he were giving away an important secret.

The meeting went on for a long time. But there was no more talk of punishment. Mangold relapsed into silence. He had been thoroughly deflated, but Schwarzenbach had managed it in a way which made them all feel sorry for him; no one felt any desire to gloat over his defeat. Rita even felt she disliked him less than before.

"Perhaps things have gone wrong so often that he has no faith in people any more," she said to Manfred that evening.

"And what about you? Do you still believe in people?" Manfred asked. "Let me tell you something. I didn't tell you about it before because I wanted to forget it myself. You know, Martin isn't the first friend I ever had. Years ago I had another, just as good a friend as Martin. He was older than I and I used to look up to him. We used to stay up all night and talk about everything under the sun. He gave me all sorts of books to read and nothing came between us for years, there were no girls, no quarrels ... until one day it was all over for good, because he didn't help me when I needed him.

"He was a journalist in Berlin. We hadn't seen each other for some time, then we met again at a university conference. We met as good friends and parted again for good a few hours later. Nothing much happened, actually. I spoke at the conference about some mistakes they were making at the university, about all the useless ballast we were carrying, about hypocrisy being the best policy if you wanted to get on."

"You actually said all that?" Rita asked, astonished.

"Do you think I was always as dumb as a fish?" Manfred asked. "Well, when I stepped down off the platform they all turned against me. Told me how dangerous and corrupt my views were. I just looked at him. He knew me, he knew exactly what I meant. I scribbled him a note asking him to speak up. If only I hadn't written it! If only I hadn't asked him to help! But how was I to know that he was just another Mangold? I'm still ashamed for him, after all these years.

"He slipped away and wrote an article about the meeting. I've read that article over and over again, the way some people can't keep away from the poison that will kill them. He said I was out of touch with real life, blinded by false bourgeois intellectual prejudices, the sort of prejudices which would drag our universities down into an ideological morass.

"I wouldn't even shake hands with him if I met him again now. And he would wonder what was wrong and why I should bother about all that, now that the papers are full of just the things I talked about then. And I wouldn't even take the trouble to answer. He's the man who pushed me into being the sort of person my conscience tells me is wrong.

"I don't know why I'm telling you all this," he said after a while. "Why should you be dragged into it?"

Rita put her hand on his shoulder. She felt she ought to argue with him about it, but did not know how to help him. This was a time when she should have been older and more experienced, she thought miserably.

21

Rita smiled as she looked at her landscape on the wall. She would miss it, she thought.

Two letters came – in one envelope with Martin's writing on it. But one of the letters was important. She felt herself turn cold. Manfred had written it. A brief flash of hope – even now, after all these weeks. How could she have thought it was all over. . . .

She had to wait for a moment before she could read it. She looked up at the picture. Don't desert me now, she thought. And the pale, delicate woman seemed to smile down at her reassuringly, although she could not possibly know what it was all about.

The letter, written to Martin a few days earlier, began without preliminaries.

Just for the record I should like to let you know that I've actually met Braun in one of the offices here. That's what you suspected all along. How right you were. And I want you to know, too, that I realise you were right, for why shouldn't we be honest with each other, even at this distance? In any case, it makes no difference to me now, although you know I could have wrung his neck then. Now I don't even want to speak to him. Why should I bother to find out whether he made all that trouble for us on purpose or whether he simply wasn't up to his job? It wouldn't change anything.

I'm not one of those who make pilgrimages to the Wall just for the thrill of it, but I still listen to your radio and I haven't been away long enough to forget everything. The 1960's – do you remember our argument? Do you still think these years will go down in history as the years when humanity gave a great sigh of relief? I know one can deceive oneself about many things for a long time (you must, if you want to go on living), but it's hardly possible that you don't feel some horror at what human nature is capable of after what came out at the last Moscow Party Congress. What's the use of talking about social orders when history is built up everywhere on individual misery and fear?

I can hear you saying something about this idea not being new or inspiring, the sort of remark you generally make, so I shan't start all over again. I've said all there is to say long ago.

I wish you happiness.

Manfred.

It was not all finished for her yet. She could still feel pain. She had to sit down quietly. She read the letter over and over again until she knew it by heart. She lay down. She usually went out for a walk with the other patients about this time, but she stayed behind alone that evening. She felt better when the room was empty and the sound of footsteps faded away in the corridor until the house was silent.

She lay quite still with her eyes shut for a while. Then she picked up Martin Jung's letter.

Dear Rita, he wrote, *I wondered for a long time whether I should send you this letter or not. It's the only letter I've had from Manfred. He's just like all the others who go away to the West; they always try to prove they were right to go, because they know in their hearts that it wasn't right. But this letter is meant more for you than for me.*

Just for the record – that used to be our battle-cry,

you know. I don't know how much he told you about that trip we made together, but believe me, it was tough. We simply could not get past a sort of wall of vague, underhanded obstruction. This Braun, for instance, who is now in West Berlin. He was an expert in our branch; he knew perfectly well how good our design was, he can only have wanted to make trouble. But nobody would believe us. Braun went to the West four months ago – he was ordered away, people say here.

I'm in a terrific hurry. There's a commission looking over our works just now. They're asking about our machine. Couldn't Manfred have held out just these eight months? That's what bothers me most of all. If only he had hung on, even if we'd had to keep him here by force. If he were here now he would simply have to face up to things. He wouldn't be able to avoid taking sides.

But what's the use of writing all this now?

Get well quickly!

Martin.

Rita lay quite still, with Martin's letter in her hand, looking up at the ceiling, tracing the pattern of cracks and damp stains which she already knew so well.

Martin would have been a good friend to him, and she a good wife, she thought; for always, too, she felt sure. He must have known that, otherwise he would not have been so wretched when he came back from the factory – without a shred of belief in the future.

But he had been so miserable that he had confided in her, tiredly but not yet entirely without indignation. He described the conspiracy of silence they had come up against, the suspicious way people had tried to trip them up when they explained their ideas. Curiously enough, it had been Martin, not he, who had got ruder and ruder and put himself in the wrong when he saw that they were not getting anywhere. Rita guessed why: Martin was desperate because he knew just where this kind of treatment would drive Manfred, who had no armour of faith to protect him. But she had been worried for Martin when she heard about his outbursts of rage against everybody, even against people in high positions.

Manfred had stayed at home for a couple of weeks after that, with an attack of influenza which seemed to have come at the right moment. He read a great deal, especially Heine's early works.

"Heine had no luck with his good Germans, either," he said.

"It was the other way round," said Rita. "The Germans didn't succeed with him."

Manfred smiled. He often smiled at her in the way grown-ups smile at children. But she said nothing, for she had still not been worried about their relationship. Perhaps he had made up his mind at that time, she thought. Even then he might have been trying to make things impossible for both of them.

His mother's smugness should have made her suspect something. He could hardly have told his mother all the details of what had happened, but she must have understood instinctively what was going on in his mind. When Rita was away she used to slip into his room as he lay in bed. She enjoyed having him helpless and depending on her again. Rita often found him in a bad temper, like a spoilt child, when she came home. She made fun of him, but he was apt to be sorry for himself and resented it.

It was after Martin had been dismissed from his re-search job at Manfred's institute that his despondency turned into real bitterness and anger. The last concession he made to Rita was to go to Rudi Schwabe to put in a word for Martin.

"I'd never do it for myself!" he said.

He came back in a mood of despair mingled with glum satisfaction and cynical resignation, for he was sure now that Schwabe was just as spineless as he had suspected.

"You should have seen his face when I said that Martin was my friend! As if there were something very queer about being friends with an outcast. 'Your friend? Is that so? . . . Unfortunately, we can't use him here. The recent incidents at the works . . . In any case, he's not mature enough for this type of work. On the other hand, of course, we never abandon anyone' . . . and so on and so forth. All the usual phrases.

"He doesn't even listen when you try to talk to him. I talked myself hoarse. But of course he's not allowed to listen. It's not just a matter of a chap called Martin Jung. Do you suppose he could keep his job if he couldn't do the one thing – carry out orders without asking questions?"

"But what's it all about? What's Martin done wrong?" Rita asked.

"He couldn't keep his mouth shut, that's all. He got up at a factory meeting and told them to their faces what he thought of them. He said they were intriguing, incompetent little busybodies who were holding everything back. That had to be punished, and Herr Schwabe was just the man for the job. The whole thing makes me sick!"

Martin's dismissal caused very little excitement,

since hardly anyone except Manfred really knew him. But they left him in his job at the works. These eight months must have been terribly difficult for him, Rita thought. It was splendid of him to stick it out. Manfred hadn't managed to stick it out; eight months had been too long for him.

Rita did not know exactly when he had decided he could not go on, nor did she know exactly when they had begun to talk a different language. She must have missed the first signs, for she had been so sure of him and he had always insisted that whatever happened they loved each other. And he had good reason to believe she loved him.

Evening drew in. Rita sat up and laid Martin's letter in the drawer of her bedside table. She was oppressed by the feeling that she had not done enough to help Manfred.

22

Manfred was soon well again and outwardly hardly changed. Shortly after he had started work again at the Institute Wendland rang him up and invited him and Rita to go on a trial run with the new light-weight railway wagon. Manfred hesitated. Wendland wanted Rita, not him, he thought. But in the end he decided to go with her.

Rita sensed that he was longing for her to say she did not want to go, but she said nothing.

It was a cool, grey April morning in 1961. They drove to the works early and walked side by side down the poplar-lined road – together here for the first time. The road was deserted, for the early shift had already started. The wind always cut sharply down the road here. Rita turned up her coat collar and put her hand in Manfred's pocket. He put his arm round her shoulder. She walked close beside him, keeping step with his long stride, and rubbed her head against his shoulder. A little boy on roller skates took a long run and let out a yell of sheer joy as he passed them. Rita felt an echo of it inside her. She took a deep breath.

"It's really spring again," she said.

"You sound surprised," said Manfred.

She nodded, but did not tell him how much she had been longing for warmth, open spaces, movement, light, or how tired she was of the monotonous winter days, the walk to lectures, discussions, quarrels, examinations, the long, dull afternoons in the library amongst the same group of readers, the greenish lights turned on one after the other in front of them, signals from which she had sometimes fled as if it were all a bad dream.

"I can feel one of your famous unfulfillable wishes coming," said Manfred.

"Yes. I want to be driving off, wearing a pretty dress, going a long, long way."

"And without me, of course," Manfred added quickly.

That was the sort of thing that worried her – he had begun to feel that any little complaint she made was a criticism of him. She said nothing. They were already in the factory grounds. With a wave of the hand she showed him the narrow lane between two buildings which was a short-cut for those who knew their way about. They walked on, still not speaking.

"Can't you even talk to me any more?" Manfred asked.

Rita felt she had been caught out and tried to find an excuse.

"You needn't bother," Manfred answered. "I know how you feel."

"What do you mean?"

"You think I'm getting unbearable."

"Oh, you're imagining things."

"No, no. I know how you feel," he repeated. "You don't think I like myself just now, do you? I've struck a bad patch."

"People only strike lucky in stories," she said. "And even then they have to go through all sorts of dreadful adventures first."

"That's all very well. But this isn't a story. This is us. But why should I remind you of that, and spoil what I like best about you?"

She had often thought about this little incident later on. Tears could not drown the memory of it, although she had not been anywhere near tears at the time. They halted for a moment in the narrow lane between two high, red-brick walls and looked up at the tiny strip of cloudy sky above. Machines clattered, but there was not a soul in sight.

"Give me a kiss," said Rita. Strangely touched, Manfred took her face between his two warm hands and kissed her.

"We do belong together, you know," she murmured. "Your hands are just right for me – your mouth, too."

He laughed and tapped her on the nose, as he always did when he felt much older than she. They walked on to the end of the lane. Rita's nose already registered the acrid smell of welding; seconds later she drew in a deep breath of it. She did not like the smell, but it was satisfyingly familiar. She explained to Manfred

142

what was going on in each workshop as they passed it; here they were building revolving stands, there the side and end walls of the coaches. . . . She pointed out how narrow and awkward it was, and how impossible it was to do anything on assembly line principles. As they passed the forge the ground vibrated under the rhythmic strokes of the heavy hammers.

They turned a corner, and the wind swept down against them again. Here the tracks started and, a hundred yards away, drastically foreshortened in perspective, stood the train, waiting to set out on its trial run. Its ten newly-painted green coaches gleamed in the early morning light – the result of long days of hard work by two thousand people. One of these was the new, light-weight model, looking no different from the others from the outside, and they had all emerged from the dust, dirt and noisy confusion of the workshops.

Rita noticed small signs of tension in the people standing about in groups, smoking and talking. She knew no one there and was beginning to feel shy and gauche when she felt a touch on her arm. She turned and saw Meternagel. He was pleased to see her.

"You've got thin," said Rita.

"Why, so have you."

They were friends again, immediately, as if she had been there every day. Ernst Wendland waved to them from a group farther away, and motioned to the train. They were to get in at once.

Rita had not forgotten how to swing herself up on to the high step. She pushed open the coach door and looked in. How empty it was!

"Like in church," said Meternagel.

Rita thought of the way he always cursed towards

143

the end, when the coaches were crowded with workers putting the various finishing touches to them.

"Take your cap off, then," she said.

His shabby, brimless cap was like a part of him, for he wore it all the time at work. He took it off, shook out his flattened-down hair, beat the dust out of the cap against his thigh, folded it up and shoved it into his overall pocket. His fair hair showed no signs of going grey, although he was already forty-eight years old.

They walked along the corridor, past three compartments, pushed open the door to the fourth and went in. There was a smell of new paint, foam rubber and plastics.

"No more wood," Meternagel remarked. "Why we still call ourselves carpenters... Plasticians would be better."

They ran their hands over the dust covers and sat down. A gust of rain drove those still standing outside into the train. Wendland looked in and asked them to keep a seat free for him. The control team spread out through the train and began their work. Music came through the loudspeakers, for they were testing the radio equipment. The wind blew harder.

At seven o'clock sharp, without any whistle, station signal or waving handkerchiefs, the train set off slowly through the northern suburbs. The trial run was to take five hours.

At that early hour the day had not yet revealed its great secret.

The track cut across the countryside; every-day life went on around them, whizzing by in second-long cross-sections. Rita saw it, but paid little attention until the great news came through and snatched the every-day mask off everything.

They were moving across a plain fringed by poplars. A road snaked through it, alive with tiny cars. A field of red and green pylons and a black filigree of wires against a grey sky turned slowly around them as the train took a curve. Then, quite suddenly, they were in the chemical and coal region. A diesel locomotive pulling open freight cars loaded with dark brown clumps of lignite crossed their track. A moon landscape of coal dumps appeared. A farmer with a cart-load of potatoes waited at a level crossing. Here and there pillars of smoke rose up from burning grass. A couple of lads lying in the scrub were smoking their first pipe. Old people were already out in their gardens, which were carpeted with green at this time of year.

None of these people had heard the great news yet. They were busy with their small daily jobs on a day which would end like all others, content with the little they had accomplished – insignificant but necessary.

Rita was sleepy. It was warm in the train (so the heating worked all right, she thought). She half listened to the electricians' criticism, which the controlman wrote down in his little notebook. She leant back and looked out of the big window and saw that the clouds had thinned and paled, ready to split open and reveal an endless expanse of blue.

The earth is gay with colour, a delight to the eye. A pale blue aureole surrounds it. This band gradually darkens, turns turquoise, blue, violet and then pitch black. The transition is a beautiful sight....

But I couldn't have known that so early, she thought, as she lay in her white hospital bed. It was night and she lay awake thinking; but she was no longer afraid

145

of sleeplessness. Shadows of branches stirred on the ceiling.

How was it possible to compare what she had seen – the delicate spots of blue appearing through a thin blanket of cloud – with what that one man had seen for us all for the first time? And yet, she thought, could not our glances have met at some point in the skies during those seconds?

Time passed at tremendous speed up there. The ninety breathless, momentous earthly minutes had begun, although they had still not heard the great news.

They rode along in their comfortable new coach, past the old, weatherbeaten back walls of city houses, past new houses with gay balconies, past flooded meadows and a grass-bordered field, past hills clothed with birch and pine woods, and again and again through villages whose houses, once gay red-brick, were now ugly, shabby and grey, huddled together to protect themselves against the laws of fear and greed, but not of sense and beauty.

"Just look at that," Manfred was saying. She had hardly noticed that Wendland had been sitting with them for some time, nor had she heard what they were talking about. But that was before they heard the great news, she was sure; for later on the tone of their conversation changed.

"As a realist, now, honestly. Do you want to make the sparks fly with material like that?"

"What are you getting at?" Wendland asked.

"I'm just trying to make a small point," said Manfred. "All this comes too late, you know. There's a time lag. We Germans ought to realise that."

"Socialism is just the thing for the eastern peoples," he went on after a pause. "They can enjoy the simple

benefits of the new society, they're not spoilt by individ-
ualism and higher civilisation. But we can't turn back.
You need unbroken heroes and what you've got is a
broken generation. It's a tragic contradiction, an irrec-
oncilable contradiction."

"That's a lot in one sentence," said Wendland. He
did not greatly enjoy straightening this man's picture
of the world, but he answered politely.

"Perhaps you're confusing the ruling classes in the
Western countries with the ordinary people," he suggested. He realised that this was just the sort of
stereotyped answer Manfred had expected. He could
feel himself getting angry.

"Hundreds of years ago one of your predecessors in
alchemy – and in the humanities, too – called Mephisto
a monstrosity born of filth and flames. He said it
in anger, though, not in gloomy resignation."

"But that's just what I mean. Centuries lie between
our generation and Faust's rage," Manfred retorted.

They subsided into an awkward silence.

Meternagel had been staring at Manfred. But he
noticed at once when the train slowed down. They had
been on the move now for over an hour. They all went
out into the corridor to find out what was causing the
delay. Leaning far out of the window, Rita could just
see the "Halt" signal in front of the locomotive. They
should have been putting on speed, for this was just the
time to start the brake tests. Everybody grumbled, although they really had no objection to a halt, for it was
the engine driver's business to get up speed again. They
were in the middle of meadowland here, with a village
to the right and a gently rising wooded slope to the left.
A solitary figure, black against the sky, stood at the top
of the hill above the woods.

Later on, she never heard the song about the sailor which came through the loudspeaker just at that moment without thinking of the young railway worker repairing the neighbouring track fifty yards behind them. The others in the gang were older men and they had barely looked up when the train halted. This young chap had stuck his pick into a heap of earth and walked slowly along to the train.

And he brought them the great news. He stood on the loose stones between the tracks, looking up at them – a complete stranger, whom they would never meet again.

"Have you heard?" he asked casually. "The Russians have had a man in the cosmos for the last hour."

I saw the clouds and their faint shadows on the dear, distant earth. The peasant stirred in me for a moment, for the deep black sky looked like a freshly-ploughed field, and the stars were seeds of corn. . . .

There was a long silence after the lad spoke. But then people began to call out and ask questions. Somebody whistled – the sort of whistle one hears at a football match. Delighted with the sensation he had made, the lad laughed, showing strong, white teeth. The same song still sounded over the loudspeaker.

But behind it all there was a sense of expectancy, of waiting for a new sound which would soon be added to the old, familiar earthly sounds.

Surely the shadow of that shining capsule above would cut like a scalpel right through all the meridians and through the earth's crust, right down to its boiling, glowing heart? Would the earth still be the same round, leisurely globe moving quietly through the universe with its living cargo? Surely it would suddenly be rejuvenated, glow more strongly, because of its son's challenge?

Would her world which she knew so well, which was still the only possible boundary to her existence – whatever it had done to her – be torn completely out of its course? This tugging at the bonds which had so far confined her world. ... Could she bear the sudden liberation from the old ideas of what was possible? Would human warmth be enough to withstand the cold of the cosmos?

That village over there, the busy repair gang, the lonely figure on the hill-top – were they still the same? The news, flying round the earth, scraped the mouldering skin of centuries. ...

The train, starting up again quietly, left behind it forever that little stretch of meadowland, the villages, the gently sloping woodlands with the solitary figure on the hill-top.

A curious shyness fell upon them and prevented them from expressing their feelings. The compartment emptied. Rita went out and stood behind the brakeman. She watched him writing in his notebook:

12th April 1961, 08.15 hours. Just heard that a manned Soviet space ship is in the cosmos.

He drew out his stop-watch, unwrapped it out of its old, soft rag and laid it down beside his notebook. The engine-driver knew what this meant. He got up speed quickly. There was only a short straight stretch before them and they had to take this chance to test the brakes. The brakeman took up his watch. He stared out at the milestones as they flitted by, faster and faster. He had been testing brakes for ten years and hardly needed his stop-watch, but he conscientiously entered the increasing speeds in his notebook. The tests could not be made at less than eighty kilometres an hour. Rita noticed his horny, ridged finger-nail as he pressed the button on the stop-watch. Time raced. He pressed the button each time they passed a milestone. Time was quickly transformed into speed.

Ernst Wendland applied the brakes himself that day. He was there, his hand on the emergency brake and his eyes on the brakeman. He had nothing to do now but wait for the brakeman's signal. At last, satisfied with the speed, the brakeman raised his arm. Wendland waited tensely. "Now!" The brakeman dropped his arm just as the next milestone flitted past. Wendland jerked the brake hard. An ugly screeching began and went on and on. . . .

The brakeman stared out of the window. There was a longer gap now between the telegraph posts; the train, slowing down unwillingly, came to a halt at last. The brakeman shook his head, even before they had measured the distance it had taken to pull up. All the old hands knew that it had not been quick enough. It was the first time in years that such a thing had happened.

Not much was said, but Rita shared their uneasiness. She had inside knowledge and knew what went on under the surface of these wagons, and she felt a thrill at being a part of the whole thing.

The braking distance had been two hundred metres too long. One of the fitters grunted disapprovingly and motioned with his thumb in the air.

"Supposing that had happened to him!"

Rita's distress dissolved in a laugh. Manfred saw it

and knew that this was a laugh which he could not share. She noticed the hurt look on his face and wondered what she had done wrong this time.

In the meantime that other man, whose great day it was, had shot down to earth again in the midst of a fiery ball and landed safely, with a "good conscience". His wife, a little girl and a speckled calf welcomed him back to his own corner of the earth again.

But they had turned homeward again, braked successfully using a different brake-stick, and now lay in the midday sun on the bank beside the tracks, for their old locomotive had stopped in its tracks.

Manfred could bear the silence no longer.

"I know what's coming now," he said, closing his eyes against the glare of the sun. "There'll be a tremendous propaganda campaign about the first cosmonaut, they'll burn up the telegraph wires and there'll be floods of news print – and people will go on living just the same as they always did. That farmer over there," he said, pointing to a man ploughing behind two horses, "he'll harness his horses again tomorrow. And our worn-out old locomotive, a relic of the last century, has left us in the lurch – today of all days! All those mountains of useless daily plodding! And brilliant extravaganzas in the stratosphere won't help, either. . . ."

Nobody answered. Wendland kept quiet out of tact, for he never liked to attack anyone weaker. Rita was speechless with shame and anger. That wasn't the real Manfred, she thought. Why did he have to behave like that?

She understood better later what was going on in his mind. History was built up on the misery of the individual, he had said, and he was already searching for evidence which would prove that he was right.

"Has your father got used to his new job?" Wendland asked after a while.

"What new job?" Manfred asked, surprised.

Wendland cursed himself. It was impossible to find the right thing to say to Manfred that day. So old Herrfurth had told some other story at home. That would be just like him, he thought. But what was he to say to his son now? What could he say to this awkward chap who put up such silly arguments?

"Oh well, you know, it isn't everybody who has to hang on to a job till it's got to be too much for him – the way I have to," he added jokingly. "As far as your father's concerned, I expect he's happier now."

He was building a bridge for Manfred, but Manfred had no intention of crossing it.

"Aha! The old story again. *The Moor has served his turn. The Moor may go.* Of course, I don't want to defend my father. That would be silly. All the same, I suppose I'm allowed to ask the reason for all this suspicious caution nowadays?"

"You're getting things mixed up," said Wendland in a conciliatory tone. But this was just what Manfred could not accept at that moment.

"So I'm mixing things up. Good. Perhaps I'm lacking in the crystal-clear logic of scientific thought. But I'm not lacking in understanding for the fine distinctions – the distinction between means and ends, for instance."

"Yes, it's often difficult to reconcile the two," Wendland agreed.

"You may as well admit that it's impossible," said Manfred. "Honesty is a good quality in anyone."

"And it would be a good quality in you, too," Rita burst out indignantly.

"I try to be honest," he said coolly.

"It looks to me as if you haven't understood what I mean," he went on, turning to Wendland again. "People seem to think I'm accusing them of something. Nothing could be further from my mind. I'm only sorry that such quantities of illusions and energy are wasted in trying to do the impossible – to make people good. That's what you want, isn't it?"

"It's absolutely necessary," said Wendland.

"That's it – the last hope for humanity. But in fact it's hopeless, the way things are now. And you'll have to admit it one day."

Wendland sat up.

"Why are you always drawing in your horns?" he asked sharply.

"What do you mean? I'm speaking from experience. Experience of the way people behave. Honesty and goodness always peel off when it's necessary. But you can always count on greed, selfishness, distrust, envy. The good old habits. But where's the humanity?"

"People only carry dirt about with them until they're able to wash it off," said Wendland. "Hate we shall need for a long time yet."

"And love?" Rita asked shyly. "The other side of hate?"

Wendland flushed. "Love is sufficient unto itself."

"I'm not the man for great feelings, I suppose," said Manfred harshly.

Wendland talked about this conversation with Rita long afterwards.

"You always think there's plenty of time to put things right, you know. I ought to have known better. . . ."

*

The substitute locomotive arrived and they climbed back on the train. Manfred turned and looked at the two of them, making no attempt to hide the bitterness he felt. It grated on his nerves to hear love talked about, no matter in what connection.

"We shall have to drop all these high-sounding phrases, all this talk of noble feelings."

Rita felt weak with grief and pity. She knew he was hurting himself most.

When they arrived home that evening they went straight up to their own room. Manfred drew Rita over to the window, which framed a rosy, clouded sunset sky. He took her face in his hands and looked into her eyes. All his pride and defiance had vanished.

"What are you looking for?" she asked anxiously.

"The fixed spot I need if I'm not to lose myself altogether."

"And you think you'll find it in me?"

"Where else should I look?"

"And you're not even sure of me any longer?"

"Oh yes, my little brown girl. . . . And you'll always let me keep that certainty, won't you?"

"So long as you want it," she said.

They closed their eyes. How long could their love keep them safe? How many blows of fate could it withstand?

23

May was cold that year. People went on lighting their stoves, resignedly, too long deprived of the warmth they longed for. The wind swept the blossoms into the gutter. But it was not only the cold, the sadly swirling, useless snow of blossoms and the biting wind which chilled the soul and filled hearts with fear.

Rita knew the town well by this time. She could picture its streets and squares with her eyes shut; but there was something disquietingly strange about it that May. There was an ugly threat about the low-hanging clouds, and a muddy stream of lies, stupidity and treachery, still unseen, seemed to be waiting to trickle through cracks in the walls or through cellar windows.

Suppressed uneasiness burst out sometimes in curses and irritable grumbling in the crowded trams. Rita noticed Erwin Schwarzenbach's tense watchfulness when he came to class – as if he were prepared for some kind of struggle. He was more sensitive to atmosphere than ever and he demanded more from his students than ever before, reacting with unusual severity against any signs of slackness.

But the most terrible thing was the change in Manfred. Worry and a sense of imminent danger prevented him from thinking coherently. When he was with Rita, he often found himself longing to suffer sharp pain.

He no longer attempted to hide his contempt for his parents. Rita was prepared for trouble every evening when she sat down to supper at the brightly-lit table. She could not taste her food or follow the scraps of conversation, for everything was drowned out by the smooth, superior voice of the radio announcer – ("A Free Voice from the Free World") – from whom Frau Herrfurth received her inspiration. Rita wondered how soon that voice would lose its politeness and go over to the attack, how soon threats would replace promises.

She looked at the faces around her – Frau Herrfurth's nervous, blinking eyes, her husband's look of weak resignation, Manfred's pent-up hatred.

None of them bothered to conceal their feelings any longer. They sat together like strangers, but not even attempting to make casual conversation.

The hatred exploded just once more. Manfred forced his father to admit that he had lost his job and was now only book-keeper. Frau Herrfurth clutched at her heart and rushed out of the room. Manfred went on abusing his father. Rita pulled him up sharply. He broke off in the middle of a sentence and left the room.

Rita was left alone with his father.

He glanced at her miserably, making no effort to retain even a shred of his manhood or gallantry.

"Fräulein Rita," he murmured. "I know you're a good girl. Just tell me what I've done to deserve all this?"

"And you let all that upset you?" Manfred asked her later. "All this endless moaning from toothless old people who don't want to harvest what they've sown? And even want to inflict their helplessness on us now? Pity? Not me!"

"Your mother seems really ill," said Rita. "She's taking drops all the time now."

"She's been hysterical as long as I can remember."

"Let's move out of here," she begged.

"Where can we go?" he asked. "One house is as good as another."

"You're simply breaking up your family," she said, but what she knew she should tell him was that she was afraid of losing him in that atmosphere.

"Well, I won't stand hypocrisy at home."

"You only behave like that because you know you're stronger than they."

"Maybe," he said, looking at her in surprise. "I'm no hero."

"That's just what I said to Martin about you."

"Clever girl. But don't forget that we're all just as unheroic as this unheroic age."

"And what about Martin?"

"Martin's young. Everybody goes through his rebellious period. But they've put him on ice now. He'll look before he leaps next time."

"But supposing he doesn't? Supposing he goes on fighting, because justice means more to him than anything else?"

"Then he's just a blockhead, not a hero," said Manfred curtly.

"What do you want, then?"

"I want peace and quiet. I just don't want to be bothered any more."

Oh no, Rita thought. He was not really like that. She had seen him at work with Martin. It was only afterwards that he had lost interest.

Manfred seemed no longer to believe that she could help him. The hardest thing to bear now was the tortured look he sometimes gave her. His need to be near her, the intensity of his love-making, his insatiable need for tenderness, did not deceive her. Sometimes, when they came to themselves again – in their own little room faintly lit by the green glimmer of the radio light, it seemed to her as if they looked past each other. My God, she thought, don't let him get lost! Don't let us drift apart!

One evening – one of the few warm, damp May evenings – Rita came out of the institute after passing an examination. She looked round for Manfred, who was to have come for her. She walked slowly along, expecting to meet him.

A car drew up beside her in a quiet side street, and Ernst Wendland got out.

"I'm so glad to see you," she said impulsively.

"Me? You're glad to see me?" he asked, surprised, then went on quickly, in his everyday, friendly tone, to suggest that they eat together somewhere out of town. Rita hesitated.

"A lonely chap like me sometimes wants a bit of company for an hour or two, you know," he added.

Well, why isn't Manfred here, Rita thought, and got into the car.

They must have passed the corner where Manfred had been waiting over an hour for her. He had watched them from a distance.

Rita knew why she had gone with Wendland – not for his sake, but for her own. She wanted a rest, not to have to think or be responsible for anything. But she knew quite well that she could not get rid of her responsibility.

"I don't believe you've even noticed it's spring," said Wendland. "You're just too tired."

She told him about the examinations. He stopped once and bought flowers, narcissi with fresh birch leaves. She told him all the questions she had had to answer in each subject, why she had done better in one subject than in another.

"But are you really interested in all this?" she asked doubtfully.

They had left the chemical factory behind them and were driving along the straight road south, caught in a queue of over-night lorries, oil tanks and cyclists.

"Do you know where I'm supposed to be just now?" he asked after a while. "I'm supposed to be speaking at a meeting."

She wondered why he was telling her this. He ought to have gone to his meeting. . . . All the same, it was nice to feel that this reliable man was being unreliable for once on her account.

"What will you say tomorrow?"

"I'll tell them I had to find out whether it was true that the fruit-trees are in blossom, the birds are singing and there are some happy people in the world, like the radio tells us. Well, it is true, I shall say, and now we can get on with our meetings. By the way, it's the first time I've done it," he added.

"Me, too," she said quickly, and they laughed.

He took her to a little village inn with nut-trees in the garden and a view over blossoming slopes on either side of a stream.

"Plenty of people don't even know this place exists," he said. "You would never expect anything so pretty so near the town."

He ordered for both of them without asking her what she wanted, and then looked across at her without speaking. He had grown thinner, but she thought it suited him, and there were little tired lines round his eyes.

"You probably don't sleep enough," she said.

"I've got used to that. It can't be helped. We're in the middle of a sort of tug of war just now, especially in the works."

He began to tell her about it. Why, these are still the same old troubles, she thought. But Wendland said their troubles were even bigger, because the works was bigger.

Rita asked about Meternagel. She said she had not seen him for some time, because she had been busy with her examinations.

"Oh, he's pulling away at his end of the rope, putting his team through their paces."

"Well, I hope he's not overdoing it," she said. "I'm coming back to work in the holidays."

"Do you really mean that?" he asked.

She was relieved to have made up her mind. It would be something definite to look forward to.

"You don't always have an easy time, do you?" he murmured, hoping not to break the fine thread of understanding and intimacy between them.

Rita said nothing, but she did not snub him, either. I'm simply taking advantage of her mood, he thought. Supposing somebody had said that to me a couple of years ago!

But she began to talk about Manfred. She felt she should not, that it was a kind of betrayal, but then it was too late to stop. Wendland went on smoking quietly and said nothing until he had himself well in hand. She told him all about what was going on in Manfred's institute, his friendship with Martin and the work they had done together, and about the new machine and the fight they had had in the factory in Thuringia.

"You ought to have told me all this long ago," he said at last. "Some people will want to hear about it, you know."

"Oh, don't tell anyone," she said. "You can't think how angry he would be!"

"But supposing we got the machine tested in the end?"

"You mean you would help?"

"Why not?"

He looked away, for the sudden joy and the trusting look in her eyes seemed to sear into him.

"And you don't think he ought to give up?"

Wendland shrugged. It was hard to say. Some people had run their heads against brick walls before without getting anywhere.

"But if you give up you just lose your self-respect, don't you?" she said.

That was what had been worrying her since she had seen how Manfred was changing.

We're too much alike, Wendland thought. I'd be sure to bore her in the long run.

"You know, there's such a thing as being drawn into a void," he said slowly, when they were back in the car. "I think that may be a real danger for him – getting drawn into an ice-cold emptiness, where he can't feel anything."

Now how does he know that? Rita wondered.

The nearer home they got, the guiltier Rita felt. She wanted to ask Wendland to stop at the corner, not just in front of the house, for she could imagine Manfred listening to the brakes screeching, and the car doors slamming. . . .

Wendland gave her a sidelong glance. He wondered what excuse she would make.

But no, she thought. I'm not going to pretend this hasn't happened. She wanted Manfred to take it in his stride, not to take it as if she had done something terrible which turned her into a stranger.

"Thank you," she said, and rushed upstairs as if her life were at stake. The room was empty.

Manfred came home at midnight. He did not look at her at all. He went over to the washstand, took a long time washing and rubbing himself dry. Rita followed him with her eyes.

"I'd have slept elsewhere tonight if I'd found some-one to take me in," he said coldly.

Rita jumped up and stood over him. He could see the pain and anger in her eyes. She was so angry that she forgot everything else – her pity for him and the habit of making things easier for him. She grabbed him by the shoulder and shook him as hard as she could.

"What did you say? Say that again!"

She was shouting down her own feeling of guilt, screaming after the long hours of waiting, afraid of what might happen to Manfred and, behind it all, angry at having the memory of the few quiet hours with Wendland spoilt.

It gave her a grim satisfaction to see how horrified Manfred was. He's never seen me like this, she thought. I'll let myself go for once. I'll keep on and on till he's afraid for me, for a change. I'll just let him see what it's like to be worried all the time, the way I'm always worried about him.

She could feel her anger subsiding, but she did not let him see it; she went on shaking him until he snatched at her hands, and began to soothe her and tell her how sorry he was. She broke away from him, sat down on a chair and wept. Let him think he's hurt me terribly, she thought. But how unimportant it was – what he said or left unsaid, for she knew now that she could not really help him. Things would come to a ter-rible end. . . .

He begged her to stop crying, begged her to tell him what he could do for her, if only she would stop.

Rita calmed down. But he went on excusing himself, for he had no idea what she was really weeping about.

"I saw you getting into the car. I was standing at the corner. I'd bought a little bunch of lilies of the valley. . . .

How was the exam? Did you get through all right? And then I gave them to a little girl. . . .

"Do you remember the funny little cinema we went to once? They've opened a new petrol station next to it. I stood there and watched them washing cars. They were doing a good job, too. I went up and asked if I could get my car washed and the garage man looked me up and down and said 'When do you want to bring your car, young man?' After that I just walked about. I don't know where I went. Yes, I really did meet an old girl friend. But she didn't want to have anything to do with me. . . ."

"You know I couldn't bear to lose you," he said after a while. "I'll try to pull myself together and stop behaving like a madman. And I'll try not to be jealous any more."

She smiled. She knew he would never change, that he would go on being jealous. He thought they would go on loving each other for ever, but Rita knew that they were not safe, that they were exposed to the same dangers as everyone else. Anything that happened to other people could happen to them, too.

Her acute fear subsided. But the thought recurred from time to time that disaster was only just round the corner.

24

They had had a few weeks together after that. However hard she tried to remember them, they seemed to be blotted out of her memory. The days must have passed, they must have talked to each other, they must have lived; but she could remember nothing about it. Then Manfred went to a chemists' congress in Berlin.

She could not even remember whether she had been lonely, or whether she had had a presentiment of disaster.

All she knew was that Frau Herrfurth had met her at the door one evening (What's she so pleased about now, Rita had wondered anxiously) – and handed her a letter from Manfred. She opened the letter, read it, but could not take in a single word.

"At last he's learnt some sense. He's not coming back," said Frau Herrfurth smugly.

I'll write as soon as you can come, Manfred had written. *I'm longing for the day to come. Remember that always.*

"Of course you can go on living with us," Frau Herrfurth had said. She could afford to be sympathetic now. "We'll leave everything as it is, except for a few of his things – his clothes and books. . . ."

In the evening the tortoise Cleopatra, who had wakened up out of its winter sleep, came out of its box and wandered back and forth across the bare floorboards. Rita watched her until her eyes hurt.

She stood up and put the little animal back in its box. She suddenly hated touching it. The dumb, sad look in its age-old eyes was eerie. She went to bed and lay with her arms behind her head, staring at the ceiling. She felt quite calm, as if a deadly cramp were stealing over her. And it came at the right time. She did nothing to stop it.

He was gone. He had left the house like any casual acquaintance and closed the door behind him. He was gone, never to return. People smiled over old stories about terrible abysses and ghastly temptations which could only be overcome by heroic deeds, she thought. But they were true, after all.

Rita talked to nobody. She gathered together the last shreds of strength and retreated into silence. She let Sigrid – eager, grateful Sigrid – drag her along through the fever of the examinations. She did what people told her.

She sometimes wondered vaguely how it was possible to drift, to die bit by bit, in the midst of people, without anyone noticing. But she did not complain. She hardly suffered. She was only a shell. She moved like a shadow across a stage and was not surprised that the real things – walls and houses and streets – slipped noiselessly away from her.

Touching people hurt her. She avoided it.

A bitter quarrel broke out in the Herrfurths' part of the house (living coffin, sleeping coffin, eating coffin, as Manfred had called it). This time it was a life and death struggle, as she realised later. Frau Herrfurth could only interpret her son's flight to the West as a signal for her. She urged her husband to burn his boats. She had everything prepared, they could leave in two hours, she said.

"Leave?" said Herrfurth. "But why? Where to?"

God, didn't he understand? They could escape to freedom at last! And in any case, they ought to be with their son.

"Who knows whether this particular son attaches any importance to his parents," said Herr Herrfurth.

He was tired out. His wife had spent a good part of her life making him tired, subduing him to her will. Now, on the one occasion when it really mattered, he could not be overruled. He was just tired.

Try as she would, Frau Herrfurth could not force him to make up his mind one way or the other. He was just tired.

He realised how tense she was, how frightened she was of the complications she herself had engineered. He saw how blue her lips often turned and how often she went to her little bottle of heart drops. He knew she was not play-acting when she clutched at her heart.

But what could he do for her now, so late in life, which he had enjoyed as best he could – without her, as things had turned out?

He sat with Rita in her little bare room, one evening late in June. For most people the nights already smelt of the lakes and summer meadows. Manfred had been gone six weeks. Herr Herrfurth had had to telephone for an ambulance and strange people with unsmiling, disinterested faces had carried his wife, gasping for breath, out of the house on a stretcher. Unused to silent patience, he had climbed the stairs to ask Rita, the only person left in the house, what he could do for his wife.

He huddled awkwardly on the edge of a chair. He glanced round the room. He had never once entered it all the time his hate-filled son had lived in it.

"And these horrible dreams at night!" he groaned, clutching his head in his hands.

Rita sat up in bed and looked at him. His grief and self-reproaches did not touch her now. She did not dream at night, she told him.

She wondered why he had come to her.

"And what have they done to you, child?" he murmured.

But she could not respond. Her head was droning from the blow she had received and she had no feeling left over for the blows that fell on others.

Herr Herrfurth began to talk to himself.

"But what could I do over there? Who wants elderly

people in the West? And what's to happen to me here? Oh, leave me in peace ... She always loved the boy more than me."

He realised that he was talking about his wife as if she were dead already. He fell silent and stared sadly in front of him.

Rita fell asleep. He was still there when she woke up again at early dawn, murmuring confusedly to himself. She felt that this man and the night she had just lived through were the most horrible she had ever experienced.

"Can't you go away now?" she exclaimed abruptly.

He got up obediently and went out.

She lay awake until day came and the air filled with the ringing of bells. Whit Sunday, she thought, and put her fingers in her ears.

Herr Herrfurth came up to see her once more, a week later. He was wearing a black tie and told her with tears in his eyes that his dear wife suddenly and unexpectedly passed away in the night and would be buried in three days' time. The conventional role of sorrowing husband helped him to get a grip of himself for a time.

There were few mourners behind the swaying coffin as it moved along the twisting paths between the gravestones. Ernst Wendland walked beside Rita without speaking.

It was lucky that all this did not really concern her, she thought. It was other people's business. But one thing did worry her; she felt she had been through it before, perhaps without the smell of decay. But she distinctly remembered the long street and Ernst Wendland beside her. So she must be dreaming now, too.

Everything seemed real – that was the trick. It was hard to grasp at first, but once she knew it was all a dream the queerness of it struck her anew. Frau Herrfurth, who had been so energetic and so greedy for life, was being buried and her son was not there; another man was walking beside her daughter-in-law. . . .

Later on, when she woke up, she would have a good laugh over it, she thought.

They came to the little mound of earth, somebody spoke the funeral service and there was a thin trickle of singing. Then the men picked up the light coffin and lowered it into the grave.

Earth to earth, ashes to ashes, dust to dust.

Rita, still smiling over her dream, looked up into the sky. Behind the trees she saw the little tower of the cemetery chapel and a swallow perched on it. She saw the swallow take to flight again when the bell began to toll; it flew up and circled round the grave. She followed it with her eye, heard its thin, shrill cry above the gentle tolling of the bell, and saw it fly, straight as an arrow, towards a far-away cloud, screaming shrilly again as it clove the blue arch of the sky with its slender wings.

And she was left alone below.

The stunned feeling, pierced by the bird's call and its flight, gradually receded and she began to weep, bitterly, forlornly.

Wendland, who had not taken his eyes off her, held her arm, led her silently through the winding paths back to the cemetery gates. He told his chauffeur to drive Herr Herrfurth home and walked with Rita down the long, chestnut-lined avenue until she was calm enough to talk.

Wendland had not heard of Manfred's flight from

Rita, but from the cautious Herr Herrfurth, who considered it expedient to express his disapproval.

They did not speak of him.

Rita felt that no one else could be such a comfort to her just then. And she told him so. Wendland understood so well what she needed. And even now he did not allow a spark of hope to light his heart.

25

It was a rainy summer. In July the sun shone upon the just and the unjust – when it shone. August began well, with high, clear blue skies, but no one took much notice of the weather, except when they looked up at the planes which flew over more frequently than usual.

"If we can just get through August and September," people said. "They never start a war later than that."

It was impossible to talk even about the weather without thinking of war. Looking back later on, Rita thought, they would all wonder how they had been able to bear that summer. It was not just a question of getting used to things, either, for it was impossible ever to get used to this tense atmosphere.

It was the first Sunday in August. Rita took the early train to Berlin, for Manfred's letter had come the day before.

"It's all arranged," he wrote. "I'll be looking out for you every day now. You must remember that. . . ."

No one had known where she was going. That was the advantage of living alone and not being responsible to anyone. She did not even know whether she would come back, although she took no luggage with her. She waved a tentative farewell to the chimneys as they flew past, to the villages, woods and solitary trees, to the groups out in the fields. She had been out harvesting with Hans and the others the Sunday before, so she knew the harvest was poor and that they were having trouble getting in what there was of it. But were those her worries now? There were trees, chimneys and cornfields everywhere in the world. . . .

It was going to be a hot day. Rita took off her jacket. The only other passenger in her compartment was a tall, slim man with a long, pale face, spectacles and brown hair, quite ordinary-looking. His glance was a little too friendly, perhaps — or was she imagining things? He made her feel uncomfortable, so she got up and stood at the open window in the corridor, watching scene after scene, colourful and ever-changing as they flitted by. Only the sky did not alter for some time — a pale morning blue lit by the low-lying sun, with a few grey-white clouds which gradually dispersed as the day advanced.

Something was worrying her, she did not know quite what. Manfred had written quite plainly and unmistakably. He was waiting for her, as if he were waiting to be let out of prison, or as if he were hungry and thirsty and waiting for food and drink. All she had had to do was to pack her little over-night bag and go to him. She had only two hours' journey before her. And wasn't it the most natural, the most sensible thing to do? So what was she worrying about?

"Aren't you happy, child?"

Oh, mother, she thought, it isn't just a question of happiness. . . .

She suddenly realised what had seemed wrong about Manfred's letter. The words which had always been enough to clear up a misunderstanding or dispel a shadow between them were not enough now. If she could only have felt that he knew exactly what he was asking of her; he thought there was no other choice. But this almost casual departure – *(They've offered me chances which I can't possibly miss)* – this reliance on quite new acquaintances who were suddenly supposed to be his friends ... there must surely be something not quite right about it all, she thought. He must be simply drifting with the current, not really taking things into his own hands.

And had he any idea of what the past eleven weeks had been like for her? She must not let him think everything was settled as soon as he saw her. He would have to give her time to think while she was with him. If she could only begin to think clearly again, if only she did not lose her head as soon as he touched her and forget everything that had happened since he left.

The train stopped only once on the way. Half time, she thought. She would have to pull herself together and think things out more quickly. But her mind was in hopeless confusion. . . .

Rita went back into her compartment. She took out a cigarette and the man offered her a light. She leafed through an illustrated paper he handed to her.

Perhaps she ought to have spoken to Wendland after all, she thought. She had seen him only the day before. She should not have tried to decide this thing alone.

She had been on late shift the night before and had been the last to leave the workshop. She had looked round as usual, counting the wagons waiting to be finished off the next morning. She had felt she could not bear to part from those dull grey, heavy objects. But she had had Manfred's letter since midday and had already made up her mind to go to Berlin.

She turned away at last and as she walked across the yard she saw Ernst Wendland standing on the steps of the office building. He lit a cigarette and walked slowly over to the gate. She followed him. There was no one else about. She wondered why Wendland was still there so late at night. He walked very slowly, glancing at the buildings on either side.

The silence struck her as sad and unnatural. Light and shadow was distributed differently at night, for the floodlights shone into the corners which were darkest by day. Even the narrow alley between the bogie shop and the forge was lit up.

Wendland turned into it. He reached the spot where Manfred had once asked her whether he must destroy what he loved most about her.

Rita quickened her step, although she was not sure whether she wanted Wendland to see her. She could hear the sharp hissing of the flames in the welders' shop, and bluish rays flickered across the path.

Wendland was already going through the gate when she called out to him. He turned round quickly and went to meet her.

"Why, Rita, you're just the person I wanted to see!" he exclaimed.

He told her he had just been through a sort of examination. He still felt weak at the knees after it. And he hadn't come through it very well, either.

Rita remembered that the yard had been full of strange cars that day, for there had been a big conference there.

"Did they haul you over the coals?"

"Yes. And I can't take criticism in my stride. I know

quite well that we haven't been making much progress lately. But you know how it is – the people who come and criticise don't know half of what's really going on – the good or the bad. And they praised me for the wrong things, so it wasn't much comfort. But the worst came afterwards. It was so awful that I forgot all about the criticism. We shan't be able to build the new coach."

"But why? We've been talking about nothing else for weeks."

"It's like this. Some of the metals we need have to be bought in the West and they've stopped delivery. They know very well over there how to make things awkward for us. We shan't just give up altogether, of course, but we'll have to reorganise everything, and that will take time."

"And what about Meternagel?" Rita asked. "Shall you tell him yourself?"

Wendland nodded. He had until Monday to think over what he would say at the department heads' meeting. He would have to tell them with as much assurance as he could muster that they would build the new coach later on, and explain what would have to be done to replace the metals they could no longer import from the West.

The clock struck midnight as they turned into Rita's street.

The short walk with Rita had done him good; all his worries and disappointment seemed to have been swept clean out of his mind, although he knew they would be there again the next morning or even, perhaps, in a few minutes.

"This is where I first met you, remember? We ran into each other at the door here. It was just after I'd been made director."

"Yes, but it wasn't really the first time, you know. I saw you first at Ermisch's birthday party."

"That's right. But did you really notice me there?"

Rita laughed. "I couldn't help it. You spoilt all their fun."

That was when she ought to have told him about Manfred's letter, she thought. He would never understand why she hadn't told him.

"I often can't bring myself to say what's in my mind," he had said. "I'd be sorry if you felt like that, too. You know you can rely on me, don't you?"

But neither of them had been able to say more just then – he because he did not know that this might be his last chance, and she because she knew it. They stood there a moment in silence, then Wendland said goodbye and Rita went up to her room. She packed her little bag quickly, then went over to the window and, for the first time for many weeks, looked out at the stars for a while. It will be fine tomorrow, she thought. She set her alarm and lay down in bed. . . .

"Well," said the man opposite her in the train, "I didn't think you'd find my magazine so interesting."

Rita blushed. She glanced at the page in front of her. Three black letters – OAS – and below them the torn corpse of a woman. She turned the page. A smiling child and black letters again – USSR.

"The Medusa's head of our times," said her companion. "Everybody has his troubles – some have plastic bombs, others this toothpaste smile, if we're to believe the illustrated papers."

"But rather different troubles, don't you think?"

"Oh, certainly. As you say. Are you on a visit to Berlin?"

"Yes, I'm going to see my fiancé," she said, hoping to choke him off.

But he went on talking cheerfully. He was interesting and amusing, too, but she did not know quite what to make of him. He told her he was a teacher and did not seem surprised when she told him she was training to be a teacher.

"You have the typical German teacher's expression," he said with a laugh. "The improver's expression. We all get it – to make up for the bad pay, I suppose."

Rita had an uncomfortable suspicion that he guessed where she was going and was trying to draw her out.

"Are you visiting relatives?" she asked.

"Well, yes, you might call it that," he said, laughing again.

She began to tire of this rather involved conversation. He noticed it, drew a book from his pocket, leant back in his corner and began to read.

She could not quite remember afterwards exactly when she had begun to steel herself to go through with what she felt she must do.

She had often been in Berlin before, but she felt that this was the first time she had really seen it. They passed little allotment gardens, a park and then the first factories. It was not a beautiful city, she thought, and it had a closed-up, secretive look about it.

The man looked up.

"Where does your fiancé live?" he asked politely.

"Why do you ask?"

"I suppose I'm allowed to ask?"

"Oh, well, I guess so," she shrugged. "He lives in Pankow."

"That's all right, then."

Was he spying on her or trying to warn her? she

wondered. Suppose he asked her exactly where her fiancé lived in Pankow? She was no good at this sort of thing. But if she said Manfred lived in West Berlin nobody would believe she was simply going to see him.

The train stopped at the frontier control post. A policeman came in and asked to see her identity book. If they ask me any questions now I shan't be able to make up a story, she thought. I shall just blurt out everything. The policeman leafed through her book and handed it back to her. Her hand shook as she put it back into her bag. Not much of a check-up, she thought, almost disappointed.

The man sitting opposite her mopped his forehead with a freshly-laundered handkerchief.

"My goodness, it's hot," he said.

Rita noticed that he left the station with a woman who had got out of another compartment. They seemed to be very friendly. Then she forgot all about him, for she had her own worries. She found the big city map and stood in front of it for a long time, memorising the names of the strange streets and stations, for she could not ask anyone to help her find her destination.

She went up to the ticket office. For the first time now she would have to reveal where she was going.

"*Zoologischer Garten*," she said.

The woman pushed her ticket through, indifferently.

"Twenty pfennigs."

"And return?" Rita was not sure whether she could buy a return ticket with East German money.

"Why didn't you say so at first? Forty, of course," said the woman crossly, snatching the ticket back and pushing another through the little window.

Two different ways of life for forty pfennigs, Rita thought, looking at the ticket in her hand. That was one of the things which made Berlin different from any other city. She put it away carefully in her purse, for she had to keep her mind free for other things.

Tired already, she joined the Sunday crowd and let herself be pushed up the steps to the platform. For these people the day was just beginning – with the usual Sunday outing atmosphere, pretty dresses, children's chatter and laughter.

Rita did not sit down in the train. For the first time in her life she wished she were someone else – one of these harmless trippers, for instance – anyone but herself. It was a sign that she had got herself into a situation which went against the grain.

She stood by the sliding doors, afraid that she might miss something important. When she had time to look up at the sky she saw that it was now absolutely cloudless. She repeated the names of all the stations and streets which lay along her route. She had not the faintest idea what lay on either side of these names and she was not curious, either; for her there was a fine line drawn through the big, strange city, and this was the line she had to follow. If she wandered away from it there was no telling what might happen.

She got out at the right station and forced herself to walk slowly, looking at a few kiosk windows on the platform. There were those oranges and chocolates, the cigarettes and cheap books people talked about so much, she thought. Things looked very much as she had expected them to look.

She was amongst the last to get to the barrier, where a group of people stood talking excitedly, the man who had been in the train with her amongst them. The woman who had joined him now hung on his arm, weeping with two other women who had apparently

come to meet them. The man caught her eye and
waved, smiling ironically, but did not speak.

Rita ran quickly down the steps. It couldn't have
started worse, she thought. Why did I have to see that
man again? Does my bad conscience show as clearly
as his?

26

She closed her eyes, trying to review clearly and calmly
what she had memorised on the map. First to the right,
across the wide street where you have to wait for the
policeman to hold up the traffic and let foot passengers
cross. Then along the famous Kurfürstendamm, the
legendary shopping street, so-o beautiful, so-o wealthy,
so-o bright and glittering, she had heard, that the
reality did not quite come up to the legend, as far as
the fifth cross-road. Then turn to the right, where the
streets are quieter. She walked on, keeping to the thin
line she had drawn for herself on the map; she saw it
more clearly in her mind's eye than the houses and
streets she passed.

At last she stood in front of the house where Manfred lived, without having once had to ask the way.

This was where her thoughts had been for days, and
now she was really here. She was surprised that anyone
could have longed for this house or fled to it, for it was
an ordinary apartment house in a grey city street.

She had been quite unconscious of the heat until she
turned into the cool, dark hall and walked up the worn,
polished linoleum-covered stairs. The harder her heart
thumped the more convinced she became that she was
doing something not quite right. She ought not to have
taken this step alone. But it was too late to turn back.

She found the door, with its shining brass plate. The bell rang, thin and tinkling. Steps approached. This must be Manfred's aunt, she thought, as a tall, thin woman in black opened the door.

The house had the sour smell of poverty-stricken respectability. It seemed to balance precariously on the edge of an abyss; the working class quarter began just behind these streets. The sour smell and the linoleum penetrated into the dark hall into which the woman rather grudgingly admitted her. She walked shyly into a room which was light enough for her to see the woman clearly. After a few words of explanation she was shown into Manfred's room.

The memory of her first glance into that room brought the tears to Rita's eyes every time she thought of it for a long time afterwards. Manfred sat with his back to the door at a table drawn up to the window. He was reading, with his elbows on the table and his head in his hands. His narrow head, short-cropped hair standing up a little at the crown, and his boyish, rounded shoulders showed up against the light. When the door opened and someone came in (his aunt, he thought), he sat perfectly still, stopped reading and stiffened defensively, then turned his head slowly. The cold, forbidding look in his eyes told Rita more about how he lived there than he could ever have described to her.

Then he saw her.

He shut his eyes. When he opened them again there was disbelief, apprehension and yearning in them. He jumped up and held out his arms.

"Rita," he murmured.

Relief spread over his face. Its intensity hurt Rita, but she smiled and stroked his hair gently.

It had been right to go to him, after all, she thought. But she still did not know what was to happen next. She shrank from what had to be said and done before the day was over. And Manfred knew what was going through her mind, too.

These thoughts flashed through their minds and were forgotten at once. Anything seemed possible again.

"But you've changed," said Manfred, as she sat down on the only chair in the room and he on the bed.

She smiled. All at once she knew exactly why they loved each other. As she had expected, all those nights full of pain and days full of difficult decisions were dissolved in a single look, in a single light, perhaps unintentional touch of his hand.

Rita looked round. His aunt had achieved in a matter of weeks what his mother had not succeeded in doing in years. The room was painfully tidy – a small, desolately bare quadrangle. The little bit of dust which could penetrate danced in the long, narrow ray of sun which shone in for half an hour at this time of day. In a moment, she thought, it would slip silently from the table to Manfred's motionless hands.

They sat quite still for a long time. Then they both got up together, as if they had heard a signal. They went into the aunt's room – the ante-room to hell, Manfred whispered. The woman sat at the window, in the same pale, narrow strip of sunshine, knitting a black shawl. She had no interest in life now except to mourn for her sister, but the tiny quirk of triumph, mingled with self-pity and pious regret, which hovered round her mouth hinted that she had at last got the better of her more fortunate sister, for she had at least managed to survive her.

When she realised where Rita had come from she was suddenly eager to offer her coffee. A touch of colour crept into her cheeks at the thought of finding out what it was like to live "over there in the Zone."

They excused themselves politely. Outside, as the door closed behind them, they stood looking at each other. Had she expected it to be like that? Of course not. Well, what had she expected?

Manfred looked away. He seized her hand and pulled her down the stairs behind him, swinging her round the turns. They ran through the cold, echoing hall and out into the warm, bright midday sunshine.

"Take a good look round now," said Manfred. "The free world lies at your feet."

Twelve o'clock struck from all the tower clocks round about.

27

"Am I to stay here all winter?" Rita asked the doctor when he paid his daily visit. October was over and November promised to be dull and cold.

"Oh no," he said. "You can leave any time you like."

"Now, at once?"

"Well, let's say tomorrow."

Erwin Schwarzenbach came to see her that afternoon. The central heating was on for the first time. Rita sat with him in the winter garden at the end of the landing. The luscious green pot-plants in the big glass windows stood up against the grey skies.

What does he want? Rita wondered. He knows I'm leaving soon.

Schwarzenbach was silent and thoughtful. He smoked and watched her. She asked him all the questions she could think of and he answered quietly until there was nothing more to say. All right, she thought, let's not talk, then. She leant back in her arm chair and listened to the rain beating against the windows and the wind howling through the trees in the park. From time to time the wind dropped and it was very quiet.

"Listen," said Schwarzenbach at last, "didn't you ever think of going after him?"

Rita understood at once.

"I did go after him," she said quickly.

"And what happened?"

Perhaps it would be a good thing to tell him, especially him, about it – and today – for tomorrow she would have her every-day worries to think about. The doctor had had the insight to let her longing to get back to every-day life grow until it was enough to tide her over the first difficult days. Nobody would be likely to ask her later on why she had done this or that. She would probably never again have time, either, to think over what she should say.

"I remember how hot that Sunday was," she said, "although I hardly noticed it at the time...."

The streets must have been hot to the touch. The few people who were not at home at lunch crept along the shady side of the pavement where the houses would only radiate their pent-up heat later in the afternoon.

These houses all looked alike. They were the same in both parts of Berlin, built for the same kind of people, with the same joys and sorrows. And they would be the same in other cities, too, she was sure. Of course, there was more glass and more glitter in the shop windows in West Berlin, and there were things to buy which she had never even seen before. But she had known that already. She had liked all that, too, and had thought it would be fun to go shopping there.

Still, all those things were connected with eating and drinking, clothes and sleeping. But why did one eat? What did people do in those beautiful houses? Where did people go in those huge cars? And what did people think about before they fell asleep in this part of town?

"Tell me everything just as it happened," said Schwarzenbach. "That's only what you think now, isn't it?"

"No, no. I thought all that at the time. I remember perfectly."

Why did he think she was anticipating things? If only people knew how much she had always thought about the meaning of living, she thought. She had not worried so much about it while she was with Manfred, because she thought she had found the answer. But it had all come back to her that Sunday. Everything had reminded her of it.

They had walked silently along side by side, but not holding hands. Once he touched her bare arm and she glanced at him quickly. She caught the hurt look in his eye and had to smile.

"Do you know what jumpology is?" he asked harshly. They were standing in front of a hoarding and he pointed out a poster on it.

"No," said Rita.

"Well, I do. It's a science. They let people jump up in the air and then estimate their characters according to the way they jump."

She shook her head, puzzled. It was a pretty poor joke, anyway, he thought. The best thing would be not to try to talk.

"Let's go and eat first," he said. "You needn't hold back. I'm earning good money now."

He realised at once that he had said the wrong thing. Suppressing his irritation, he began to point out the various buildings to her.

"You don't have to do that," said Rita. "You never used to."

"Oh, but I did. You've just forgotten."

His face beside mine in the water, she thought. How can he compare the two things?

"I haven't forgotten anything," she murmured. . . .

"Have you ever been in West Berlin?" she asked Schwarzenbach.

"Yes, years ago."

"Then you know what it's like. Lots of things are fine, but they're no fun. There's always the feeling that there's something wrong. And it's worse than being in a foreign country, because people talk the same language. It's like being in a foreign country, familiar, yet horrible."

That was what she had said to Manfred as they sat at lunch. He had only been thinking of the restaurant, which was new and pretty; he knew she was thinking of other things. It irritated him, but he tried to hide it.

"Oh, you're still wearing your political spectacles," he answered. "I know it isn't easy to break away from everything. But it will all be different in West Germany. It's not so hysterical as this mad Berlin. I was there for a fortnight. They've stuck to their promise. My new job starts on the first of the month. Everything is settled and we can leave very soon. I was over there when Mother died," he added, for he knew they would have to speak about it. "I only got Father's telegram when I got back."

It had made no difference, of course, for he could not have gone back to attend the funeral in any case. They had put a wreath from him on his mother's grave: "To my dear mother with love".

Rita remembered the swallow. He knew nothing about that, and she would never tell him. How many things he did not know. . . .

"We're having a tough time just now," she said.

"Who's we?"

"All of us," she answered, "especially at the works. You know I'm working there again these holidays."

"They were having a tough time when you went there first, remember?"

He means things never get any better, she thought angrily. He means it's hopeless to wait for things to get better.

"Well, that's all behind me now," said Manfred bitterly. "I don't want to think about it any more. Those senseless difficulties. Those exaggerated hymns of self-praise when some little thing happens to work out. Those self-flagellations. I'm getting a job now where other people are paid specially to get rid of all those obstructions. That's what I've always wanted. I'd never get it over there – not in my lifetime, anyway. You'll see how pleasant everything will be for us."

Us? thought Rita. Or should I be a teacher over there? And why does it seem impossible to me? She had herself sometimes thought that Meternagel was working himself to death uselessly. He took on more than he could manage. But that was just why she could not go off and leave him in the lurch. . . .

"Just think," she said to Manfred, "they were going to throw two of the men out of the brigade because they were doing too much!"

"Imagine that!" said Manfred, but he could not even pretend to be interested and she did not bother to explain what had happened.

Schwarzenbach waited patiently when she paused between sentences. He asked no questions and let her tell things in her own way, but he seemed to be waiting for something.

"I told him about everything that had happened since he went away," she went on, "and I had no idea then how it would end."

She had recalled the quarrel between Meternagel and Ermisch. To an outsider it had seemed as if they were always quarrelling about the same thing. Meternagel was fighting to help the works and Ermisch was trying to get all he could for the brigade. Things seemed to be repeating themselves. Meternagel had said a year ago that they could finish ten instead of eight window frames a shift, and now he wanted them to do twelve.

"And next year it'll be fourteen," Ermisch had said.

"Of course, it'll be at least that many," Meternagel insisted.

But if you looked more closely there were some little differences, too. Meternagel had not been trying to annoy Ermisch and Ermisch was quieter than he had been. Perhaps there was more in it than just window-frames, after all.

"I couldn't understand what was going on," Rita said to Schwarzenbach. "When should you speak up and when is it better to hold your tongue? One day I actually stood by and watched Horst Rudolf – that's the tall, handsome chap who earned the most and was always such a hit with the girls – while he put in a frame in fourteen minutes flat. I asked him what he did in the other sixty-six minutes. 'For God's sake, shut up,' he said. 'Don't you let on to a soul.' And I really didn't tell anyone."

"Not even Meternagel?" Schwarzenbach asked.

"Oh, I didn't need to tell him. He knew all about it. He knew about all sorts of things that were going on. But I felt uncomfortable all the time after I'd seen that. I used to go past the work-benches and wonder how much time was really being wasted. Later on, I noticed that I wasn't the only one who was worried about it. I didn't tell Manfred about that, though, because I didn't know how it would end. But I told him how worried I was because they were all beginning to avoid Meternagel. Even the Party secretary told him to go easy or he'd drive them all away to the West, I told Manfred. . . ."

"Rita!" Manfred whispered. "Not so loud, for heaven's sake!"

She looked at him. "You've certainly changed," she said.

All the noises in that pleasant little restaurant seemed very loud. She could hear a mother mildly scolding her little daughter. "Ingrid, dear, don't say she. You should say Auntie." "Never mind," said Auntie, indulgently, "she's only a little girl." She could hear the plates rattling in the kitchen and the light footfalls of the waiter. The light fell softly through the lime-green curtains. It was hard to believe that the sun was beating down on the street.

"What are you thinking about now?" Manfred asked; he could not bear it when the silence lasted too long.

"Do you remember when you were a kid how awful

the grown-ups' habits seemed? I'm sometimes afraid I might get used to the most awful things. And you, too."

"What sort of things?"

"Oh, all sorts. Not saying what you think. Working as little as possible. Getting used to having more bombs in the world than would be needed to blow us all up. Or losing someone you belonged to, forever, and having nothing but a letter left over – 'You must always remember that. . . .'"

"Rita!" Manfred exclaimed. "You don't think it was easy for me, do you? Do you think I've had an easy moment since then? I know it's all been too much for you, but you're getting everything mixed up – the works and the bombs and me. I'll make up to you for everything if you stay with me. You still can't make up your mind what's the right thing to do, can you? But couldn't you trust me just this once? 'I'll follow you where'er you go, through enemy host, through ice and snow', as they say."

Rita said nothing. What did people who wrote songs like that know about real life? What would they have written about the two of them sitting there so close together and yet so hopelessly far apart?

The meal they ate must have been good, but she had no idea what they ate. She refused wine so early in the day, and Manfred agreed at once.

They went out into the hot street again. Rita felt that things were getting beyond her.

"Isn't there a park somewhere near, where we can sit down?" she asked.

"A garden. Not exactly a park."

"Let's go there, then."

Afterwards she wished they had gone on walking through the streets, for this little garden would never be a park. The few flower-beds and bushes, snowball and lilac, and young birches and lime-trees were all past their best, grey with dust and their leaves curling up like thin parchment in the heat. They could hear them crackling, too, although there was not a breath of wind. The only splashes of colour were the brightly painted benches crowded with old people and young mothers with their prams.

Where do lovers go? she wondered.

They sat down at the end of a row of tired, silent people. They dared not look at each other. It hurt to remember the simple pleasures of the previous summer – now lost and gone forever.

"Where are people to go, anyway?" said Manfred, "in a city without a hinterland. It's cruel!"

"But you can't blame me for that," said Rita.

Manfred pulled himself together at once.

"I'm sorry. I'm going crazy myself. It makes you crazy. Let's stop blaming each other as if we were enemy politicians. It's simply ridiculous."

He was really frightened, for he saw how far things had gone, and his fear made him honest.

But his honesty was what killed all hope in her. She knew now that he had simply given up the struggle and if he had given up loving or hating he could live anywhere. He had not gone away out of protest, but had just given up. This going to the West was not a new experiment but the end of all experiments. . . . It did not matter any more what he did.

And for weeks afterwards she was tortured by the thought that all this had been in his mind while they were still together and she had not been able to help.

There was nothing very unusual about a girl losing the man she loved most, she thought. There was no need to get absolutely desperate about it. If he had left her for another girl her pride would have pulled her through, she was sure. No, that was not the worst part of it.

"I love you and no one else, and I'll always love you," he said. "I know what I'm saying. No one ever belonged to me before you. Is it too much to ask you to go with me? I know how you feel now. But shut your eyes for a minute and think of the Schwarzwald, the Rhine, the Bodensee. Don't those names mean anything to you? Aren't they in Germany, too? Or are they only a legend, a page in your geography book? Isn't it unnatural not to want to see them? Not even to want to see them? Just to sweep aside the very thought?"

Every word he said sapped her strength. She felt weaker than ever before, and full of bitterness. A wave of longing for all those strange landscapes and faces, longing for a full life with Manfred, swept over her and almost engulfed her. Why must she be forced to make this choice? She would lose a part of herself whatever she decided.

She felt as if she knew this little corner of a strange city as well as if she had lived in it for years. Ordinary people lived in it, but it was no ordinary city. Its days and nights were made of different stuff, it lived only in the present, trembling before the inevitable advance of reality. Things tried out and found wanting were being offered here as solid wares and the people forced to buy them did not notice that there was no substance in them. . . .

"What are you thinking about now?" Manfred asked. "Don't take it all so seriously. I was here in any case, and they offered me a good post, so I stayed here. There's nothing very unusual about that."

"It wouldn't be unusual anywhere else," Rita answered. "But here in West Berlin it is, you know. Did you know that your mother boasted about having got in touch with those two men who persuaded you to stay? And do you realise why she did it? She did it for herself. She wanted you to think she had been right, after all, so that you wouldn't despise her any more. You know what Wendland said when he heard you'd gone? He said he could have forgiven many people, but not you, because you knew very well what you were doing."

"Huh! Wendland again!" said Manfred with hatred in his voice. The silent agreement not to hurt each other more than they need was forgotten now. "Wendland indeed! Wendland of all people! He knows exactly what's going on. He doesn't have to rely on the newspapers. He can see behind the scenes. Do you think I wasn't full of optimism once, too? That I didn't believe that if you tore up the roots of evil you'd get rid of evil altogether? But evil has thousands of roots. You just can't get rid of it. It may be noble to go on trying. But you can't be noble if you have no faith. Do you think it's fun to be cheated? You've seen it happen once, but I've seen it many times. That's the difference.

"Here I know where I am, at least. I'm prepared for anything here. Over there it'll take who knows how long before facts get the better of big words. The fact is that man's not made to be socialist. If you force him into it he twists and turns until he's back where he belongs – at the best-filled trough. I could feel sorry for your Wendland, I could really."

"Why are you so mad at him?" Rita asked.

The question made him so angry he could have hit her. She had never seen him in such wild despair. He knew at that moment that the life he had left behind him would never leave him alone, and this was what infuriated him. All he wanted now was to shift the blame on to someone else for the despair he felt at having failed to stand up to the pressure of that harder, sterner life.

I should be harming myself, and him even more, if I went with him now, Rita thought.

"Everything would be so simple if they lived like cannibals, or if they were starving, or if the women looked as if they'd been crying," Rita said to Schwarzenbach. "But they're quite happy. They're sorry for us. They think everyone can see at a glance who is richer and who is poorer in Germany. You know, a year ago I would have gone with Manfred anywhere he wanted. But now...."

That was what Schwarzenbach had been waiting for. "And now?" he asked.

"The Sunday after I'd been to see Manfred was August 13th," she said after a long pause. "I went over to the works as soon as I heard the news. It was queer to see so many people there on a Sunday. Some of them had been sent for and others had come of their own accord."

"Perhaps you didn't really love him after all," Schwarzenbach suggested. "Lots of girls think of that and nothing else. Why wasn't it like that with you?"

If she could have done only that, she thought. She had tried and tried, lying awake at night, torturing herself, trying to get used to the idea of living over there in the West. But it was all too strange and far removed from her daily life and thoughts.

"Yes, it's the attraction of a great historical movement," said Schwarzenbach, nodding to himself. Rita smiled. Perhaps she had felt something of the sort as she sat beside Manfred in that dreary little garden.

They walked up and down for a while, then stood in a niche surrounded by clipped hedges. Rita was dead tired. She leant against a tree and Manfred stood before her, his hands against the trunk on either side of her head. They gazed at each other, hearing nothing of what was going on around them.

"How's Cleopatra?" he murmured.

"She doesn't eat much."

"You might try her with bits of tomato."

"That's a good idea. I'll try that."

They smiled at each other. The parting had already begun, but they could still smile. Yes, she thought, this is just how I remember you on the wind-swept meadow at home. I knew what you were like even then, but I wasn't faced with this kind of decision. If a thing like this can only happen once in a lifetime – and surely it can only happen once – then it's happening to me now and I shall have it behind me, and you, too.

They smiled. Manfred rubbed his face against her hair. He pressed her hands. Rita began to tremble. She craned her head back until she could see the hot, bleached summer afternoon sky through the sparse leaves. He's still there, she thought. These are his hands. This is the smell of his skin. This is his voice, strange to me now.

A silent green wall between us and the world. Is there a world? But we're here. Oh God, we're still here!

But a voice, a child's voice singing, was enough – after a long, long time, it seemed to her – to break through that wall. *Get well, get well, little goose,* it sang. *In a hundred years it will all be over. . . .*

In a hundred years! There was no wall, she thought bitterly, only the two of them and a little girl singing a silly song. She walked quickly back through the little garden and out into the street, where Manfred caught up with her.

They crossed over to the shady side and walked silently along side by side. They must have wandered through several streets before they stopped at a clean little garden café and sat down at a small round table under a sunshade that looked like a huge mushroom. It had done its work for the day, for the sun had already disappeared behind the roof of a four-storey house.

They ate ice-cream and watched the people coming and going, preoccupied with their own affairs. They were too tired to think about themselves any more. They knew that the pain would come again – soon, or tomorrow or the day after, to shake them through and through and tear at their hearts. But at that moment they were numb and exhausted. A ball rolled under their table and they threw it back to its owner, listening politely to the mother's apology. A man at the next table was preparing for a big family gathering and he came and borrowed the third chair from their table.

The silence between them lasted so long that they felt they might never be able to speak again. They sat there so long that it seemed as if they might never move again. They knew what had to be done, but could not make the first move.

There was a great deal of noise at the next table.

"Waiter!" the hearty man called out loudly.

There was only one waitress and she had her hands full attending to all the tables, but she hurried over.

"We're giving our Uncle from the Zone a special treat," he said. "Do you think we want him to see how bad the service is here?"

"From the Zone?" She peered at the uncle. He was up from the country and was sweating in his heavy, dark suit. "Where are you from?"

"Hermannsdorf," said the old man.

"Well I never!" she exclaimed. "I come from round there."

Flushed and excited, she told him the name of her village and asked him about old friends, about the harvest and whether he was going back.

"I know how you feel, miss," the hearty man broke in, "the world's a small place. But poor old Uncle needs a drink."

Rita leaned back in her chair. A ragged, semi-transparent sickle, shining palely in the greenish, late afternoon sky. Night would soon draw in around them.

The air had been changing while the moon had risen. She could breathe more freely now – much too freely, so that she felt she must draw deep breaths to fill her lungs. It rose between them, no waves of joy or pain could pass from one to the other. It was as if the deaf, silent city were suddenly under water without knowing it. The moon, a pale lamp in the real world, hung over her; there was no other sound, no other light. Neon lights, like secret signs, sprang up here and there.

BUY SALAMANDER
YOU CAN DO IT WITH NECKERMANN
NEVER BE WITHOUT 4711.

Dusk fell over the city.

28

The rain tapped lightly against the window panes.

"It's letting up," said Schwarzenbach. "I can go now." But he made no move to get up.

"I sometimes wonder whether we ought really to judge the world by our standards – of good and evil, I mean," Rita went on. "Shouldn't we just take it as it is?"

But if that were really true, she thought, it would have been silly not to have stayed with Manfred; any sacrifice would be silly. Manfred had always insisted that the game was the same, only the rules changed. And the augurs' smile might fall on anyone. . . .

"Do you know why I came to see you today?" Schwarzenbach asked. He had understood what she meant, but did not answer directly. "I wanted to find out if there were any sense in telling the truth as one sees it in all circumstances."

"And you thought you could find that out from me?"

"Yes, and I have, too. I was beginning to have my doubts. You know how it is, sometimes too many things happen all at once."

And he told her about an article he had had published in the teachers' journal. He had written about dogmatism in teaching and bad teaching methods, giving some examples from his institute. It was no use dictating people's opinions to them, he had written. The thing to do was to convince them that socialism was right, not to make yes-men of them.

"Of course that's true," said Rita. "There can't be any doubt about that, surely?"

Schwarzenbach smiled. He felt better already. There had been objections to his writing that particular article at that particular time, when it was supposed to be better not to discuss these problems openly. Mangold had popped up again, thinking this was just the time to accuse Schwarzenbach of being a political romantic.

The people who were against him had the upper hand just then, Rita thought.

"Well, let them hold meetings and pull me to pieces. Now I can always remember how honest you've been. We are in a special position just now, of course; we're in a position to face the truth, not to pretend difficult things are easy, not to call black white, not to take advantage of people's belief in us – the most precious thing we've gained. Tactics are all right, but only if they bring us nearer the truth.

"Socialism isn't a magic formula, after all. Sometimes we think we're changing something when all we're doing is giving it a different name. You've convinced me today that you can only get to people's hearts by giving them the pure, naked truth. We can afford to do it, too."

"Oh, but my story isn't as important as all that!" Rita protested.

"Well, I see exactly what you were trying to tell me," he said with a smile.

He stood up. It was already dark outside. A nurse came and switched on the lights in the corridor. She looked in, nodded and went on. The big house was very quiet.

"Will you come down and see me off on the bus?" he asked.

"We ought to drink a glass of wine now, oughtn't we?" Manfred had said. She watched him take the bottle from the busy waitress and pour it out himself.

The greenish-yellow colour anticipated its aroma and light dryness. Moon wine, she thought, night wine, remembrance wine. . . .

"What shall we drink to?"

She said nothing.

"To you – to your little mistakes and their big consequences."

"I'm not drinking to anything," she said.

They emptied the bottle and left the café, leaving the noise of the family party behind them. They walked down the street to the big square, almost deserted at that hour. They paused before crossing it, half afraid to disturb its calm. The sunset colours above it were curiously mixed. Exactly above their heads, stretching right across the square, ran the frontier between night and day. A veil of cloud stretched across the night-grey half, and the clearer half ended in unearthly colours, with a strip of glass-green merging into blue just above the horizon. The little corner of earth on which they stood – one square of pavement no bigger than a square metre – fell within the shadows of the night.

Long ago lovers used to search for a star where their eyes might meet after they had parted. What should they search for?

"They can't divide the sky, anyway," said Manfred.

The sky? This whole arch of hope and longing, love and grief?

"Oh yes," she murmured. "The sky divides first."

They walked through a narrow side street and came out quite close to the station. Manfred stopped short.

"Your bag!" he exclaimed, knowing she would not go back for it. "I'll send it to you."

She had all she needed in her handbag.

They were pushed and jostled in the busy main street

and he had to hold on to her so as not to lose her too soon. He held her arm lightly and pushed her gently in front of him. They did not see each other's faces until they stopped again in the station hall.

Anything she did not decide now she would never be able to decide. Anything she did not say now would never be said. What they did not know of each other now they would never know.

All that was left now was this lifeless moment, empty of hope and not yet coloured by despair.

Rita picked a thread off his jacket. A flower-seller who had made a study of the right moment to interrupt parting lovers came up and offered them a bunch.

Rita shook her head violently. The man retreated. You never knew what to expect.

Manfred looked at his watch. She had only a few moments longer.

"Go now," he said.

He went up to the barrier with her. They stopped again. They stood on an island between the crowd pushing up to the trains on the right and down to the exit on their left.

"Go!" said Manfred. "Go now!"

She moved on, still looking at him.

He smiled. (She should remember him smiling when she thought of him.)

"Goodbye, little brown girl," he murmured.

Rita leant her head on his breast for a moment. For weeks he could still feel the light pressure of her when he closed his eyes.

She must somehow have got through the barrier and up the steps. She must have taken the right train and got out at the right station. She was not surprised now that everything went smoothly. Her train home stood there waiting, almost empty. She got in slowly, found a seat and the train moved out of the station. That was how things had to be, for she would have had no strength to deal with the slightest hitch or make the smallest decision just then.

She did not sleep, but she was not fully conscious, either. The first thing she really saw was a quiet, shining little lake which caught the waning light in the sky and reflected it back more strongly.

Curious, she thought, so much light in so much darkness.

29

The day Rita returned from the sanatorium to the sooty town was cool and indifferent, a day like any other in early November, suspended between the sad decline of autumn and the translucency of winter.

Hardly changed after her two months' absence, she moved back into her old room in an almost solemn mood, as if renewing or reaffirming a decision taken long before.

She knew what lay behind her and what the future held in store; this was all that had changed, but it gave her confidence.

She did not mind walking through the streets alone, seeing no one she knew. It was midday and the shops would soon be closing. She had forgotten about the noise and the crowds and she was almost afraid to plunge in. She would have to get used to the penetrating noises, colours and smells again. How could people bear it all their lives, she wondered, smiling at her country girl's notion, for she would probably see things with a townswoman's eye again the very next day.

There was no doubt that Rita had been through a terrible experience. She was well again but, like many people, she could not know how much inner courage she would need to look life firmly in the face again, day after day, without deceiving herself or being deceived. There may come a time when people will recognise that the fate of countless ordinary people depended on their inner courage – for a long, difficult, threatening but hopeful moment in history.

Rita stood at the window of her attic room again. She pulled the curtain aside, sniffed the familiar smell of smoke and autumn, put her elbows on the window-sill and cupped her face in her hands – a chain of habitual movements followed inevitably by thoughts broken off here long ago. She noticed again, just as she had done on that far-off August evening, that the willows on the farther bank of the river were all bent by the wind in the same direction – away from the water – and she even thought she heard the train's whistle which had been engraved on her memory that evening.

She felt today as if she had been hearing that whistle all day long. She remembered how, on that other day, only three weeks after she had parted from Manfred, she had had the sensation of being followed by the indifferent glance of some unavoidable being. She had known even then that lovers in poetry had chosen death not because they were separated but because they dreaded the return to the grey dreariness of life. Leaden normality paralysed their limbs, beat down their spirits, hollowed out their will to live. The circle of confidence, hitherto unlimited, closed in painfully. She measured it cautiously, always waiting for new inroads. Where would it hold firm?

That train's whistle had seemed to snatch away all

her remaining will to live. She no longer shrank from admitting to herself that the place and the time she had collapsed had been no accident. She had seen the two heavy green coaches rolling towards her, inexorably, quietly, certainly. They're coming right at me, she had thought, and she knew quite well that she was bringing it upon herself. Instinctively, she allowed herself one last attempt to step out of their way, not out of despairing love, but in despair because love is transitory like everything else. That was why she had wept when she awoke out of unconsciousness. She had wept because she had been saved.

Today she felt something approaching distaste at the thought of that sick state of mind. Time had done its work and had let her regain the strength she needed to call things by their right names.

Rita moved away from the window and began to unpack her bags. She spread her things about the room. She took a sudden dislike to many of them. She still had money from the work she had done in the summer and she made up her mind to go out and buy a skirt and a couple of new blouses the next day. She would take Marion with her, she thought, so as not to choose the wrong colours.

She took out the mirror which was lying at the bottom of her suit-case, sat down on the edge of the bed and looked at her face closely, thinking it had been far too long since she had looked at herself; she smoothed her eyebrows – they were all right, she thought. She peered at the corners of her eyes. Tears had left no traces there. She examined every inch of her face, the line of her cheek, the chin. And unconsciously she began to smile. But the new expression remained in her eyes, that was where experience showed.

The door opened cautiously, although she had not heard the step on the stairs. She looked up and saw Herr Herrfurth standing in the doorway. He turned to leave again quickly, for he had not expected to find her there so early. But he thought better of it, came in and hastily handed her a note. He had brought Cleopatra with him, too, in a cardboard box. She had managed to survive her absence fairly well, he said.

The note was from Meternagel.

"Come over and see me. I'm ill in bed at home."

"He's just about done up," said Herr Herrfurth. "They've made him foreman again. So he'd got what he wanted and could have taken things a bit easier. But no, he went on working like a demon, till they had to fetch him away in an ambulance."

She must go to him at once, she thought.

She took the tortoise from Herr Herrfurth and set her down in the corner.

"Sit down for a minute, won't you?" she said, lifting her suit-case off a chair.

Herr Herrfurth sat down apologetically.

Well, he certainly hasn't looked in a mirror for a long time, either, she thought. She had known him for so long that she could see all the little signs of neglect quite clearly. And the tears a man never weeps leave their traces.

"I'll pay rent for my room now, of course," said Rita.

"Oh, no, that wouldn't do at all!" he protested. He couldn't possibly take rent from a girl who had been almost. . . . She should not insult him in that way.

"But I'd feel much easier, you know," she said.

Herr Herrfurth slumped back in the chair.

"You're a queer girl – forgive me for saying so. There was a great deal that my wife didn't understand about you, either. She had her little peculiarities, too, of course. . . . But I can honestly say I took you into my house without any hesitation. Only I never seemed to get any response from you."

Rita understood that, like other weak people, he longed for an audience to his constant embellishment of facts. Once, the night before his wife died, she had heard him being really honest – honestly admitting defeat. But his honesty had not lasted long.

"That Sunday when you went away I really believed that things would be all right again between you and Manfred," he went on. "I began to feel hopeful again. You can't imagine what it meant to me to lose my wife and my son at one blow!"

But how long is it since your son was a real son to you? she thought.

"It's a mystery to me why you came back," he said. "You may think me old-fashioned, but love was more romantic in my day, and more permanent. Yes, much more permanent."

Rita remembered his wedding group. She said nothing. What could she say?

"Don't think I would ever mention your trip to Berlin to anyone who ought not to know about it," he added, putting a wrong interpretation on her silence.

"Oh, you needn't worry about that," she said. "I'm sure you wouldn't want to get me into difficulties."

"Why do you think my son hated me so?" he asked after a while.

Rita looked at him in surprise. Did he really want to know, or was he only worrying about what he felt was an undeservedly solitary old age? But she could not possibly tell this old man the truth.

"Anybody can make a mistake, you know," he went

on. "You can't always know beforehand whether you're putting your money on the right horse. It's easy enough to accuse older people of making mistakes afterwards. Believe me, dear Fräulein Rita, I've had a great deal of experience in life. Sons always repeat their fathers' mistakes. And in the end we all go the same way to the grave."

So now that he had tasted the bitterness of life he thought he understood it. You couldn't prevent men like that from having children, she thought. It'll be my job to protect children from such fathers.

"Well, he doesn't hate you any more," she said, "he really doesn't."

Herr Herrfurth got up, groaning faintly. These blows of fate were hard to bear and he was a sorely tried man; he held out his hand resignedly to the girl who refused to understand him. Grief would overcome him again, he knew, in his big empty living-room downstairs. But for an instant longer he tried to be his old self, a man with a thoroughly good opinion of himself.

Another thought occurred to him before he left.

"You remember Herr Schwabe, don't you? The Dean of Studies' secretary, an old school friend of Manfred's. Not a bad fellow, really. He's had a little trouble since Manfred left. He'd certainly be glad to take back some of the things he said to him. It's one of those cases which show very clearly how much depends on whether a person is in a good or bad temper at the time."

Rita remembered what Schwabe had said to Manfred when he went to see him about Martin. She remembered how they had teased him at that party at the Professor's house, too. She wondered whether he had learned anything since then, or whether he was still marching cheerfully forward under a new slogan?

That was what she thought, but she did not say anything.

"And what about Rolf Meternagel? Have they deleted that bit from his file about how he came to spend three thousand marks too much?"

"Well, I should hope so," said Herr Herrfurth in a friendly tone. "After all, it was only three thousand marks."

And he went away at last.

Rita went to see Rolf Meternagel. He was flat on his back again, as he had been so many times before. A man like that, who had never sat back in a quiet corner and waited for his food to drop into his mouth, who had never bothered to reckon up what stood to his credit but had always given other people plenty of time to pay their debts to him, who had never saved up the only thing he had – his health and strength – would certainly get many knock-out blows and have to pick himself up and start all over again many times, she thought.

Rita remembered how, all through those weeks when Meternagel was trying to step up production and nobody knew how it would affect the men's wage packets, Herbert Kuhl had kept his eye on him and never missed a chance to irritate him. Something seemed to be boiling up inside him until one day, at last, things came to a head. He and Kurt Hahn, a new man, had each put in fourteen frames during the night shift, three nights running, while the others were still only putting in ten.

The others pushed past Meternagel to their lockers, for they were still avoiding him like the plague, but Kuhl stopped in front of him.

"Well, how about it?" he said challengingly.

"About what?" asked Meternagel in a friendly tone.

"I shall go on putting in fourteen a shift," said Kuhl.

"That's fine."

"You're not keen on a chap like me breaking the norm, are you?"

"Don't be silly! Why shouldn't you? But I'd like to know why you're doing it," said Meternagel, looking him squarely in the face.

"Well, I'll tell you," said Kuhl, gritting his teeth. "Other people can do far less and be praised to the skies for it. But all you ask me is, why do I do it? You don't trust me because I was an officer in the Wehrmacht – that's why you ask. You don't ask anyone else. Let me tell you, I put all I had into being an officer. I was never one to do things by halves. If they'd stood people up in front of me and told me to shoot them I'd have shot them, and no qualms of conscience afterwards, either. The difference between me and some other people is that I say so straight out, but they shut up about it. You can make a swine out of anyone, I tell you. Well, what are you all staring at?" he looked round belligerently.

"Well, but just think, man. You're giving yourself the lie," said Meternagel in his every-day voice. "Why, for sixteen years now you've been trying to convince yourself that you're a swine. But you're not a swine after all."

He chuckled and the men all turned to look at him. Kuhl was sweating as if he had been hauling a heavy load. The muscles in his face twitched. He was still angry with himself for giving himself away. He took no further part in the argument that followed and Rita was not even sure he was listening.

Horst Rudolf, the handsome chap whom Rita had

seen with her own eyes putting in a frame in fourteen minutes, began to protest loudly.

"But look here, everybody in our brigade's earning good money, because we're all good pals. I don't feel like working with chaps who stab me in the back. It's a case of them or me!"

"I'd be sorry to lose you," said Meternagel placatingly.

"Well, we can't stop now," said old Karssuweit sadly. "We've gone too far already, believe me."

Nobody spoke. Did they really want to slow down and start juggling with figures again as they had done when Ermisch had run the brigade?

Meternagel tried another tack.

"I don't know whether you've noticed, but things look to me to be pretty tricky just now. Something's going to happen. Maybe we can help to tide over if we raise our norms a bit. That's not so dumb as it sounds, you know. And supposing they ask us first? Are we just going to tell them to leave us alone, we're earning good money?" he added, looking Ermisch full in the face.

Ermisch had been expecting this for weeks. He turned brick-red.

"What do you take us for?" he shouted, spluttering with rage. "Do you think because we cheated you once we're going to go on forever cheating? Yes, if you want to know, we did play a trick on you with those three thousand marks. Of course I knew those jobs we kept on filling in on our pay slips just weren't being done any more. Most of us knew it. You lost your job. Good. But does that make us swine for good and all?"

Meternagel turned so pale that Rita thought he was going to faint. He bent down and picked up his shabby leather brief-case.

"Let's break it up. Meetings don't have to go on forever," he said.

Just as they were leaving Ernst Wendland appeared.

"We're terribly short of carpenters," he said to Ermisch. "Are we going to get more window frames from you or not?"

"Maybe," said Ermisch sullenly.

"Maybe is a pretty roundabout word."

"Not really," said Meternagel. "You know what generally happens when a girl says maybe."

Wendland grinned and offered them cigarettes.

"You're in clover," he said to Ermisch. "It's easier to be a famous brigade leader than works director."

"But you can't hang on to the job so easily," said Ermisch.

They laughed and pounded each other on the back.

Rita knocked at Meternagels' door. She was afraid he might have changed in these eight weeks.

As usual, his wife opened the door. Her face lit up when she saw Rita.

"He's asleep," she said, "but I can wake him up."

"Don't let him notice if the sight of him gives you a bit of a shock," she said, as she opened the door.

"Well," she said, "whoever told you it was your turn to go sick after me?"

He saw that she had not been prepared to find a very sick man, but he passed it off. He could only do one thing at a time – raise his head, smile or speak, so he did all that in turn. His smile was the only thing about him which had not changed. And that simply made her feel worse.

"Sit down, child," he said. "It's caught up with me this time at last – heart, nerves, circulation and God knows what else. I shall have to go away and be patched up."

"And who's to be foreman while you're away?" she asked.

"No use shutting my eyes to facts," he said. "I'll never be able for that job again. Ermisch'll take my place."

What could she say? Rita gave up pretending. They had known each other long enough not to have to beat about the bush. It was eighteen months since she had followed him shyly round the works for the first time, desperately anxious not to let him catch her making a mess of her job.

"It's a good thing we don't know beforehand what's going to happen to us," he said. "I used to think I'd reached rock bottom sometimes, and nothing worse could possibly happen. I guess I've really and truly reached rock bottom this time. Nothing'll ever surprise me again."

"Oh, they'll never really get you down," said Rita.

They both laughed. Frau Meternagel stuck her head in at the door, pleased to hear them laughing. She had known at once that Rita would do him good. She called her into the sitting-room for a cup of coffee.

The coffee was thin. Rita had never seen this room without Meternagel in it. Without him and his eternal cigarette smoke it seemed desperately empty. She noticed now how shabby the sofa was. And there was no carpet on the shining linoleum.

Meternagel's wife was glad to have someone to talk to.

"He's not like other people, you know," she said sadly. "I've had to sit by and watch him driving himself to this. Other people have TV sets and washing machines and refrigerators. But do you know what he's done with his money ever since the girls left home? He's been saving it up. He thinks I don't know what for, but I do. He wants to pay back the three thousand marks he paid out by mistake that time. As if a big factory like that would miss three thousand marks! But I miss them terribly."

Rita drank her weak coffee. She ate a sandwich with it.

"I was a maidservant and he was an ordinary carpenter when we married. We'd known each other ever since we were children together."

Rita knew the old block of flats where they had lived.

"Where it's clean there can't be any serious need," the almoner had said, and refused to grant Meternagel's widowed mother and five children an allowance.

"I often used to go over and clean up when his mother was away doing up people's laundry. They were all boys and Rolf was the eldest," she added.

And she had grown old by his side. She must have been very pretty when she was young, Rita thought, but now her face was lined and sad. She had on a dress which might have been new five years earlier, for she had had to count the pennies all their married life.

"You just can't imagine how hard your husband has worked and how much he has done," said Rita, trying to find words to comfort her. "And they think so highly of him, too. I don't know what they'll do without him."

"Oh yes, of course I know that," she answered softly. "He just can't be any other way."

Meternagel was asleep when she peeped into his room again. She avoided looking at his tired face. She closed the door softly behind her.

The day – the first day of her new-found freedom – was drawing to a close. People were on their way home from work. Squares of light sprang up in the dark walls. All the little private and public activities of evening began – the thousand and one small tasks, setting tables, lighting fires, a song for the children at bed-time. A man might look up at his wife as she cleared the table after supper and she might not see the look of gratitude on his face. A woman might lay her hand gently on her husband's shoulder, something she had not done for a long time, feeling that this was the moment when he needed it.

Rita went a long way out of her way, walking along many streets and glancing in at many windows. She saw how inexhaustible supplies of kindliness, used up during the day, were renewed each evening. And she was not afraid that she would miss her share of kindliness. She knew that she would sometimes be tired, sometimes angry. But she was not afraid. And what made up for everything was the feeling that people could learn to sleep soundly again and live their lives to the full, as if there were an abundance of this strange substance – life – as if it could never be used up.

BIBLIOGRAPHY

SELECTED BIBLIOGRAPHY

This bibliography is based to a large extent on the valuable compilation of works gathered by Alexander Stephan in *Text und Kritik,* 46 (1975). I have eliminated those references which I thought were insignificant and have updated the bibliography. In addition I have endeavored to include numerous English references which Stephan omitted in order to aid the English-speaking reader. For those who read German, Stephan's bibliography and Martin Reso's book *'Der Geteilte Himmel' und seine Kritiker* are important reference sources. The best short critical study of Christa Wolf to date is Stephan's recently published book, *Christa Wolf,* included in this bibliography.

Primary Works by Christa Wolf.
Arranged chronologically.

1. BOOKS

Moskauer Novelle. Halle: Mitteldeutscher Verlag, 1961.

Der geteilte Himmel. Halle: Mitteldeutscher Verlag, 1963.

Nachdenken über Christa T. Halle: Mitteldeutscher Verlag, 1968.

Lesen und Schreiben. Aufsätze und Betrachtungen. Nachbemerkung von Hans Stubbe. Berlin: Aufbau, 1971. (Includes "Deutsch sprechen," "Eine Rede," "Fünfundzwanzig Jahre." "Probe Vietnam," "Blickwechsel," "Zu einem Datum," "Brecht und andere," "Der Sinn einer neuen Sache — Vera Inber," "Tagebuch — Arbeitsmittel und Gedächtnis," "Glauben an Irdisches," "Bei Anna Seghers," "Ein Besuch," "Lesen und Schreiben").

Till Eulenspiegel. Erzählung für den Film. Berlin: Aufbau, 1971. (With Gerhard Wolf).

Unter den Linden. Drei unwahrscheinliche Geschichten. Berlin: Aufbau, 1974. (Includes "Unter den Linden," "Neue Lebensansichten eines Katers," "Selbstversuch").

Kindheitsmuster. Berlin: Aufbau, 1976.

2. TRANSLATIONS.

Divided Heaven. Trans. Joan Becker. Berlin: Seven Seas, 1965.

The Quest for Christa T. Trans. Christopher Middleton. New York: Farrar, Straus Giroux, 1970.

"An Afternoon in June." Trans. Eva Wulff. *Cross-Section.* Ed. Wieland Herzfelde & Günther Cwojdrak. Leipzig: Edition Leipzig, 1970. 256-272. (Anthology of the PEN Centre German Democratic Republic).

"Change of Perspective." Trans. A. Leslie Willson. *Dimension* (Special Issue 1973), 180-201.

3. SCREENPLAYS.

Der Geteilte Himmel with Gerhard and Konrad Wolf, 1964.

Fräulein Schmetterling, 1966.

Die Toten bleiben jung. Co-author, 1968.

4. REVIEWS, ARTICLES, ESSAYS, EDITIONS.

"Komplikationen, aber keine Konflikte." Review of Werner Reinowski's *Diese Welt muß unser sein* in *Neue Deutsche Literatur,* 6 (1954), 140-45.

"Probleme des zeitgenössischen Gesellschaftsromans. Bemerkungen zu dem Roman *Im Morgennebel* von Ehm Welk." *Neue Deutsche Literatur,* 1 (1954), 142-50.

"Um den neuen Unterhaltungsroman." Review of E. R. Greulich's *Das geheime Tagebuch* in *Neues Deutschland,* 169 (1952).

"Achtung, Rauschgifthandel." *Neue Deutsche Literatur,* 2 (1955), 136-40.

"Die schwarzweissrote Flagge." Review of Peter Bamm's *Die unsichtbare Flagge,* in *Neue Deutsche Literatur,* 2 (1955), 148-52.

"Menschliche Konflikte in unserer Zeit." Review of Erwin Strittmatter's *Tinko* in *Neue Deutsche Literatur*, 7 (1955), 139-44.

"Besiegte Schatten?" Review of Hildegard Maria Rauchfuss' *Besiegte Schatten* in *Neue Deutsche Literatur*, 9 (1955), 137-41.

"Menschen und Werk." Review of Rudolf Fischer's *Martin Hoop IV* in *Neue Deutsche Literatur*, II (1955), 143-49.

"Die Literaturtheorie findet zur literarischen Praxis." *Neue Deutsche Literatur*, II (1955), 159-60.

"Popularität oder Volkstümlichkeit?" *Neue Deutsche Literatur*, I (1956), 115-24.

In diesen Jahren. Deutsche Erzähler der Gegenwart. Ed. Christa Wolf. Leipzig: Reclam, n. d.

" 'Freiheit' oder Auflösung der Persönlichkeit." Review of Hans Erich Nossack's *Spätestens im November und Spirale, Roman einer schlaflosen Nacht* in *Neue Deutsche Literatur*, 4 (1957), 135-42.

"Autobiographie und Roman." Review of Walter Kaufmann's *Wohin der Mensch gehört* in *Neue Deutsche Literatur*, 10 (1957), 142-3.

"Vom Standpunkt des Schriftstellers und von der Form der Kunst." *Neue Deutsche Literatur*, 12 (1957), 119-24.

"Unsere Meinung." *Neue Deutsche Literatur*, I (1958) 4-6.

"Botschaft wider die Passivität." Review of Karl Otten's *Die Botschaft* in *Neue Deutsche Literatur*, 2 (1958), 144-45.

"Kann man eigentlich über alles schreiben?" *Neue Deutsche Literatur*, 6 (1958), 3-16.

"Eine Lektion über Wahrheit und Objektivität." *Neue Deutsche Literatur*, 7 (1958), 120-3.

"Erziehung der Gefühle?" Review of Rudolph Bartsch's *Geliebt bis ans bittere Ende* in *Neue Deutsche Literatur*, II (1958), 129-35.

Wir, unsere Zeit. Prosa und Gedichte aus zehn Jahren. Eds. Christa und Gerhard Wolf. Berlin. Aufbau, 1959.

Proben junger Erzähler. Ed. Christa Wolf. Leipzig: Reclam, 1959.

"Vom erfüllten Leben." Review of Ruth Werner's *Ein ungewöhnliches Mädchen* in *Neue Deutsche Literatur,* 3 (1959), 7-11.

"Literatur und Zeitgenossenschaft." *Neue Deutsche Literatur,* 3 (1959), 7-11.

"Sozialistische Literatur der Gegenwart." *Neue Deutsche Literatur,* 5 (1959), 3-7.

"Die Literatur der neuen Etappe. Gedanken zum III. Sowjetischen Schriftstellerkongress." *Neues Deutschland,* 167 (1959).

"Anna Seghers über ihre Schaffensmethode. Ein Gespräch." *Neue Deutsche Literatur,* 8 (1959), 52-7.

"Auf den Spuren der Zeit." Review of *Auf den Spuren der Zeit. Junge deutsche Prosa.* Ed. Rolf Schroers in *Neue Deutsche Literatur,* 6 (1960), 126-9.

Review of Dieter Noll's *Die Abenteuer des Werner Holt* in *Sontnag,* 46 (1960).

"Deutschland unsere Tage." Review of Anna Seghers' *Die Entscheidung* in *Neues Deutschland,* 77 (1961).

". . . wenn man sich durch Arbeit mehrt." *Berliner Zeitung,* 95(1961).

"Land, in dem wir leben. Die deutsche Frage in dem Roman *Die Entscheidung* von Anna Seghers." *Neue Deutsche Literatur,* 5 (1961), 49-65.

"Ein Erzähler gehört dazu." Review of Karl-Heinz Jacobs' *Beschreibung eines Sommers* in *Neue Deutsche Literatur,* 10 (1961), 129-33.

"Schicksal einer deutschen Kriegsgeneration." Review of M. W. Schulz's *Wir sind nicht Staub im Wind* in *Sonntag,* 50 (1962)

"Diskussionsbeitrag auf der 'Konferenz Schriftsteller in Halle.'" *Neue Deutsche Literatur,* 8 (1962), 132-35.

"Nachwort" in Anna Seghers, *Das siebte Kreuz.* Berlin: Aufbau, 1961.

"Rede auf der Zweiten Bitterfelder Konferenz." *Protokoll der von der Ideologischen Kommission beim Politbüro des ZK der SED und dem Ministerium für Kultur am 24. und 25. April im Kulturpalast des Elektrochemischen Kombinats Bitterfeld abgehaltenen Konferenz.* Berlin: Dietz, 1964. 224-34.

"Einiges über meine Arbeit als Schriftsteller." *Junge Schriftsteller der Deutschen Demokratischen Republik in Selbstdarstellungen.* Ed. Wolfgang Paulick. Leipzig: Bibliographisches Institut, 1965. 11-16.

"'Notwendiges Streitgespräch.' Bermerkungen zu einem internationalen Kolloquium." *Neue Deutsche Literatur,* 3 (1965), 97-104.

"Christa Wolf spricht mit Anna Seghers." *Neue Deutsche Literatur,* 6 (1965), 7-18.

"Gute Bücher — und was weiter?" *Neues Deutschland,* 19 December 1965. Diskussionsbeitrag auf dem 11. Plenum des ZK der SED.

"Abgebrochene Romane." *Situation* 66 — 20 *Jahre Mitteldeutsche Verlag.* Halle: Mitteldeutscher Verlag, 1966. 156 ff.

"Vorwort," in Juri Kosakow. *Larifari und andere Erzählungen.* Berlin: Kultur und Fortschritt, 1966. 5-11.

"Juninachmittag." *Nachrichten aus Deutschland.* Ed. Hildegard Brenner. Reinbek: Rowohlt, 1967.

"Auf den Grund der Erfahrungen kommen. Eduard Zak sprach mit Christa Wolf." *Sonntag,* 7 (1968), 6-7.

"Anmerkungen zu Geschichte." Anna Seghers. *Aufstellen eines Maschinengewehrs im Wohn-*

zimmer der Frau Kamptschik. Neuwied: Luchterhand, 1970. 157-64.

"Wortmeldungen. Schriftsteller über Erfahrungen, Pläne und Probleme: Gegenwart und Zukunft." *Neue Deutsche Literatur,* 1 (1971). 68-70.

"Autoren — Werkstatt: Chrita Wolf. Gespräch mit Joachim Walther." *Die Weltbühne,* 9 January 1973, pp. 51-55.

"Fragen an Konstantin Simonov." *Neue Deutsche Literatur,* 12 (1973), 5-20.

"Dienstag der 27. September 1960." *Tage für Jahre.* Ed. Elli Schmidt. Rostock: Hinstorff, 1974. 84-98.

"Hans Kaufmann. Gespräch mit Christa Wolf." *Weimarer Beiträge,* 6 (1974), 90-112.

"Das wird man bei uns anders verstehen. UZ-Gespräch mit der bekannten Autorin Christa Wolf." *Unsere Zeit,* 11 February, 1974.

"Ueber Sinn und Unsinn von Naivität." *Eröffnungen. Schriftsteller über ihr Erstlingswerk.* Berlin: Aufbau, 1974. 174.

"Max Frisch, beim Wiederlesen oder: Vom Schreiben in Ich-Form." *Text und Kritik,* 47/48 (1975), 7-12.

"Alltägliche Befindlichkeiten." *Neue Deutsche Literatur,* 8 (1975), 121-28. (Correspondence with Gerti Tetzner).

SECONDARY WORKS

1. GENERAL STUDIES

Beckermann, Thomas. "Das Abenteuer einer menschenfreundlichen Prosa. Gedanken über den Tod in der sozialistischen Literatur." *Text und Kritik,* 46 (1975), 25-32.

Brettschneider, Werner. "Christa Wolf." *Zwischen literarischer Autonomie und Staatsdienst. Die Literatur in der DDR.* Berlin: Schmidt, 1972, 120-30.

de Bruyn, Günter. "Günter de Bruyn über Christa

Wolf Fragment eines Frauenporträts." *Liebes-und andere Erklärungen. Schriftsteller über Schriftsteller.* Ed. Annie Voigtlander. Berlin: Aufbau, 1972. 410-16.

Cosentino, Christine. "Eine Untersuchung des sozialistischen Realismus im Werke Christa Wolfs." *German Quarterly,* 2 (1974), 245-61.

Crips, Lilane. "Darstellung von sozialen Konflikten in der Romanliteratur der DDR." *Deutschland Archiv,* 8 (Sonderheft, 1975), 157-176.

Durzak, Manfred. "Ein exemplarisches Gegenspiel. Die Romane von Christa Wolf." *Der deutsche Roman der Gegenwart.* 2nd. rev. ed. Stuttgart: Kohlhammer, 1973. 270-93.

Feitknecht, Thomas. "Das Problem der Selbstverwirklichung." *Die sozialistische Heimat. Zum Selbstverständnis neuerer DDR-Romane.* Bern: Lang, 1971. 71-80.

Franke. Konrad. *Die Literatur der Deutschen Demokratischen Republik.* Munich: Kindler, 1971. 373-78.

Fürnberg, Louis. "Brief an Christa Wolf." *Fürnberg, Ein Lesebuch für unsere Zeit.* Ed. Hans Böhm. Berlin. Aufbau, 1974. 420-1.

Gugisch, Peter. "Christa Wolf." *Literatur der DDR in Einzeldarstellungen.* Ed. Hans Jürgen Geerdts. Stuttgart: Kröner. 1972. 395-415.

Herminghouse, Patricia. "Wunschbild oder Porträt? Zur Darstellung der Frau im Roman der DDR." *Literatur und Literaturtheorie in der DDR.* Ed. Peter U. Hohendahl. Frankfurt am Main: Suhrkamp, 1976. 281-334.

Huebener, Theodore. "Christa Wolf." *The Literature of East Germany.* New York: Ungar, 1970. 112-115.

Jäger, Manfred. "Auf dem langen Weg zur Wahrheit. Fragen, Antworten und neue Fragen in den Erzählungen Christa Wolf." *Sozialliteraten. Funktion und Selbstverständnis der Schriftsteller in der DDR.* Düsseldorf: Bertelsmann, 1973. 11-101.

Jäger, Manfred. "Die Literaturkritikerin Christa Wolf." *Text und Kritik,* 46 (1975), 42-49.

Kaufmann, Hans. "Zu Christa Wolfs poetischem Prinzip. Nachbemerkung zum Gespräch." *Weimarer Beiträge,* 6 (1974), 113-25.

Köhler, Hermann. "Christa Wolf erzählt." *Weggenossen Fünfzehn Schriftsteller der DDR.* Eds. Klaus Jarmatz and Christel Berger. Leipzig: Reclam, 1975. 214-32.

Köhn, Lothar. "Erinnerung und Erfahrung. Christa Wolfs Begründung der Literatur." *Text und Kritik,* 46 (1975), 14-24.

Kunert, Günther. "Von der Schwierigkeit des Schreibens." *Text und Kritik,* 46 (1975) 11-13.

Lennartz, Franz. "Wolf, Christa." *Deutsche Dichter und Schriftsteller.* 10th rev. ed.. Stuttgart: Kröner, 1969. 761-2.

Nawrocki, Joachim. "Christa Wolf, die Frosche und die Grundsatzfrage." *Das geplante Wunder. Leben und Wirtschaft im anderen Deutschland.* Hamburg: Wegner, 1967. 268-71.

Promies, Wolfgang. "Dass wir aus dem vollen Leben . . .' Versuch über Christa Wolf." *Positionen im deutschen Roman der sechziger Jahre.* Eds. Heinz Ludwig Arnold & Theo Buck. Munich: Boorberg, 1974. 110-26.

Raddatz, Fritz J. "Eine neue sozialistische Literatur entsteht." *Traditionen und Tendenzen. Materialien zur Literatur der DDR.* Frankfurt am Main: Suhrkamp, 1972. 379-90, 627, 671-72.

Salisch, Marion von. *Zwischen Selbstaufgabe und Selbstverwirklichung. Zum Problem der Persönlichkeitsstruktur im Werk Christa Wolfs.* Stuttgart: Klett, 1975.

Schuhmann, Klaus. "Aspekte des Verhältnisses zwischen Individuum und Gesellschaft in der Gegenwartsliteratur der DDR." *Weimarer Beiträge,* 7 (1975), 5-36.

Stephan, Alexander. "Die 'Subjektive Authentizität' des Autors. Zur ästhetischen Position von Christa Wolf." *Text und Kritik*, 464. (1975), 33-41.

Stephan, Alexander. *Christa Wolf. Roman, Essay und Kritik*. Munich: Beck, 1976.

Wilmanns, Gerda. "Christa Wolf." *Deutsche Dichter der Gegenwart. Ihr Leben und Werk*. Ed. Benno von Wiese. Berlin: Schmidt, 1973. 605. 18.

Zipes, Jack. "Growing Pains in the Contemporary German Novel —East and West." *Mosaic,* V/3 (1972), **1-17.**

2. *Moskauer Novelle*

Mieth, G. "Komposition, Erzählperspektive, Gattungsproblematik." *Deutschunterricht* (DDR), 4 (1966).

Schultz, Gerda. "Ein überraschender Erstling." *Neue Deutsche Literatur,* 7 (1961), 128-31.

3. *Der geteilte Himmel*

Autorenkollektiv. "Gestaltung der Perspektive im Menschenbild. Zu Christa Wolf: *Der geteilte Himmel,* (1963)". *Literatur im Blickpunkt. Zum Menschenbild in der Literatur beider deutschen Staaten*. Ed. Arno Hochmuth. 2nd rev. ed. Berlin: Dietz, 1967. 193-211.

Barthel, K. *"Der geteilte Himmel — zur fiilmischen Umsetzung." Film,* 3 (1964).

Bonk, Jürgen. "Christa Wolf: *Der geteilte Himmel." Junge Prosa der DDR*. Eds. Willi Bredel & Jürgen Bonk. Berlin: Volk und Wissen. 1964.

Brandt, Sabine. "Annäherung an die moderne Literatur?" *Frankfurter Allgemeine Zeitung,* 8 October, 1963.

de Bruyn, Günther. "Christa Wolf. 'Rita und die Freiheit.' " *Maskeraden. Parodien*. Halle. Mitteldeutscher Verlag. 1966. 9-13.

Caute, David. "Divided Hearts at the Wall." *The Nation,* 13 February 1967, pp. 215-16.

Dittman, G. "Auseinandersetzung mit der Gegenwart. *Der geteilte Himmel* im Literaturunterricht." *Deutschunterricht* (DDR), 6 (1966).

Geisthardt, Hans Jürgen. "Das Thema der Nation und zwei Literaturen. Nachweis an Christa Wolf — Uwe Johnson." *Neue Deutsche Literatur,* 6 (1966), 448-69.

Geisthardt, Hans Jürgen. "Weltanschauung und Romanaufbau." *Konturen und Perspektiven. Zum Menschenbild in der Gegenwartsliteratur der Sowjetunion und der Deutschen Demokratischen Republik.* Berlin: Akademie, 1969. 167-89.

Gerlach, Ingeborg. "Christa Wolf: *Der geteilte Himmel." Bitterfeld. Arbeiterliteratur und Literatur der Arbeitswelt in der DDR.* Kronberg. Scriptor, 1974. 125-133.

Hamm, Peter. "Der Blick in die Westdeutsche Ferne." *Die Zeit,* 27 March 1964.

Halsken, Hans-Georg. "Zwei Romane: Christa Wolf *Der geteilte Himmel* und Hermann Kant *Die Aula." Deutschunterricht* (BRD), 5 (1969), 61-99.

Karl, Günther. "Dialektische Dramaturgie. Ein Versuch zu Gestaltsproblemen des Films *Der geteilte Himmel." Filmspiegel,* 4 (1964).

Karl, Günther. "Experiment im Streitgespräch." *Neues Deutschland,* 5 September 1964.

Kloehn, Ekkehard. "Christa Wolf: *Der geteilte Himmel.* Roman zwischen sozialistischen Realismus und Kritischem Realismus." *Deutschunterricht* (BRD), 1 (1968), 43-56.

Leonhardt, Rudolf Walter. "German Literary Letter," *New York Times Book Review,* 12 September 1965, pp. 18-19.

Reso, Martin, ed. *'Der geteilte Himmel' und seine Kritiker. Dokumentation.* Halle: Mitteldeutscher Verlag, 1965.

Reinig, Christa. "Der ungeteilte Hades." *Der Spiegel,* 3 (1965), 70-71.

Reitschert, Gerhard. "Die neuen Mythen." *alternative,* 35 (1964), 11-13.

Tippkötter, M. "Die Förderung individuellen Lektüre und Christa Wolfs Erzählung *Der geteilte Himmel.*" *Deutschunterricht* (DDR), 2 (1964).

Wolf, Konrad. ". . . das ist hier die Frage. Regisseur Konrad Wolf nimmt Stellung." *Sonntag,* 6 (1965), 9-10.

4. *Nachdenken über Christa T.*

Anonymous. "Nachdenken über Christa T." *Times Literary Supplement,* 24 July 1969, p. 8809.

Anonymous. "The Quest for Christa T." *Times Literary Supplement,* 13 August 1971, p. 961.

Beckelmann, Jürgen. "Der Versuch man selbst zu sein." *Süddeutsche Zeitung.* 26/27 July 1969.

Franke, Konrad. "Ihre Generation Voraus." *Frankfurter Hefte,* 7 (970), 524-5.

Haase, Horst. "Nachdenken über ein Buch." *Neue Deutsche Literatur,* 4 (1969), 174-885.

Hammer, Jean-Pierre. "L'individu dans la société socialiste (Christa T.).' *Allemagnes d'aujourd' hui,* 21 (1970), 61-70.

Huyssen, Andreas. "Auf den Spuren Ernst Blochs — Nachdenken über Christa Wolf." *Basis,* 5 (1975).

Kähler, Hermann. "Christa Wolfs Elegie." *Sinn und Form,* 1 (1969), 251-61.

Kersten, Heinz. "Christa Wolfs *Nachdenken über Christa T.*" *Frankfurter Rundschau,* 21 June 1969.

Mayer, Hans. "Christa Wolf/Nachdenken über Christa T." *Neue Rundschau,* 1 (1970), 180-6.

Michaelis, Rolf. "Der doppelte Himmel. Christa Wolfs zweites Buch: *Nachdenken über Christa T.* Der umstrittene Roman aus der DDR." *Frankfurter Allgemeine Zeitung,* 28 May 1969.

Mohr, Heinrich. "Produktive Sehnsucht. Struktur, Thematik und politische Relevanz von Christa

Wolfs Nachdenken über Christa T." *Basis,* 2 (1971), 191-233.

Moscoso-Gongora, Peter. "The Quest for Christa T." *Saturday Review,* 8 May 1971, pp. 31-2.

Nolte, Joste. "Die schmerzhaften Erfahrungen der Christa T." *Grenzgänge. Berichte über Literatur.* Vienna: Europaverlag, 1972. 176-81.

Orlow, Peter. "Der erste Tauwetter-Roman im DDR-Winter." *Die Orientierung,* 246 (1969), 11-20.

Pawel, Ernst. "The Quest for Christa T." *New York Times Book Review,* 31 January 1971, pp. 7, 33.

Raddatz, Fritz J. "Mein Name sei Tonio K." *Der Spiegel,* 23 (1969), 153-4.

Reich-Ranicki, Marcel. "Christa Wolfs unruhige Elegie." *Die Zeit,* 23 May 1969.

Sachs, Heinz. "Verleger sein heisst ideologisch kämpfen." *Neues Deutschland,* 14 May 1969.

Sander, Hans-Dietrich. "Die Gesellschaft und Sie." *Deutschland Archiv,* 6 (1969), 599-603.

Schonauer, Frank. "Selbstein und Sozialismus." *Stuttgarter Zeitung,* 22 November, 1969.

Wallmann, Jürgen P. "Christa Wolf: *Nachdenken über Christa T." Neue deutsche Hefte,* 4 (1969), 149-55.

Wallmann, Jürgen P. "Uber die Schwierigkeiten 'ich' zu sagen." *Die Tat,* 1 August 1970.

Weith, Wolfgang. "Nachrichten aus einem stillen Deutschland." *Monat,* 253 (1969), 90-4.

Whitley, John. "Quest for Christa T." *Sunday Times,* 16 May 1971.

Wiegenstein, Roland. "Verweigerung der Zustimmung?" *Merkur,* 23 (1969), 779-82.

Willett, John. "The Quest for East Germany." *New York Review of Books,* 2 September 1971, pp. 21-3.

Wohmann, Gabriele. "Frau mit Eigenschaften." *Christ und Welt,* 12 May 1969.

Zehm, Günther. "Nachdenken über Christa W." *Welt der Literatur,* 27 March 1969.

Zehm, Günther. "Rückzug ins private Glück im Winkel.' *Welt der Literatur,* 3 July 1969.

5. *Lesen und Schreiben*

Anonymous. "Lesen und Schreiben." *Times Literary Supplement,* 6 April 1973, p. 396.

Auer, Annemarie. "Geglückte Versuche." *Neue Deutsche Literatur,* 2 (1973), 118-25.

Bilke, Jörg B. "Zumutbare Wahrheiten." *Basis,* 4 (1973), 192-200.

Cwojdrak, Günther. "Nachdenken über Prosa." *Sinn und Form,* 6 (1972), 1293-9.

Hirdina, Karin. "Genau, zupackend, veränderlich." *Sonntag,* 34 (1972).

Raddatz, Fritz J. "Vom Lesen und Schreiben — drüben.'" *Süddeutsche Zeitung,* 24/25 February 1973.

Wallmann, Jürgen P. "Christa Wolf. *Lesen und schreiben." Neue deutsche Hefte,* 1 (1973), 164-7.

Weith, Wolfgang. "Verbotene Früchte gezuchtet." *Die Zeit,* 9 March 1973.

6. *Till Eulenspiegel*

Hartl, Elwin. "Nachdenken über Eulenspiegel." *Die Furche,* 12 October 1974.

Heise, Wolfgang. "Nachbemerkung." Christa Wolf. *Till Eulenspiegel. Erzählung für den Film.* Berlin: Aufbau, 1973. 217-23.

Hirsch, Helmut. "Klugheit als Aktion." *Neue Deutsche Literatur,* 8 (1974), 136-9.

Jost, Dominik. "Spiel dir den Film von Till." *Die Zeit,* 4 April 1974.

Kähler, Hermann. 'Panorama der Zeit des Bauernkrieges." *Neues Deutschland,* 13 February 1974.

Krättli, Anton. "Literatur der DDR und westliche Kritik." *Neue Züricher Zeitung,* 5 July 1974.

Lämmert, Eberhard. "Zum Sehen geschrieben." *Frankfurter Allegemeine Zeitung,* 6 April 1974.

Raddatz, Fritz J. "Narrheit als Zeitkritik — so und so." *Merkur,* 9 (1974), 889-91.

Schoeller, Wilfried F. "List der Schwachen." *Frankfurter Rundschau,* 88 June 1974.

Töpelmann, Sigrid. "Till Eulenspiegel." *Sonntag,* 6 (1974).

Wallmann, Jürgen P. "Neuinterpretation des Till Eulenspiegel." *Deutschland-Archiv,* 4 (1974), 421-2.

Weith, Wolfgang. "Der Narr als Systemskritiker." *Süddeutsche Zeitung,* 3 April 1974.

7. *Unter den Linden*

Abicht, Ludo. "Christa Wolf, *Unter den Linden.*" *New German Critique,* 6 (1975), 164-169.

Bohm, Gunhild. "Der Ausspruch des einzelnen." *Deutschland Archiv,* 8 (March, 1975), 296-99.

Krättli, Anton. "Unwahrscheinliche Geschichten aus der DDR." *Neue Züricher Zeitung,* 29 November 1974.

Last, Rex. 'Identical Issues," *Times Literary Supplement,* 10 October 1975, p. 120.

Michaelis, Rolf. "Recht auf Trauer." *Die Zeit,* 12 December 1974.

Plavius, Heinz. "Mutmassungsmut." *Neue Deutsche Literatur,* 10 (1974), 154-7.

Simon, Horst. "Zur Erfindung dessen, den man lieben kann." *Neues Deutschland,* October, 1974.

Werner, Hans-Georg. "Zum Traditionsbezug der Erzälungen in Christa Wolfs *Unter den Linden.*" *Weimarer Beiträge,* 4 (1976), 36-64.